VOW

KATHERINE BENTLEY

VOW
Copyright ©2021 Katherine Bentley

All rights reserved. No part of this book may be resold or reproduced in any manner whatsoever, or stored in any information storage system, without the prior written consent of the publisher, except in the case of including brief quotations for use in reviews and certain other non-commercial uses permitted by copyright law.

For permissions requests, contact the publisher, Kindle Direct Publishing, or katherinebentley20@gmail.com.

This is a work of fiction. Names, characters, businesses, places, events, locales, and incidents are either the products of the author's imagination or are used in a fictitious manner.

Front cover image by Alejandro Colucci, Epica Prima: The Art of Alejandro Colucci.

ISBN: 9798524280114 (Paperback)
ISBN: 9798483621911 (Hardback)

To Amy, for all the reading and listening over the years.

To Nicola, I could not have done this without you.

To Christopher, Olivia and Mark, for all the encouragement and support.

INTRODUCTION

I first learned of the Vestal Virgins in a Roman history textbook in school. Since then, I have always wanted to write about them, the most privileged and influential women in Greco-Roman society.

The Order of the Vestals was an all-female religious sect that dated back to Rome's young monarchy. For thirty years of their lives, these women lived in luxury, were treated like royalty, and were hailed as heroines. They could vote, own property and had the best education available. The two conditions to this lifestyle were that they remain virgins for the entirety of their servitude and that they watch over the Flame of Vesta, making sure it never died. It was believed that if a Vestal lost her virginity or if the Flame of Vesta went out, the goddess Vesta would no longer protect the Roman empire. The punishments for failing in these duties were either some form of torture or death. Their vow of chastity, believed to safeguard Rome, invited obsessive and hypocritical public scrutiny and was often used as a scapegoat for political failures.

The limitations on the Vestal Virgins seemed to be of an entirely sexual nature. However, in a religious context this made sense. Only the most spiritually uncontaminated were allowed to directly serve the gods. Purity was essential in ancient rites and is still an aspect of many religions today. Thus, innocence was considered vital in women who held religious positions. As a result, a new Vestal Virgin was selected between the ages of six and ten, before she reached puberty. As the loss of virginity was considered the pollution of the mind, body and soul, the Vestal priestesses maintained that true innocence was a state of all three; that a priestess must be, essentially, psychologically chaste.

CONTENT WARNING
This book contains discussions, themes and scenes of sex, sexual oppression and sexual violence.

I welcome you to the world of the Vestal Virgins during the Golden Age of Rome under the reign of Emperor Augustus. Finally, the tale of these women can be told.

I
ARIES ET AUGUSTUS
-The Ram and the Revered One-

We made our way towards the arena where the games were taking place after Vestalia, a midsummer festival honouring Vesta, the goddess of the home and hearth.

When we arrived, the crowd parted. As always, they fell silent when they saw the six Vestal Virgins approaching. My father had once told me that many people could thrill a crowd. When the Emperor clattered through the streets in his chariot, the city jumped to life. People stretched out their arms, screaming so loud that it could be heard across the Mare Nostrum. He also said that there were very few who could silence it. We were those few. When they saw us, it was holy. Figures froze as we passed by. Their hearts leapt into their mouths or skipped a beat. People gasped and voices died. Throats closed as if the very act of breathing was sacrilegious. When they finally remembered themselves, they shoved each other out of our way, not daring to touch us.

We took up our seats in the imperial box. Not long after, the clamour of the mob grew in a loud crescendo. The speaker had announced the Emperor's name: Augustus. We stood and looked around to see him approaching in the splendour of his purple toga.

The Emperor of Rome was in his sixties, fleshy and grey. His toughened leathery skin told the tales of his youth, building the empire. It was hard to reconcile the idealised muscular build of his statues with the man that shuffled into the imperial box now. However, the din of the masses signalled that we were still in the presence of divinity, no matter how old. Head adorned with a laurel wreath and toga hemmed in purple, Augustus came to the ledge and raised his bejewelled hand to greet the crowd. They went wild for him – the man who had destroyed the traitor Mark Anthony and his barbarian enchantress Cleopatra, conquering Egypt and expanding the empire. The son of deified Julius Caesar, Augustus was Rome's first Emperor.

In his shadow followed his wife, Livia. She was an elegant lady and tall, even in her old age. She was her husband's elder by a year or so. She glided along, glamorous in her flowing, dark emerald stola with a turquoise palla wrapped around her shoulders. Her arms were lined with silver bangles, her hands and hair covered with various gems. Her serpentine eyes looked in our direction, surveying us. Then she reclined on her golden throne next to her husband's.

Following Augustus and Livia was a middle-aged man I had never seen before, but I had heard of him. He was Tiberius, Livia's son by a previous marriage. He walked with his hands behind his back and did not raise either one to greet the crowd. He was lean and tanned. His eyes, narrow and dark like his mother's, scanned the scene around him with obvious distaste. When he caught sight of us, he did not even bow his head as was common courtesy.

'Ugh, Tiberius,' Val retched quietly. 'What a killjoy.'

Valeriana, or Val as we liked to call her, was my closest friend. Taller than me by just a forehead, her hair was a rich chestnut colour, her eyes brown like autumnal leaves, and there was a beauty mark in the right upper corner of her mouth. She had a small, ovular jawline. She could have been the daughter of Venus, the goddess of beauty.

'Why?' I asked.

'People despise him. He doesn't get on with anyone. All he ever does is sulk and scowl,' she complained. 'As Augustus' heir, you would think he has much to smile about.'

'Sometimes one does not wish to inherit such a vast amount of responsibility, Val,' Rufina cut in behind us.

We turned around to face a tall girl with raven-black hair and huge, dark eyes. Her lids were lined with thick, long lashes. She had a tanned face, sculpted cheekbones and a full mouth.

'I doubt Tiberius ever desired his fate,' she continued. 'Why should he when Augustus took all he ever wanted from him?'

I frowned. 'What do you mean?'

She gave me a sad smile. 'Tiberius' first wife. They say it was true love.'

I looked back at the heir to the empire, slouching in his throne and looking down at his hands.

Rufina's words floated into my ear. 'But he was forced to divorce her for Augustus' daughter, Julia, and that marriage failed catastrophically.'

'Rumour has it that Augustus works him harder than a slave,' Picia added. She was a petite girl and the third of my friends, with a curvy figure and mousy brown curls. Her olive-green eyes sparkled whenever she spoke.

The Emperor leaned over, jabbing a finger into Tiberius' stomach, making him sit up straight.

Rufina hummed in agreement. 'He should be pitied, not despised.'

Val huffed. 'Hardly. He's still the heir to a colossal fortune and power.'

Escorting the imperial family was Prefect Gnaeus of the Praetorian Guard, the Emperor's bodyguards. He was big and bulky under his white toga, the attire for the Praetorian Guards when they were stationed within the city of Rome. Middle-aged with a short, dark beard and stormy-looking eyes, he bowed when he saw us.

'Vestals!' Emperor Augustus greeted, coming towards us.

I curtseyed along with the others.

He frowned. 'Word has reached me about what happened at the Baths of Agrippa,' he began, shaking his head.

My heart jumped in fear.

'That slave, spying on you all in the tepidarium. The insolence!'

I relaxed a little. *So he had not heard*, I thought.

'Well, never fear. I have him fighting today in the arena as his execution. He will die painfully for his offence.'

I glanced around at the rowdy rabble who were taking their seats, roaring for the games to begin. A queasy feeling settled in my stomach. The thought of a man's last moments being jeered at while desperately fighting for his life disgusted me.

'Thank you, Caesar,' I forced myself to say.

He smiled. 'Well, enjoy the games, girls,' he said, leaving the conversation to return to his throne.

We curtseyed in farewell.

After a short while, once the Emperor was ready to begin, the speaker announced the first battle. The games were filled with bloody and gruesome skirmishes between men and men, and then men and animals. The crowd reacted enthusiastically to the spectacles.

Picia and Val leaned on the ledge of the imperial box to see the action more clearly. Rufina and I stayed in our seats while the slaughter reigned below us. Neither of us took great delight in this sort of entertainment. I found it generally distasteful and horrible, while she just found the whole matter a waste of time.

'And now, ladies and gentlemen,' the speaker announced, 'your next warrior: Aries Gloriosus Iovis!'

The arena erupted with noise. Every man, woman and child was on their feet. Such a name was notable: 'The Glorious Ram of Jupiter'.

The gates opened, and a man walked into the sandy arena. He was dressed in a tunic and lorica segmentata, a breastplate made of two circular metal plates laced together around the torso. He was carrying a bronze galea, a helmet, under his arm. There was a gladius, a sword, hanging from its sheath around his waist.

When I caught sight of his dark curls, I was filled with dread. There was no doubt in my mind. 'Oh, Vesta,' I murmured. I stood up and went towards the ledge, Picia and Val parting to let me stand in between them.

Rufina, following, stood behind me, easily able to see over me. 'Is this the one who spied on us earlier in the baths?'

'Indeed,' Occia's stern voice sounded from behind us.

Occia was our mistress, known officially as the Vestalis Maxima. She was a middle-aged woman, imposing yet elegantly poised with a serene, matronly aura. She had a square face and some smile lines were beginning to appear around her dark eyes. Her hair was concealed beneath her headdress, like the rest of us.

'Will he fight another gladiator or an animal?' I asked.

'I don't know,' she replied. 'At any rate, he deserves whatever is coming to him.'

My head began to ache.

Aries turned towards the imperial box as he put on his galea. The people in the stands roared at him, bloodthirsty.

I felt a wave of regret wash over me. *Would it have been kinder to have let him die earlier in the baths?*

'Is he looking at us?' Picia asked.

'It is perfectly natural for condemned souls to turn to the Emperor and his Vestals in search of good fortune or salvation,' Occia sneered. 'Pathetic.'

I had to close my eyes at her words.

'Aries Gloriosus Iovis,' the speaker declared, 'has committed crimes against the state and the gods. He will face four beasts from the deserts of Africa!'

The crowd bayed in response.

My stomach lurched.

Aries drew his gladius, gripping it firmly and readying his stance.

Just then, about a dozen or so slaves ran out of the gates and opened up giant trapdoors in the ground of the arena, one by one.

The first animal was a great male lion, an enormous creature with a magnificent mane. The king of the beasts prowled out to greet the games, low and alert.

'Did you know that they starve the beasts to make them hungrier?' Val said, grinning.

No one replied. Everyone's attention was on the lion, but I had listened to her and my blood ran cold.

From the next trapdoor sprang a large, yellow, black-spotted cat.

'Good gods, what is that?' Picia gasped.

'A leopard,' Rufina said.

The third animal was another lion, smaller than the first, while the last was a huge hound, black and white.

'A hyena,' Rufina muttered as if transfixed. 'I've read about those. They have jaws that can crush a man.'

Aries spared no time. He turned to the hyena which was nearest to him. He ran at it straight on and slashed at the air between them. The wild dog, bearing its teeth, lunged at him, but Aries leapt to the side and the beast attacked the space where he had been. Then he brought up his gladius and decapitated the hyena in one swipe.

A mixture of boos and cheers echoed throughout the arena.

My pulse was frantic.

'Executed perfectly,' Val joked, and Picia giggled.

The limp carcass of the hyena caught the attention of the starving lions, its head rolling off to the side, with its blood spreading around it in a puddle and seeping into the grains of sand.

For the moment, Aries left them to fight over their meal. He turned just as the leopard was leaping at him from behind. In one swift motion, he jabbed his gladius upwards, cutting through the cat's neck as it attacked. Blood spattering onto his face and armour, he withdrew his weapon and the leopard collapsed.

The tumultuous noise of the mob, greatly impressed by his antics, filled my ears.

He turned back towards the lions, slicing off the tail of the nearer, smaller one. It yowled in pain as it leapt around to face him, whining terribly with its head bowed. Without hesitation, he brought down his gladius and the lion's head tumbled to the ground.

I tried not to vomit. *Barbaric.*

The larger lion growled ferociously as it faced the gladiator, baring its sharp fangs. Then, taking its chance, it jumped at him, claws out and jaws wide, but Aries flung his blade like a spinning wheel of death towards it, impaling the cat between the eyes. It teetered on the spot until it fell to the ground.

Aries removed his gladius from the large feline's skull and backed away from the bodies of the dead animals. He looked up expectantly at the imperial box.

I could hardly hear my thoughts over the thunder of the audience. With relief coming over me, I turned to Occia. I had to fight the smile forming on my face. 'He survived,' I said, trying not to sound too excited.

She nodded, eyes narrowing. 'Yes, indeed.'

My gaze landed on the imperial couple sitting a short distance away. Emperor Augustus seemed disquieted by Aries' victory, but not as annoyed as I had expected. Livia, on the other hand, wore a sly grin. I turned back, grabbing the ledge. Her expression told me that this was not over yet.

Gates on either side of the arena were pushed open.

Aries' head turned and almost immediately he began ducking and jumping around.

'Arrows!' Someone, nearby, shouted from within the audience.

Everyone craned their necks to see.

I scanned the scene, but I could not see the missiles shooting through the air from this height. What I could see was a second gladiator, small and wide, charging into the arena while furiously loading his bow as he fired mercilessly at Aries. My heart jumped each time he released an arrow, but Aries deftly dodged them all.

Then from the other set of gates trudged out a much larger and more muscular gladiator. He was holding an axe over his shoulder. His flesh was deathly pale.

'A Goth,' Rufina informed us, 'from the cold lands beyond the northern borders of our empire.'

Aries looked from one man to the other. He settled on the archer and went for him. His opponent abandoned his bow, throwing it to one side, and drew his sword. Their blades met.

The crowd was in an uproar as they fought in fast fury.

The larger gladiator came up behind them, his axe ready to cleave their skulls apart. Neither of them seemed to notice him, too focused on each other.

It took all of my willpower not to lose control and scream at Aries to watch his back.

Then unexpectedly, the large Goth stopped and stood, watching them just like everyone else. He lifted his axe and looked down at it. Then he glanced up around him, searching the crowd until his gaze fixed on us.

'He's going to throw it at one of them,' I whispered. 'Is he looking for the Emperor's permission?' I asked no one in particular. I looked between Aries and his opponent, wondering whom the Goth would end first. They were near enough for the axe to easily find its mark.

He drew back his arm and flung the blade, but not at Aries or his opponent. *At us!*

'Aemilia, get down!' Rufina exclaimed.

A shriek escaped me and my hands flew to my face. I ducked, my eyes remaining fixed on the flying axe.

Slicing through the air, it was heading straight for the Emperor's throne, but the blade missed Augustus by the breadth of one of the silvery hairs on his balding head.

Livia, who had flung herself down on the ground, hurried over to him.

Prefect Gnaeus, after checking that Augustus had not been harmed, then wrestled with the axe embedded in the top of the throne.

The crowd was going wild with panic for their Emperor.

Augustus, holding onto his wife for support, slowly got down from his seat. His dark eyes were wide with fear. He raised a shaky hand to his forehead, feeling for a wound that wasn't there.

His wife pressed her lips to his temple, saying something softly. Then she led him to the ledge of the imperial box where, holding hands, he stood to his full height, managed to smile and raised his hand in a calming wave.

Instantly, the air filled with cheers.

I shared relieved looks with my friends before peering down into the arena below at the three gladiators. I remembered how in the baths I had begged for Aries to be spared. I wondered if I had made a tremendous mistake. *Did I save a would-be conspiring assassin of the Emperor?*

Suddenly Aries bellowed, flinging his blade at the Goth's back. It stuck, and the huge pale man dropped to his knees, collapsing onto the ground face-down. Then Aries swept up the bow and an arrow off the ground and shot it straight through the other gladiator's forehead. His second victim fell backwards, sprawled across the sand. Both were dead.

Silence settled on the arena at what Aries had just done. However, as the spectators broke out into annoyed yells and shouts, I realised that Aries had made a dreadful mistake: he had killed without imperial consent.

All eyes turned to Augustus, still standing with his wife beside him. Expectation and anticipation filled the air. Slowly, the Emperor drew his thumb up, pointing to his neck. *Death to the loser.* The crowd became ecstatic, deafening in their approval, and Aries bowed to the imperial couple.

I breathed a sigh of relief.

Augustus turned towards us. and we curtseyed before him. He seemed shaken. 'Vestals, do you still wish for the slave to die? The choice remains yours.'

I glanced at Occia, who was about to speak, but I got there before her. 'Caesar, does his earlier crime in the baths still matter now when he has just avenged an attack on you? Does that loyalty deserve an execution?'

He hummed, considering my words.

'Caesar,' Occia interrupted, coming forward. 'That slave pried upon us all earlier this morning. While Aemilia may choose to forgive him, others might not. I certainly will not. You must execute him.'

He gave her a stern look.

She bowed her head. 'We would be most grateful if you did, great Caesar.'

He glanced back at me before facing the Chief Vestal again. 'Vestal Aemilia is right. The slave has shown loyalty to Rome today,' he said. 'He is thus pardoned from any previous offences against the state.'

She clenched her jaw. 'Yes, Caesar.'

He sent her a reassuring smile. 'Never fear. He will most likely be dead within a few days of these games anyway.'

He turned away as we curtseyed in farewell.

I glanced over the ledge to see Aries walking out of the arena. Then I remembered the risk he still posed to me, to my reputation.

Meet him, an inner voice told me, *before it's too late.*

II
VIRGINES VESTALES
-The Vestal Virgins-

Earlier that morning, there had been a brush of lips on my bare shoulder. I detected the scent of mint leaves and smiled, opening my eyes. The morning heat caressed my face.

Standing by the windowsill, I could see the summer sunlight beaming down on Rome around me. The city glowed gold. The Forum Romanum, a large marketplace across the road, was crowded with people cloaked in white. The sky above was aquamarine.

'Aemilia, take your face out of the sun,' a soft voice whispered. It was Picia. With her light, airy words, she could sweeten anyone, just like Iberian honey. 'It is not yet midday, but you still risk browning.'

I turned around, giving her a peck on the cheek.

Picia was three years my junior and, like me, a novice within the Order of the Vestals. She giggled musically and enveloped me in a soft hug. She was the perfect height for me to rest my chin on the crown of her head. 'I am so happy for you,' she said.

'Oh, please. It's not like I'm getting married!'

We broke our embrace.

'No, but if you stay at that windowsill, you will certainly give men something to consider,' a deeper voice sounded.

We turned to see Rufina. The oldest of my friends at nineteen, she was in her second decade of servitude as a Vestal Virgin. Lips pursed and arms folded, she raised an eyebrow. 'You're not some lady of the evening,' she scolded as I stepped back from the windowsill and approached her.

I stood on my tiptoes to kiss her cheek and felt the corner of her lips fail to resist a smile.

'Relax, Rufina,' Picia said behind me. 'It is her birthday, after all.'

'Indeed,' she agreed, sighing in resignation.

I looked around my bedchamber, a pretty little room. Four slaves were setting out my clothes for the day on the small bronze bed. It had a feather-stuffed mattress and wool blankets rolled up beneath it for the winter months. There was a turquoise Egyptian chair near the window. The walls were covered with tapestries. One depicted the goddess Vesta by her hearth. Another showed her in conversation with Dionysus, an amphora of wine in his arm. In a third, she was defeating Saturn with her siblings.

At that moment, the door swung open, and Val swanned in. 'Good morning, Aemilia!' she greeted in a sing-song voice.

At eighteen, she was also in the second decade of her servitude along with Rufina. They carried out the duties that Picia and I were still just learning to do.

Rushing forward, she embraced me enthusiastically. 'Happy birthday, my dear!' She placed a kiss on the top of my head. Standing back, she caught sight of the slaves at my bed, staring at us all while they awaited orders. 'Well?' she demanded sharply. 'Don't just stand there. Get out.'

'Val!' Rufina hissed with a disapproving look.

The beautiful girl rolled her eyes. Just as the slaves were rushing out of the door, she cleared her throat loudly.

They halted in their steps, glancing back at her.

'Thank you,' she said, her tone now sweet. 'We will not need you again this morning.'

They bowed and dashed from the room. Only Metallia remained, my maidservant, with skin, eyes and hair darker than ebony, with her attention on a glass box of utensils in her hands. She knew she was to stay.

Val turned to me, her face bright with excitement. She clasped her hands. 'Well then, shall we begin?' She splayed them for dramatic effect. 'We have quite the day planned, so you must dress quickly, my dear.'

As I raised my arms over my head, they lifted the nightdress off my body. Picia folded up the garment and put it on my bed. Rufina brought over the clothes in which they robed me. They wrapped my chest in a breast cloth. Then they tied a fresh loincloth in place and slipped a white tunic over my head. It reached my knees. I stepped into my stola, a long, white dress which they pulled up and bound in place, fastening it at my shoulders. They tied a ribbon beneath my chest and another around my waist. The hem of the stola brushed against my ankles.

'We shall now leave her hair in your care,' Rufina said kindly to Metallia, who nodded, not meeting her eyes.

One by one, they kissed my cheeks and left my bedchamber.

After Metallia brought over the Egyptian chair for me to sit on, she began by arranging my hair in the traditional bridal fashion of the Vestals. She divided it into six separate plaits which she wrapped around the crown of my head and supported them in place with a white vitta, a woollen ribbon. She interwove the braids above my forehead with even more ribbons, and she placed the infula, a headdress, over my hair. It covered my plaits with small white ropes hanging down over my shoulders. On this, she laid a white veil covering everything, fixed in place with a clasp.

It was a complicated and intricate process, sometimes even painful when she accidentally tugged my hair too tightly. My head and neck would ache by the end of the day, but I always felt confident after she worked her magic.

She helped me with my sandals and draped my palla over me. She held up a looking-glass so that I might approve the finished look. Although I was more attractive than usual, I would never declare myself a great beauty.

'Thank you, Metallia,' I said gratefully.

'Happy birthday, domina,' she said, bowing and avoiding my eyes.

After putting her tools away, she held the bedroom door open for me as I left, going out into the first-floor corridor where Picia, Rufina and Val were waiting near the staircase. They were all dressed the same as I.

'Stunning, as always,' Val said. 'Shall we go?'

I smiled and allowed her to link arms with me, going down the stairs with Rufina and Picia following behind, already chattering.

'Thank you for planning today, Val,' I said.

She beamed at me and squeezed my arm tightly. 'Of course, my dear. You deserve it. It is not often we get a day off, and I swear that you will enjoy every moment of it, even if it kills me,' she laughed.

I giggled. 'I am sure.'

The House of the Vestals was a mansion of three floors. All the Vestals slept on the first, the slaves housed above us. On the ground floor were the living spaces, including the main hall - the atrium - and a public space for meetings, a kitchen, some storage rooms, a banquet hall and a decorated interior courtyard with two large impluvia, pools within the floor which collected the rainwater that fell from above.

Occia was standing in the atrium, awaiting us as we approached. Her pale skin glowed under the sunlight from a large opening in the roof. She spread her arms, and I embraced her fondly. 'Happy birthday, Aemilia, my dear.' Her voice was deep. 'How old are you now?'

We parted.

'Eighteen, domina,' I replied, grinning.

'I am glad,' she said. 'How long until you are no longer an initiate?'

'I have two years left of my first decade, domina. Then I can join Val and Rufina by the fireside.'

She smiled. 'Excellent. Pray, tell me, Aemilia, what is the first thing that any good day of pampering requires?'

'I do not know, domina.' I shrugged.

'And you call yourself a Roman?' She raised an eyebrow. 'The Baths of Agrippa, my dear,' she said, lightly tapping my nose with her forefinger. 'Are we ready then, girls?'

We all nodded, squealing excitedly.

She led the way out of the House of the Vestals into the street. As we departed, guards at the doorway lined up around us in a square formation.

One heard the city before seeing it, the din of voices in the air. There was the smell of the Forum Romanum, a mixture of meat, fish and fruit, so potent that one could almost taste it. I could already feel the drumming of feet on the earth. Rome was the centre of all that mattered. It was the beating, booming heart of the world.

We progressed through the crowded streets in relative silence, the heat bearing down upon us until we reached the Baths of Agrippa, an imposing complex of several buildings built by Marcus Vispanius Agrippa, a deceased son-in-law of the Emperor. It was usually heaving with people, but, when the Vestals were visiting, no one else was permitted inside, not even the patrician men of the Senate. No one was allowed to see the Vestals naked. Thus, throughout the whole site, only our little party and a few slaves were present.

The heat outside was even more powerful than usual. Sweating and panting as we reached the changing room, I couldn't understand why the others had the strength to move with such zeal as they did, giggling and joking as the slaves peeled their clothes away. A slave girl came over to me as I sat down on a bench, catching my breath, but I waved her away, not ready to be pawed and pulled.

'Aemilia, are you alright?' Val asked, frowning at my sedentary state.

I nodded and gulped, but my throat was dry. 'I'm fine.'

'It's your northern blood,' Rufina told me in jest, rolling her eyes. 'Even after nearly a decade in Rome, you cannot stand the heat.'

I smiled. 'I just need to cool down. Give me a moment and I'll follow you shortly.'

Val shrugged. 'It's your birthday. We'll be in the tepidarium.'

Letting me alone, the other Vestals and the slaves departed to the steam room. Why they would go there straight after the heat of the outside world, I would never know.

Breathing deeply, I took off my veil and let it fall to the floor. Then I removed my palla and leant down to untie my sandals. Kicking them off, I stood back up and removed the stola until I was standing in my white tunic. I would have sent for a slave, but I needed to be on my own.

Unfortunately, the gods didn't seem to care about that. Otherwise, they would not have sent the intruder.

A man, a stranger to me, stepped inside. He was tall and dressed in a dirty tunic. He halted in shock once he caught sight of me, staring at me through long, dark wavy locks. His wide eyes flew over my body which, save for the flimsy tunic, was barely covered.

I assumed he was a slave. I shot to my feet, opening my mouth to order him away.

Suddenly, he lunged at me, his hand clamping down over my mouth and his other arm going around my waist. He held me in a tight grip.

'Don't scream,' he whispered.

III
SCELUS
-A Crime-

Furiously, I tried to wriggle out of his grasp, but it was no use. I was locked firmly in place, and he was too strong.

'Stop resisting!' he hissed.

I crumpled, defeated.

He glanced at the open doorway, from where he had come, and then down at me. 'I mean you no harm. I'll let you go if you don't make a sound.'

Considering it, I nodded.

His grip on me relaxed gently.

His mistake.

As he eased his hand from my mouth, I caught his index finger and bit down hard on it for all I was worth. He cried out in alarm and I shoved him away from me. It was a pathetic effort given his size and strength, but he still toppled. Landing on his backside, he groaned, face contorting.

I saw my opportunity and bolted past him, dashing for the doorway. Mid-stride, I felt his hand on my ankle as he yanked me down beside him. I cried out when my right knee hit the floor and I collapsed.

'Sorry!' I heard him whisper loudly.

Desperate to get out of there and ignoring the numbness in my leg, I propped myself up, and saw his wide-eyed gaze travelling across my skin to where the hem of my tunic had ridden up my bare legs. Burning hot with outrage and humiliation, I lashed out my foot and kicked him as hard as I could. My heel struck his right cheek.

He bellowed as his head was knocked back.

I scrambled to get to my feet, but a sharp pain shot through my knee. Yelping, I fell over once more.

I glanced over to see him lightly touching the right side of his face and wincing, glaring at me through his left eye.

He cursed under his breath and rose to his feet, approaching.

I shuffled backwards on my hands. 'Get away from me!' I snapped.

He moved past me and went to close the door, still pressing his palm against his cheek. As he turned back to me, he held out his other hand to help me up. 'I'm not going to hurt you,' he repeated.

'It's a bit late for that!' I slapped it away.

He knelt down.

I tensed up. 'What do you think you're doing?'

'Inspecting your leg,' he replied softly.

'Don't touch me!' I tried to crawl away, but my back met the cold wall.

He only drew nearer. 'It's a bit late for that,' he said quietly, looking up at me through his dark eyelashes.

I was livid. 'If you don't get out of here right now, I swear on all the gods, I'll -'

I was cut off when his fingers touched my skin. I froze, watching him as he examined my knee, his brow knitted in concern.

Thankfully, his eyes didn't wander anywhere else this time. He even pulled the hem of my tunic down as far as it could go without obscuring my knee. His long fingers gently traced my leg, and my hairs stood on end.

Despite myself, I took him in. His face was softly sculpted and his eyes were a deep, dark brown.

He glanced up at me, catching my stare.

I quickly looked away, my face growing warm.

'It will bruise,' he concluded.

'As will your face,' I muttered.

He frowned. 'There's no need to be rude.'

I scowled, wary of him, yet intrigued. 'There is every need. In case you are unaware, you're in close quarters with a nearly naked Vestal!'

There was a mischievous glint in his eye. 'Some would consider that paradise,' he replied, smirking.

I scoffed and rolled my eyes. 'This isn't a joke. If you are found in here with me, you will be killed, if not for injuring me or even touching me then at least for being alone with me when I'm wearing practically nothing.'

'There are worse reasons to die,' he said, shrugging. Then he got to his feet and held his hand out to me once again. 'Can you stand?'

'Of course I can.' I ignored the gesture, getting to my feet. I managed to take a step with a slight limp. I put my hands on my hips. 'See?'

We locked eyes.

'Who are you? No one is supposed to be here today.'

He swallowed and paused as if unsure of what to say, however something in his eyes changed and he looked away. He took a step back, but did not reply. Then he turned around, opened the door and departed immediately, vanishing.

Now alone, shock came over me as I reflected on what had just taken place. With rising panic, I realised the awful truth. This man, a complete and utter stranger, had touched me. More than that, he had seen me in my tunic! *But why had he come in here and where had he gone to now? Would he tell anyone what happened?*

Suddenly, I heard the screams and cries of my friends from the room next door. I limped towards the tepidarium where I found the other Vestals standing in the steam-filled room. They were sharing a whole palla between them, trying to cover up their bare bodies in front of two armed guards. One was restraining the man with whom I had just quarrelled several moments ago. His dark eyes met mine from across the room. The other guard was awkwardly questioning Occia, covered only by her palla.

'Aemilia!' the Vestalis Maxima called, catching sight of me.

I approached her.

'Did you see this man wandering around here?' She jabbed a finger towards the captive.

There was no way I could let slip that we had already met, given the circumstances. So I shook my head. 'No, domina.'

The guard frowned at me. 'He would have had to come from the direction of the changing room, domina.'

I shrugged. 'I would not know. I did not see anyone.'

Occia nodded, sighing. Then she noticed my leg where a bruise was beginning to form. 'What happened?'

I blinked. 'I fell.'

She huffed like it was yet another inconvenience, but turned around and continued to talk to the guard.

I faced the girls, joining their embrace underneath the palla. Even though I was the most clothed one in my tunic, I still felt very bare. 'Are you all alright?'

'We found him creeping around in here,' Picia sniffled as Val rubbed her arm reassuringly.

Occia's voice rose in an unladylike bark. 'What?'

The guard cleared his throat. 'A thousand apologies, domina. We did not mean to lose sight of the slave.'

Slave? The intruder's voice had seemed quite refined for a person of the lower orders.

Occia was shaking with rage. 'What a pathetic pair you are! He has been sneaking around, prying and spying on us. We are the Vestal Virgins.' Then she turned to the captured man. 'You could die for this.'

'Such is the punishment for many things these days - usual Roman justice. And I am already a condemned man,' he said, shrugging.

'Silence! I did not permit you to speak. Kill him,' she ordered, nodding at the guards.

Almost immediately, he was kicked in the back of his knees and he fell to the ground. One guard forced his face to the floor and the other raised his sword, ready to execute him.

A rush of fear and guilt came over me and I stumbled forward, breaking away from the others. 'Please,' I begged. 'Do not.'

Occia looked at me, perplexed. 'He has invaded our sacred privacy.'

'But he does not need to die now, not if he is already condemned, surely?' I asked, turning to the guards. 'What is his fate?'

'I am to fight in the games today,' the man replied, looking up at me from his position on the floor. 'I am a gladiator.'

Val snorted. 'No doubt running away. A coward too, no less.'

Ignoring her, I addressed Occia. 'If he survives the games then let him be executed. The gods may already have a plan for his demise and who are we to interfere?'

She clenched her jaw, considering my words. 'Very well.' Then she nodded and looked down at him. 'But should you fail to die today, slave, you will face an official execution. Justice will be served.'

The guard put down his sword.

The man was hauled to his feet.

She addressed the soldiers. 'If you're not careful, you'll both join him there.'

They bowed with pale faces, turned around and marched away with him.

As we left the baths, my mind was in torment. Being a Vestal Virgin had many benefits, including the adoration of the public, but that love quickly turned to hatred when our morals were in question, especially if men were involved. I knew I could not have had his death on my conscience, living the rest of my life knowing I hadn't intervened. For some reason, I did not want to see that dark wavy head of hair leave the broad shoulders on which it stood, but in letting him live I had now given him the

27

chance to destroy me. He could still speak of our meeting and, if he did, I would be a dead woman walking. So either I had to hope he didn't blab about meeting me or I had to find and convince him to forget that we had ever met.

IV
LUDI PECTORIS
-Games of the Heart-

I looked at him now, exiting back out through the gates of the arena. My mouth was dry. I hesitated, but I knew that this was the only chance I would likely ever get.

'Domina Occia?' I asked, turning to her.

'Yes?' she huffed, looking at me. Evidently, she wasn't pleased with Augustus' decision to let Aries saunter around with his smirking head still on his shoulders.

'May I speak to the gladiator?'

She blinked. 'Excuse me?'

'To tell him that he has been forgiven,' I said, keeping my chin up.

'Somebody else will do that,' she said dismissively. 'Or better yet, he can figure it out for himself.'

'Domina, please. I wish to carry the message personally on behalf of all the Vestals,' I pressed further. 'I would not be gone long.'

She hesitated, frowning. 'Oh, very well. Since it is your birthday, you may go.'

I grinned and curtseyed. 'Thank you.'

'You will take an armed escort,' she conditioned.

I nodded, and she asked Prefect Gnaeus, standing nearby, to accompany me with his soldiers down to the dungeons. Peering over my shoulder, I saw the other Vestals gathered, gazing at me in bewilderment.

Eight guards surrounded me, led by Prefect Gnaeus. They took me down the stone stairs, past plebeians and patricians, to the underground. A few paces further on, we entered a tunnel lit by torches. The air wreaked of blood, sweat and excrement. I was guided through noisy dungeons, past the cells of growling monsters and those of huge hulking men in armour. Their scowling eyes followed me. It was the first time I had been looked at with such deep dislike, but perhaps these poor men were beyond the point of faith.

'Here we are, domina,' the Prefect said as we approached a cell door.

The guards stood aside.

I frowned and looked around at them. 'I wish to enter.'

He chuckled. 'We cannot allow that, domina. None except the soldiers may go in.'

'None except the soldiers and I,' I insisted, glaring up at him. 'I am a Vestal Virgin, priestess of the Pontifex Maximus, Emperor Augustus. I come and go wherever I please. I do not need anyone's permission.'

He looked me up and down before nodding and bowing his head. 'Of course. Apologies.'

'Domina,' I said to him.

'Apologies, domina,' he corrected himself.

He reached for the keys at his waist and unlocked the cell door. Dragging it open, he held it as I walked inside a small room, the guards following. It was bare save for one torch burning on the wall. The gladiator was nowhere to be seen. I turned around in confusion, facing the Prefect and his men.

'He will be along in a short while,' he reassured me.

'When?' I demanded. 'I have a busy schedule to keep.'

'One cannot be sure, domina. Such unreliable creatures slaves are, especially when they have reached their baseness by criminal means,' he commented. 'Would you like to be guarded while you wait?'

I glanced at the troop of soldiers behind him. 'I will require only one of your men.'

He bowed his head. 'Please, domina, allow me the honour.'

His guards bowed before exiting the cell, closing the door behind them.

Pacing as I waited, my heart started to pound. *Oh, why did I come? I could have just summoned him instead.*

I heard the door open and spun around to see Aries being shoved inside by a guard. He stumbled into the cell, head bent, hair heavy with sweat. As he straightened up, a look of surprise passed over his face.

Prefect Gnaeus cleared his throat. 'Domina, shall I stay?'

I briefly considered his offer. I did not know Aries or what he might do. Then I realised that I could not have anyone, especially the empire's highest-ranking officer, overhear the conversation we were about to have. I shook my head, trying to seem relaxed. 'No, thank you, Prefect.'

He cast me an uncertain glance, bowed and pushed past Aries, leaving the cell.

The gladiator and I stood in silence until we both heard the door shut.

I prepared to speak, but he beat me to it. 'Aemilia,' he greeted, smiling pleasantly. 'To what do I owe the pleasure?'

I blinked, unable to answer, discommoded by his blatant refusal to acknowledge my rank.

He moved past me. 'Are you here to celebrate my win? I hope you brought wine. I daresay I deserve it.'

I frowned. 'Excuse me?'

He turned away from me and took off his blood-stained breastplate, discarding it on the floor. His tunic was stuck to his skin with sweat, revealed the muscular definition of his back. He then took that off. Thankfully, he kept his loincloth on. His sweat-soaked skin glistened under the torchlight.

'Enjoying yourself?' he chuckled, looking over his shoulder.

Indignant, I didn't reply.

'Did the games at least entertain you?' he continued, turning around to face me.

I scowled. 'No, I despise such spectacles.'

He seemed surprised as he bent to undo the cord knots of his sandals.

'But that is partly why I am here.'

'Go on.'

I cleared my throat. 'Your performance in the arena saved your life.'

'Obviously.'

I rolled my eyes. 'No, that's not what I mean. Today's games were intended to be your execution for spying on us in the baths, but since you killed the Emperor's assailant, you have been pardoned for your offences against the Vestals. You have proven your virtue.'

'Not well enough, I should think,' he grumbled. 'I'm still a slave, am I not?' He tossed his untied sandals to one side and straightened up. 'Is that it?'

I shook my head. 'No. There is one more thing.'

A cheeky glint came to his eyes. 'Oh?'

'Why were you in the baths? You had no reason to be. Vestal Valeriana was under the impression you tried to flee this fate of the games. Is it true?'

He hesitated before nodding. 'Yes, she is entirely correct,' he said as if it was obvious.

I frowned, disappointed. *Cowardice was not particularly appealing.*

'I do not ever plan to die for the pleasure of others.'

I nodded. 'Still, you fought bravely.'

'Thank you,' he scoffed. 'Now, is that all?'

My heart was beating quite fast. He was impatient to be alone, I could tell. However, there was still the matter of my reputation which at this moment was far more critical. I opened my mouth to speak, but for some reason no words came out. So I just stood there for a few moments, gaping like a fish.

Then he smirked. 'Look, as much as I hate to disappoint a lady, I am too worn out at present to continue our earlier ventures.'

Impudence! I blushed, taken aback. My hands clenched into fists at my sides. Yet somehow, his audacity gave me the courage to say what was on my mind. 'It is, in fact, the opposite I want to ensure.'

His eyebrows furrowed, confused.

I continued: 'I have reassured everyone that we did not meet alone in the baths, at all. I trust you will support this version of events since your head will be the one at stake should the truth be known.'

He smirked and slowly approached me. 'So, you want me to lie?'

Staring up at him, I stumbled backwards and felt the damp wall behind me.

'You want me to say that I never saw you in just your tunic?' He reached up and tucked a stray strand of hair back underneath my headdress.

My heart was beating fast. He was too close. With all my strength, I brought my hands up to his chest and shoved him away.

Alarmed, he lost his footing and stumbled backwards.

'I want you to forget it ever happened!' I hissed fiercely before leaving the cell as quickly as I could. My face was red hot. I cursed myself. *That didn't go to plan at all.*

'So you didn't bring any wine then?' he shouted after me.

V
CASTIMONIA
-Chastity-

Picia and I followed Occia towards the Temple of Vesta. As we went, I recalled the first time I had walked this path, eight years ago when I had just entered the Order of the Vestals. One of the first questions I had ever asked was, 'What is a virgin?' I didn't understand the term back then. I still didn't.

Occia's answer had always been the same: 'For the next thirty years, you have sworn never to let a man touch you or see you unclothed.' The only additional detail was: 'It means that a man does not have carnal knowledge of you.'

We had wrinkled our little noses in confusion. 'What does that mean?'

'You will know when you are older,' had been her reply.

She turned to us now, clasping her hands as she stood in front of the tall Temple of Vesta. 'As you well know, here we safeguard the glory of Rome.' She smiled. 'Who knows how we achieve that?'

'By keeping the Flame of Vesta burning,' Picia replied.

'Exactly! And who is Vesta?' she asked.

'Our goddess of the home and hearth,' Picia said.

'So, what does that mean for us?' the Chief Vestal inquired.

'By being her priestesses and tending to her Flame, we take care of the hearth of Rome,' I replied. 'We are the housekeepers of the empire.'

'Precisely. And how is the glory of Rome put at risk?'

'By letting the Flame die out,' I answered.

'Excellent,' she said, pleased.

'Can we see the Flame?' Picia asked, hopefully.

'Not today.' She shook her head. 'To be custodian over the Flame is one of the greatest honours ever. You will have your turn to watch over it every day when you begin your second decade of servitude. You will get enough of it, I promise you.

'In the meantime, your duty will make you rich and educated young women with the right to vote and manage your own affairs. All you must do is perform the tasks expected of you: keep the Flame of Vesta alight and, more importantly, never lose your virginity.'

*

The festival of Vestalia took place every year at midsummer, lasting just over a week. At the end, we hosted a night of festivity in the House of the Vestals. The mansion became a palace, festooned with flowers and blazing with torches. The air was thick with the aromatic scents of food and wine. It was a banquet fit for the gods, fit for Vesta.

Only the noblest in the empire had been invited to celebrate with us. The entire priesthood was there, including the Pontifex Maximus himself, Emperor Augustus, who sat at the head table. Most of the aristocracy was present and the whole imperial family of the Julian dynasty. There were musicians, poets and famous veterans who had journeyed for weeks, returning from far and wide, to be present.

The only person not there was Rufina. She was on duty, guarding the Flame this evening. However, she was the type of girl who would rather sit alone in silence than in a room crowded with drunken revellers.

'Happy Birthday, Aemilia, darling,' a voice said.

I closed my eyes, sighing in dread. There was only one person in the whole empire who had that sickly-sweet voice. Plastering a smile on my face, I shifted around in my chair to see Lavidia standing behind me. A beautiful girl from one of the noblest families in the city, like Rufina and

Val she was in her second decade of servitude, protecting the Flame and carrying out her duties which Picia and I were only learning to do. She was the sixth of the Vestal Virgins and my least favourite.

'Lavidia,' I greeted her, trying to sound happy.

She, too, wore a strained smile. Her hair was a lighter brown than any I had ever seen. Rufina was pretty sure she bleached it with lemon like prostitutes do, while Val suggested urine since it worked so well with togas. Lavidia always denied it, of course. Nevertheless, it made her the target of all gazes, as was the intention, and made the green flecks in her brown eyes glow. 'How are you?' she asked.

'Well.'

'I heard what happened.' She pouted. 'For you all to be spied on by a slave in such a place. How humiliating!' Then she looked at me, eyes widening as if she had remembered something shocking. 'I heard you begged both Occia and the Emperor not to punish him. Now, what on earth made you do that?'

I hesitated, searching for the right words. Fortunately, they came to me. 'I believed the spying was unintentional on his part; that he was simply in the wrong place at the wrong time,' I replied stiffly. 'Anyway, he showed his loyalty to Rome by avenging the Emperor's life.'

She snorted. 'I would have had him executed on the spot.'

Val, sitting to my left, joined in. 'Aemilia, at least, is merciful.'

Lavidia pursed her lips at the comment.

'But there's no need to be concerned about his fate. He's a gladiator, a slave, and will be dead within the week,' Val added.

'With the gods' blessing,' Lavidia agreed.

There was a tense silence between the three of us. I took a sip of wine from my goblet, but I barely tasted its sweetness. When I glanced down at the contents, I remembered the blood on Aries' breastplate. Val was right. Chances were that by the end of the week, he would no longer be a living, breathing, hair-flicking, smirking and thoroughly infuriating man.

'And you visited him in his cell, I heard,' Lavidia gasped, drawing a hand to her chest, feigning alarm. 'Whatever for?'

My throat closed up and I could not reply. I continued to drink and ignored her.

Luckily, Val came to my aid again. 'It was simply to reassure him that he would not be punished for any offences against us.'

'Reassure him?' Lavidia sounded horrified. 'Why would anyone feel the need to reassure a slave? A scoundrel and undoubtedly a barbarian?'

Again I had no response. My mouth was dry. I had to close my eyes. Unfortunately, that did not stop the sound of her incessant, self-righteous, nosy judgement.

'It astonishes me. I cannot deny it. Why would a Vestal need to visit such a man in his cell for that reason?'

'There were guards present,' Val interjected.

I sucked in a deep breath.

'No,' Lavidia protested, 'I heard that she dismissed them.'

Unable to bear another sound from her, I shot up from my seat and charged off through the crowd of guests, leaving the poisonous cow behind.

Val appeared at my side. 'Don't listen to her. She is just bitter. She had to watch the Flame this morning so she missed the games. That's what has crawled under her headdress.'

I didn't reply, but I knew Val was just trying to help. We made our way upstairs. There, she called for Metallia and waited with me in my bedchamber until she arrived.

'I had a lovely day, Val,' I said while taking off my headdress.

'I hope so,' she said, giving me a sad smile. 'I am sorry that rascal ruined it.'

'He only added to the excitement. You promised me an eventful day and you did not disappoint.'

'Well, I hardly planned his part in it,' she giggled. 'Did you notice how handsome he was?'

'Indeed. Very good-looking,' I said casually, trying not to blush at the memory of his face or his hair or his eyes.

'Are we allowed to admit that?' she asked me.

I frowned. 'I'm not sure.'

She raised an eyebrow. 'Surely, if everyone agrees that someone is handsome would that not make it fact instead of opinion?'

I shrugged. 'I do not know.'

'I think all women should be able to observe and recognise that some men just have Venus' blessing without being accused of thinking anything improper,' she laughed.

I smiled too.

'Looking, but no touching,' she added.

At that moment, Metallia entered the room, curtseying to us both before moving over to help with my hair.

Val walked towards the door. 'And the same applies for the men too.'

I hardly slept that night as my guilt began to grow. My mind churned with her words. He might have only seen me in my tunic, but there wasn't much else left to the imagination as far as I saw it. He had looked. He had touched. And I had let him.

*

'From the Emperor!' Occia announced, waving a small scroll in the air. She had summoned the Vestals, except Val who had taken her turn to guard the Flame this morning, to the atrium.

We assembled to hear what the great Caesar Augustus had written.

She unrolled the parchment and read it out to us. 'Dearest Vestals, who protect the empire daily with their virtue,' she began, smiling, 'tomorrow, a handful of slaves will be sent as a gift to you all. They are a reward for your wonderful work during Vestalia. Thank you, as always, for your dedication to your duties. They keep the glory of Rome everlasting. Bless you and farewell, Caesar.'

'Oh, Vesta,' Picia gasped in delight. 'Presents!'

'Well, we deserve them as he said,' Lavidia pointed out, smirking.

'I daresay some of us do.' I shot her a glare.

'Now, now, girls,' Occia scolded, struggling not to beam at the Emperor's message. 'Let us be humble. We do our work with devotion, but we must not forget to thank the gods for aiding us in our endeavours.'

'Yes, of course, domina,' Rufina agreed.

'What kind of slaves?' Lavidia inquired.

'I do not know anything except what I have just announced,' Occia replied. 'But there will probably be a mixture of skills and backgrounds. Anyone can be a slave, you know.'

'Excuse me?' Lavidia interrupted, her tone alarmed. 'Forgive me, domina. Do you mean some of them will be barbarians?'

'Why? Is that a problem?' Occia asked. 'They are just slaves.'

'We have always bought Roman slaves who have loyalty to the empire and our work,' she explained. 'Foreigners do not have such enlightened understanding and sympathies.'

'Will they be able to understand us?' Picia wanted to know. 'Will they speak Latin?'

'I do not know, girls,' Occia replied, exasperated. 'But please remember that these slaves will be a gift from the Emperor himself. We will not raise any objections about what they look like or where they come from, for he will have selected them. Furthermore, slaves are more inclined to be loyal if they have kind masters or they might maliciously spread rumours of sin, and we wouldn't want that, would we? So, there will be no more protests concerning the Emperor's very generous gift. When they arrive, you will all show gratitude no matter what.'

*

'It's a bad idea,' Rufina flustered, pacing around the records' room. 'Introducing barbarians here. What better way to put our lives at risk! At least Roman slaves would have some sense of patriotism and respect for us.' She flopped down onto a recliner and put a hand on her forehead.

'Do not bother yourself with worry. Your opinion hardly matters anyway,' Val said, reclining on a couch, but she couldn't keep a concerned frown off her face. She had long since been back from tending the Flame and had been informed of all the happenings that morning.

'I shouldn't have to be kind to a barbarian!' Rufina exclaimed, getting to her feet again. 'Why should I when they have waged war and uprisings around the empire for centuries?' She threw her hands up in the air.

'Rufina, watch what you say,' Val hissed, looking between her and me. 'There is no need to associate every foreigner with ill fortune.'

The older girl glanced at me and seemed to remember herself, stammering awkwardly, 'Oh, Aemilia. I'm sorry. I forgot.'

I smiled. 'It's alright. I understand.'

'Anyway, you'll have to be kind to them or they'll claim you've neglected your duties,' Val reminded her.

'Or let the Flame of Vesta go out,' Picia chimed.

'Or have broken your vow of chastity,' I added.

Rufina blushed.

Suddenly, Lavidia swept into the room. 'Did I hear the word 'chastity'? What good timing! Aemilia,' she said, approaching me.

I turned to face her.

'I hope you don't mind. I informed Occia earlier today that your dealings with that gladiator might warrant an inspection.' Her eyes were big and bright.

I froze. Her words took a moment to settle in as goosebumps appeared on my skin. 'Excuse me?' I gasped.

'You did what?' Val snapped, crossing the room towards us.

'Now, now.' Lavidia smiled sweetly. 'There's no need to be like that. It's just a simple inspection, that's all. A trip to the Emperor, a few check-ups and that's it.'

'I have done nothing wrong.' My voice was weak. I felt winded.

She giggled. 'That's for the Emperor to decide.'

'What possible dealings could Aemilia have had?' Picia asked.

Lavidia donned an expression as if the answer was obvious. 'She sought a private audience with a gladiator in his holding cell after the games - the very slave who spied on you all in the baths that morning.' She raised an eyebrow. 'Does that not strike you as odd?'

'How dare you! I am innocent,' I insisted.

Her pompous and confident expression didn't budge, as if it was made of stone. Her eyes landed back on me. 'Aemilia, I would hate for one of us to act dishonourably, betray everyone, disobey the gods and undermine our most noble priesthood. By insulting Vesta, it would place the glory of Rome at risk.' Her voice dropped to a whisper as she leant in. 'I am just making sure.'

'You should have saved yourself the trouble,' I hissed.

She batted her eyelids and showed me her pearly white teeth. 'If you have nothing to fear, dearest Aemilia, surely you will not have a problem complying with an inspection. It is for everyone's sake. You should be thanking me. I will stop at nothing to ensure the safety of the empire.'

Then she turned to us all. 'Now, one of you lot should go the temple. My turn for guarding the Flame is over.' Giving me one last slimy smile, she departed the room.

Val snorted once the door had closed. 'She will stop at nothing to be a lying, scheming bitch.'

'Val!' Rufina exclaimed in horror. 'Save us the vulgarity, please.'

'This whole situation is vulgar,' she argued. Then she turned to me. 'Do not despair. Occia knows how that cow loves to create trouble.'

'Anyway, we believe you,' Picia added.

I tried to smile, despite the dread within. 'Thank you.' I glanced at Rufina, who stood with pursed lips, avoiding my gaze.

'Don't you believe Aemilia?' Val asked her.

Rufina hesitated. 'Why did you seek the private audience with him?'

'I told you why. I wished to thank him for slaying Augustus' assailant.' I tried to seem as sincere as possible. 'He showed so much patriotism to the state, even after we had threatened his life, that I felt it was owed.'

Rufina nodded in thought. Then, at last, she spoke. 'Aemilia, I don't understand why you would risk being seen alone with a man, even if he was a slave, instead of just summoning him, but I don't believe you have committed any crime. You have never given anyone cause to suspect you of sin, Occia included.' Then she smiled. 'And what is more, the Emperor dotes on you.'

Picia burst into giggles.

I snorted, 'I would hardly say that.'

She shrugged. 'You impressed the old man with your talk of loyalty and the Fates.'

'Rufina!' Val gasped. 'Did you just call Emperor Augustus an old man?'

Laughter echoed from the records' room.

*

After cena, we were walking towards our bedchambers when out of nowhere Picia asked, 'I still don't understand. What did Lavidia mean by 'dealings'? What are dealings?'

'She was implying that I had lost my chastity,' I replied, stiffly.

'Really? How?'

I shrugged. 'I'm not quite certain.'

Rufina spoke up from behind us. 'It's when one has sex for the first time.'

'Sex? What is that?' Picia pressed.

'We will all be told in time,' was her reply. 'Apparently.'

We stopped outside Picia's room. After sharing a glance with Rufina, I bent slightly and pecked Picia on the cheek.

She retired into her room, appearing satisfied with the response. 'Goodnight, girls!' she called over her shoulder, closing the door.

'Look at her go,' I murmured. 'Satisfied that one day her questions will be answered.'

'I am too. You cannot say the same for yourself?' Rufina asked me.

'I don't know,' I said. 'It makes little sense to me that the matter of an unchaste Vestal is so serious to warrant its punishment yet they do not tell us what it involves.'

'Well, keep that opinion to yourself,' she advised, lowering her voice. 'And don't repeat it in public. We don't need any misinterpretations.'

However, that night, I couldn't sleep. Despite the reassurances of my friends, I was not convinced that Occia wouldn't send me for an inspection. I tossed and turned until morning came. After my lessons, I approached Occia as she was dozing in a room off the atrium away from the heat of the midday sun. I knocked gently on the door.

She opened her eyes, looking at me with surprise. 'Aemilia, what can I do for you?'

I cleared my throat. 'There is something I wish to ask you, domina.'

She sat up straighter, ready to listen. 'Go on.'

I entered. 'Lavidia said she spoke to you yesterday and asked you to have me inspected because I met with that gladiator in his cell?'

She smiled kindly at me. 'My dear, don't fret. I see no reason to have you inspected.'

Relieved, I exhaled loudly. 'Thank you.' Pausing, I queried, 'May I know why not?'

She shrugged. 'I trust that after the upbringing you have had here you know how to conduct yourself. Besides, you were not gone long enough.'

I frowned. 'Long enough for what?'

'Long enough to break your vow.'

'I see,' I replied, nodding slowly, but I didn't. *There was a timespan?*

Then, deciding it was an apt moment to do so, I took a deep breath and said, 'Domina, on that note, some of my friends and I would like to understand what breaking our vow entails?'

Her face darkened.

I was quick to explain myself. 'As important as it is for us to be chaste, we have not been told how to ensure that we always are. We know that it involves a man having carnal knowledge of a woman. But -' I broke off, searching for the right words.

'What is carnal knowledge?' she finished for me. I nodded, relieved she understood what I was trying to say. 'I know it seems illogical, but it is better for all concerned to leave that question unanswered, my dear.'

I looked down, unable to hide my disappointment. I had been foolish to hope for a more transparent response. 'Of course, domina. My apologies.'

'You are brave to ask. Curiosity is natural, but ignorance has always been the best policy here. As my predecessor put it: 'If a Vestal is unaware, she will never dare.' One day, you will be old enough to understand and will be told the truth,' she said, smiling reassuringly.

'Yes, I see that.' I did not, but I knew it would be unwise to press the matter further.

'Good.' She leaned back, seemingly satisfied. Then she frowned. 'You girls should not be discussing such a subject.' Her frown deepened into a scowl. 'Fetch the other Vestals to the atrium immediately.'

I walked away, cursing myself. I should have just listened to Rufina. *What did I just do?*

*

'What did you say?' Val demanded.

'I cannot remember!' I said, flustered.

'I swear on all the gods,' Lavidia snarled, towering over me, 'if you get me into trouble for this -'

'She will not,' Val interjected. 'It is not a crime to ask questions.'

Lavidia glared at her. 'It is if one is a Vestal Virgin and if the questions are about sex!'

'Are we all going to be inspected?' Picia asked worriedly.

'Of course not,' I reassured her, but my words were simply not enough. Looking around, it was clear that no one was convinced.

'If I am inspected, I will have you horsewhipped,' Lavidia hissed at me, seething with rage.

'Lavidia!' Val scolded her.

She turned to face her. 'Oh, don't get so high and mighty with me. You think you are so perfect!' Lavidia spat at her. 'When in reality you are not. You are just as culpable as the rest of us.'

'I have done nothing wrong,' Val whispered. 'Neither has Aemilia.'

'We are going to be late,' Picia reminded us.

We turned towards the atrium, dreading every step.

All the Vestals, except for Rufina who had eagerly gone to tend the Flame of Vesta earlier today, stood there.

'Ladies,' she began, clasping her hands. She did not look pleased, speaking in a sharp tone. 'You all know your vow of chastity and your duty to keep the Flame of Vesta alight. You all know the punishments if these are not honoured. And you should be grateful. For womankind, there is no better position than a Vestal. You have privileges as would befit the imperial family. Your lives of luxury are the envy of all.'

Her frown softened. 'But the conditions for such a life are also simple. You are here for thirty years at least and each decade serves a different purpose. First, as initiates, students, you learn what your duties are and how to perform them. Afterwards, in your second decade, you carry them out as custodians of the Flame. Finally, you pass on your knowledge and wisdom to the newest members in your last decade.

'Then you have the choice of living a normal life like other Roman women, with marriage and children, or you can remain a Vestal, like me, and I am in my forty-seventh year of servitude. But, as long as you are Vestals, you are required to be chaste. Your virginity represents the health and safety of this empire. The Flame of Vesta represents the glory of Rome. Is that not easy enough to understand?'

We nodded.

She sighed. 'I know many of you have questions about what exactly it is to be chaste and what is involved in breaking your vow. But such queries will be answered when you are ready and that moment will be decided by either the Emperor or me. It may even turn out that you will not be told until you are free from servitude and choose to wed. A Vestal must not just be pure with regards to her body. It must also concern her mind. Thus the truth is best kept from her.' Then she smiled. 'Patience is a virtue and ignorance can be blissful. You should consider yourself wedded to Vesta, to her teachings and to your duty to protect Rome and yourselves.' She shrugged. 'It truly is that easy.'

Lavidia raised a hand. 'In light of this reminder, will inspections be taking place?'

I cursed her silently. *She wanted me gone, didn't she?*

'No,' Occia said, shaking her head. 'None have acted suspiciously. But no more questions about it from now on. Let us not dwell on what we should not. It would not end well.'

VI
INTERROGATIO
-The Question-

The grove was quiet, save for the birds chirping. The morning sun shone through the green treetops, and short grass tickled my feet where my sandals failed to cover them. Apart from the strain of stretching my arms up to reach for the fruits above, plucking oranges was my favourite chore of the summer months. I savoured the silent solace. It gave me the chance to enjoy the nature around me, the birdsong and the sunshine.

'Vestal Aemilia?' a man's voice interrupted.

I jumped around in surprise.

It was Prefect Gnaeus.

My eyes widened, and I put down the basket of freshly picked oranges which I had been holding. I saw that we were the only two standing amongst the trees. I shifted on my feet and put on a smile. 'Prefect, you startled me.'

He bowed shortly. 'Apologies, domina.'

'If you are looking for the Chief Vestal, she is probably in her study,' I told him.

He shook his head. 'I wished to speak to you, domina.'

'Oh?' I asked, smiling more genuinely now. Admittedly, I was flattered. I was used to people preferring to spend their time with the older priestesses. 'Well, I am all ears. Would you like to have our audience inside?' I gestured to the house, the roof of which could just be seen over the crowns of the orange trees.

'Let us remain here,' he said firmly, nodding. 'It is more private.'

Private? 'As you wish.'

He didn't seem to be listening as he spotted the basket at my feet. He approached and bent to pick one up.

'Are these any good?' Before I could answer he grabbed one and, with a loud chomping sound, took an enormous bite straight out of it, rind and all. A beam spread across his face. 'They are delicious,' he praised through his rather full mouth.

I glanced down at the basket, the only barrier separating us, and then back at his face. 'I am glad you like them.'

He chewed, juice dribbling over his lips and seeping into his beard. The bitten orange in his hand drenched his large fingers.

I couldn't help the rising feeling of disgust and discomfort within me.

'Anyway, it seemed to be a great waste killing that gladiator,' he said slurping noisily.

I raised my eyebrows. 'Who?' *Aries? A wave of queasy grief lurched in my stomach. Was he dead already?*

'The one who was slain in the games. We all saw it a few days ago.'

'Ah,' I realised with relief. He meant the Goth. 'Well, he did make an attempt on the Emperor's life,' I reasoned.

He hummed. 'I understand, but the amount of money spent on training gladiators is no small matter.'

I blushed. 'Oh. Yes, I suppose.'

'I think it shows poor judgement on the Emperor's part,' he murmured aloud, squinting up at the tops of the orange trees. 'He should have executed the one who killed him. That one was badly-trained, in my opinion.'

'You believe that the Emperor was wrong to let his saviour get away with killing his attacker?'

'Yes. He should have waited for imperial permission before doing it, as is customary.'

I tilted my head. 'Are you criticising the Emperor's decision?'

He chewed slower and stared at me. 'No, just questioning it. If I had been in charge, I would not have let it slide.'

'You mean if you were Emperor?' I asked, now even warier. 'Prefect, that implication could seem treasonous.' I tried for a light-hearted laugh. It was hardly comforting hearing those words coming from Augustus' head bodyguard.

'You won't tell on me, will you?' he chuckled.

He spat his coloured saliva at my cheek.

I cringed, taken aback.

He stopped laughing, his dark grey eyes moving to my face. He raised a rough hand and touched my skin, wiping away the spittle with his thumb.

I did my best not to recoil, feeling a shiver run up my spine. My heart began to pound quickly. *What in Jupiter's name was he doing?*

Suddenly his hand dropped. 'Will you marry when your servitude is over?' he asked me, his tone light yet his gaze was serious.

'Excuse me?' I asked, eyebrows shooting up.

'Your service doesn't last your whole lifetime,' he pointed out.

I gulped. 'Indeed. I have many years to think about marriage. Twenty-two to be exact.'

He nodded. 'I expect I'll have had many more wives by then. I've already gone through two.'

I couldn't keep the shock off my face, but he didn't seem to notice.

'I want at least one of them to be a Vestal at some point. There are many benefits from such an alliance, not least the wealth.' He smirked. 'Aside from that, I want a wife who understands discipline, restraint, hard work, important matters and keeps her promises. I see no better candidates than those in the House of the Vestals.' He drew back. 'If you do not wish to accept my offer, I will make it to the others.'

'What offer?' I squeaked.

'To become my wife, the wife of the Prefect of the Praetorian Guard.' He smiled smugly and bopped my nose as if my shock amused him. 'You will have a lavish house and all you could ever want.' He raised his eyebrows, looking at me expectantly.

I spluttered at his speech.

He scowled. 'Are you laughing at me? After such a request? An offer of marriage will not likely come around again.'

'Of course not,' I replied, trying to overcome my astonishment. 'This is simply a surprise.' *A great one.*

He nodded, but was still frowning.

'There are things which I feel we must both consider, if I may.' I thought quickly. 'First of all, as Augustus is the guardian of the Vestals, you would need to ask his permission. And why arrange it now? I have only been a Vestal for eight years. I have two decades more to go before I am free to wed, and by then I will most likely be unable to have children.'

He scoffed. 'Divorce is easy. Marriage is an investment. So when the opportunity presents itself, I see no point in not securing the arrangement. And don't fret your pretty head about children – I do not think I will need any more. I already have enough now.'

Aghast, I had to protest. 'Prefect, we have just met!'

'I know you are the daughter of Aemilius Valerius Faustus, a great soldier in his day. Were his whereabouts known I would ask him directly for your hand.'

I blushed at the mention of my father. He was still famous decades later. 'Thank you. I will consider your offer seriously.'

'When might I expect your reply?' He tapped the handle of his sword.

I coughed nervously. 'I will need some time. An offer of marriage has never been made to me before.'

He smiled confidently and picked up my hand, kissing it firmly, the bristles of his beard scratching along my skin.

I forced a smile.

'Thank you, Vestal Aemilia. I look forward to hearing from you soon.'

He dumped the half-eaten orange back into the basket, its juices and his saliva seeping over the other oranges, through the reeds and onto the leafy ground underneath. Then he sauntered out of the grove.

Dumbfounded and utterly devoid of rational thinking, I made my way towards the house, carrying the now sticky basket and stumbling over fallen logs. I was stunned.

When I entered, I saw some Vestals in the atrium, including Occia who stood in front of a large band of men and women. I faltered as heads turned my way. *What was happening? Did I miss something?*

'Aemilia,' Occia greeted. 'Do join us. The Emperor's gift has arrived.'

I came forward, joining Rufina, Val and Picia, and looked at the new slaves. They were all dressed differently, some in rags and others in togas. They were of every age, size and complexion. Those who were clearly barbarians stood out by their oddly coloured eyes, hair or skin.

Occia addressed us all. 'As you recall, these slaves are a gift from Emperor Augustus for our work during the festival of Vestalia,' she announced, clasping her hands together. 'I trust you will all treat them with the utmost kindness and graciousness, not just because they are gifted to us by our most holy Emperor, but because of a Vestal's natural gentleness towards her inferiors.

'There are many different types of slaves, as you can see.' She gestured to them. 'Some may be knowledgeable and can help with the education of the initiates. Others may be suited to more manual labour. But many will just be house slaves, fit to fetch and carry. Any questions?'

As she finished speaking, my eyes landed on another pair across the room. They were a deep dark brown with a glint, smirking at me, unmistakably familiar.

My heart jumped in surprise, and perhaps a glimmer of delight, as Aries Gloriosus Iovis gazed back at me.

VII
PRECATIOQUE QUAESTIO
-A Prayer and a Problem-

The dead dove lay limp in my hands. Trying not to stare at the dark red blood seeping through its feathers onto my skin, I held it in front of the altar, our shrine to Vesta. I knelt before it, shifting uncomfortably on the stone floor. The altar lay in a small room off the atrium, dimly lit by the sun's light against the red-painted walls. I closed my eyes and began to pray.

'Caught you,' a male voice said.

I jumped in fright, my contemplation broken, and turned to look over my shoulder. It was Aries. *Of course, it was Aries! Why was he everywhere?*

A flurry of possible insults with which I could attack him flew through my mind at once, but I decided to be civil. 'A successful gladiator suddenly finds himself a mere house slave. Tell me, how does that happen?'

'Good fortune?' he suggested.

I raised an eyebrow.

He shrugged. 'I know not. This morning I was taken from my bed, not to the training arena, but to a cartload of other slaves headed for here. Why? Do you have a problem with it?'

I grunted, unimpressed, 'You can count on it.' I turned back to the altar. 'Leave me. I am praying. I do not require you now.'

His sandals scuffed the floor, heading further into the room. 'A slave must be there for his master or mistress, even unnecessarily. Besides, what if I require your help?'

I huffed, rolling my eyes, and looked back at him. *Maybe if I entertained him, he would leave eventually.* 'Then say it. What do you want?'

He approached and leant against the wall beside me. 'Spiritual guidance,' came his reply, softer this time. A deep dimple lay in his clean-shaven cheek.

I snorted in dry laughter. 'Then you should seek out an augur or other priest. I may be a Vestal, but I am not obliged nor trained to give such instruction. I am only an initiate, a newcomer.'

'The other house slaves say you have been here for eight years. I would have thought that long enough,' he remarked.

'Well, unless you are the Pontifex Maximus, that opinion means nothing,' I snapped back.

He glanced at my hands and raised his eyebrows. 'I am very certain that the bird is already dead, Aemilia. Any other life you could squeeze out has utterly vanished.'

I looked down and saw my white knuckles locking the bird's corpse in a fierce grip. I let go of it entirely, dropping it on the altar, mumbling, 'Sorry.' Then I scowled, getting to my feet. 'I do not have to apologise to you. You do not get to tell me what to do and I certainly do not have to obey - quite the reverse. Furthermore, never address me by my personal name alone. You must call me domina or Vestal.'

He raised an eyebrow at me, with that dimple still digging into his tanned cheek. 'What has made you so annoyed with me, Vestal Aemilia? We got on so well the previous times we met.'

'Then I see you did not listen when I told you to forget them.'

He stepped forward. 'How could I? You have not.'

He raised his hand as if to touch my cheek, but I slapped it away. He jumped back, staring at me in surprise.

'Do not touch me!' I hissed.

Footsteps moved towards the room. In the crack of light under the door, I saw a shadow approaching. I heard my pounding pulse against my chest. Then the sound of the footsteps shrunk away.

Aries touched my wrist.

I looked at him, holding my hand in an almost reassuring way.

His smirk had entirely disappeared. 'Why are you so terrified?'

I pulled myself away from him. 'Why are you not? You have attacked me. You have touched me. And you have seen me with barely any clothes on! I do not know what you want from me, but if you think you can get away with it then you are dreadfully mistaken.'

He stared at me in shock. 'I do not want anything from you,' he claimed, sounding offended.

'Yet you behave in this way? You must have a death wish,' I snapped.

Perhaps it was the rosy light in the room or maybe he did indeed blush.

Victory washed over me and I pushed past him, returning to the altar. 'You want spiritual guidance? Here it is. Don't touch me or speak to me unless invited to do so. That way, we both get to keep our heads.'

I knelt, squeezing my eyes shut and refusing to hear an answer, but he didn't say anything. Nevertheless, I felt his eyes on me. Blocking him out, I prayed, trying to let the anger leave me.

I found Vesta in candle-fire and the blood of a dove, imagining myself kneeling before her at her hearth and confessing to what I had done, and to what Aries had done also. I envisioned begging her forgiveness and receiving it, then standing and turning away from the flames.

When I came back to reality, I looked up to see that Aries was gazing out of the window. 'I have prayed that we both be forgiven,' I let him know, my voice hoarse. 'You for whatever crimes you have committed, and me for my sins.'

He didn't acknowledge my words.

I wondered if he was listening at all.

His gaze seemed to reach over the top of the city to the mountains beyond.

I stood up and spoke more clearly. 'Where are you from?'

He glanced at me, no emotion on his face. 'Here.'

I blinked in surprise. It made sense now: the lack of a foreign accent, a cultured one if anything. 'Rome? So you should know the ways of our Order.'

'I get the general gist, domina,' he said, turning to me, 'but not the specifics.'

'You have no right to know the specifics. No one outside of the Order does,' I told him. 'Common knowledge is more than enough. So do I need to explain why you cannot treat me like you are?'

He chuckled, but there was no humour in his face. 'Do not speak to me as if I was a child.'

'Well then take this seriously.'

He huffed, exasperated, running a hand through his hair. 'Forgive me. I forgot my place. I apologise.' His tone was sarcastic.

'Do not do so if it is of no value,' I said, slightly hurt at his lack of empathy.

He made no reply, looking away again and clenching his jaw.

I huffed, frustrated. 'What reason have you given me to trust you? You must understand that in this place even the slightest conversation with or about a man is regarded with suspicion. There is danger everywhere. Many would try to kill the Vestals to put Rome at risk. Many more would do the same simply to create trouble.'

'I would never wish to put you in peril,' he said, still not looking at me.

'Pardon?' My voice was tiny.

He turned to me. 'You heard me.'

'You shouldn't stare,' I murmured, looking down again. My cheeks felt aflame and I cursed myself.

'Easier said than done.'

He approached me until he was less than an arm's length away. I felt the air move when he breathed, yet, I could not say it was too close for comfort. Everything was mute save for my heartbeat. All I could see, as I looked up into his gaze, was cocoa brown. I was trapped.

A cheeky glint came to his eyes. 'You can breathe now.'

That broke the spell. I blinked and stepped away from him. Thankfully the gods did not leave me voiceless. 'Why do you constantly have to turn me into a joke?' I demanded.

His laughter died, his smile dropping at my words.

Before he could even search for a suitable reply, I turned away, infuriated and insulted. I left the room, head muddled. My eyes began to sting and my lower lip trembled. I felt a dull ache in my forehead as I went out into the atrium where the slaves and Vestals were still gathered. I ascended the staircase and went directly to my bedchamber.

The moment I shut the door, I couldn't hold back the tears any longer. My face crumpled as I bent my head into my raised hands, weeping. At some point amidst the tears I made my way over to my bed. There, I sobbed silently into the fabric, digging my fingers into the linen and hugging the cushions.

Then, as I heard the door creak open, I remembered the one problem with privacy in the House of the Vestals: it doesn't exist.

VIII
DUBITATIO
-Uncertainty-

Val's face poked around the door. 'Aemilia?'
I raised my head from the bed, aware that my hair was everywhere and my face was probably blotchy and red. 'Good afternoon.' I sat up.

She hesitated. 'I have come to fetch you. It is your turn to draw water from the spring.'

I wiped my cheeks and eyes. 'Oh, yes. So it is.'

'What happened?' she asked softly, coming to kneel down before me.

I looked at my hands, considering telling her, but I knew it would be too risky.

'We've been like sisters for nearly a decade now. You can trust me,' she said gently. 'What's troubling you?'

I slumped, sighing. 'It is nothing. I was merely thinking about all that has happened.'

She frowned. 'Oh?'

I shook my head. 'I do not know how I feel.'

She waited patiently.

I thought carefully, looking warily at her. 'What do you think of them?'

She seemed caught off guard by the question. Her eyes searched the air beside my head, in thought, before returning to mine. 'The slaves? They are new assets.' She shrugged. 'I cannot help feeling some will be troublesome.'

'How do you think they perceive us?' I shifted uncomfortably.

'Should we care? Yes, we have to be kind to them, but we don't actually have to worry about them or what they think,' she giggled, trying to lighten the mood.

I paused and, trying to sound nonchalant, asked, 'Val, what would you do if advances were made towards you?'

She pulled back in horror. 'I would tell Occia immediately and have the man executed!'

'But what if you found you began to like him in return?' I did not look at her face. I did not want to see her reaction.

I heard her silence, her hesitation.

'Aemilia, this talk is dangerous,' she whispered.

My heart clattered in sudden panic. *It wasn't worth the risk.* 'I know, I'm sorry. Forget I asked.' I stood up.

She got to her feet quickly as well. 'Wait, let me answer.'

I tried to seem calm while she thought of what to say.

'Feelings are natural,' she began. 'The gods have them too. They are a result of having hearts. So, you are allowed to feel attraction, but as a Vestal you must not let it determine your actions. For us, pursuing any man is cause for disaster.'

I nodded. She was right. *What was I thinking?*

Then her face darkened further. 'Why do you ask? What happened?'

'Nothing,' I replied quickly.

'Aemilia, I know when you are lying.' When I didn't reply, stuck for words, she sighed. 'Fine, do not tell me yet, but do when you are ready.' She was about to turn away, but then stopped herself and took a sideways glance at me. 'Is it a slave who has made advances towards you?'

I froze, unblinking, staring at her.

'It is,' she said, with widening eyes, her voice quiet. 'Oh, Aemilia. No Roman woman in her right mind would pursue a slave.'

'No,' I croaked and cleared my throat. 'It is the Prefect of the Praetorian Guard, Gnaeus.'

She put her hands on her hips and looked at me carefully. 'Really? Oh. Well, you can't execute him!'

Although her comment made me smile, I couldn't relax under the sense that I was lying. *Prefect Gnaeus may have made advances, but had not Aries as well?* I clasped my clammy hands. 'He wants me to marry him once my servitude ends, but …', I trailed off, trying to find the right words. 'The conversation was quite uncomfortable.'

She listened carefully and hummed thoughtfully. 'Well, it is a good match, Aemilia, even if it is over two decades away. There is no point in denying it,' she said and approached me, cupping my cheeks, 'but don't give him anything, not even an empty promise, and do not let him scare you. No man has the right to make a Vestal uncomfortable.' She gave me a smug smile. 'He can just wait to be graced with your answer.' She patted my arm. 'If a man truly believes you are worth it, he will wait however long it takes.'

I couldn't help but smile. 'Thank you,' I whispered, pulling her in for a tight hug.

She kissed my cheek and broke the embrace. 'Now, you really must go to the spring before it gets too dark.'

We burst into relieved giggles and, after fixing my dishevelled appearance, she grabbed my hand and pulled me from the bedchamber.

*

'Dusk is no time for a young lady to be outside,' Aries' voice said as his hand landed on the rim of the amphora.

Looking up, I saw him standing over me, a dark silhouette against the rosy evening and the setting sun. The crescent moon on the other side of the sky was reflected in his dark eyes. I was sitting on the rocky bank of a trickling stream at the base of the Palatine Hill, a distance not too far to walk from the House of the Vestals.

I sighed, tired of his presence. It was too late for me to work up the strength to have another spat with him. Still, some annoyance at his cheekiness brewed within me.

'What about a young lady revered throughout the world who is constantly escorted by her guards?' I pointed to the troop of soldiers standing a little further off, observing our interaction.

He withdrew his hand from the amphora as he caught sight of them. That dimple flashed in his cheek before he looked at me again, eyes twinkling. 'I think that it only takes one man to attack such a woman.'

'Yet several to fend him off, which I have, and a watery grave for his cadaver, which I also possess.' I gestured to the stream by which I sat.

'What a dark turn of phrase.'

I huffed, worn out. 'I am not in a good mood.'

He glanced down at his sandals. 'If I have angered you, I apologise.'

'Since when did you care about how I feel? Every moment I have been with you, I have not been happy. Who gave you the right to strut in here, saying and doing what you please? Why are you even here?' I asked wearily.

'I told you before: I do not know why. I did not choose to be here. Slaves don't have that luxury.' His brown gaze seemed sincere.

I narrowed my eyes. 'Nevertheless, you seem rather positive.'

He ran a hand through his hair. 'There is too much to be negative about in this life.'

I rolled my eyes and looked away.

'I confess that once I realised you were here, matters began to look up.'

My mouth parted as I looked at him. *Excuse me?*

'I enjoy your conversation, Vestal Aemilia. It is always rather exciting, especially our meeting at the games,' he said, raising an eyebrow.

I scowled. 'You enjoy my conversation yet you don't listen to a word I say. All I wanted, at the games, was to persuade you not to use what happened in the baths against me.'

'I endangered both our lives. I am sorry for that.' Then he smiled reassuringly. 'And I wouldn't have told anyone. We could blackmail and threaten each other until our dying days, but I have no intention of that. I never have. I meant what I said.'

'About what?'

'About not wishing to put your life at risk. You're exceptional.'

I couldn't fight a smile. 'Don't flirt or flatter.'

He shrugged. 'I merely observe and state facts.'

I bit the insides of my hot, smiling cheeks. 'How am I exceptional?'

'You care,' he said. 'Anyway, it's rather charming when you're annoyed with me.'

I snorted in laughter, despite myself, but I resisted the urge to let his compliments placate me too much. 'This must stop. Nothing good will come of it. I could be forced to have you removed for both our sakes.'

'Indeed. We wouldn't want that,' he said.

Suddenly I realised how close we were, sitting by a trickling spring in the dark evening, close enough to hold each other. For a moment I wondered if the only thing stopping us was the watchful guard nearby. Worried they might be able to hear us, I stood up, breaking the proximity and attempting to end the conversation.

He got to his feet as well. The smirk was gone, but starlight twinkled in his eyes. 'Allow me to carry that in for you.' He gestured to the amphora in my arms.

I smiled at his chivalry. 'No, thank you. I know it's large and heavy, but I'm practising because in time, I will have to do it nearly every day, not that it's a huge burden. It's a blessing. Vestals retain the right not to have to use water from the city supply. We have been given our own private source here - one of many privileges.'

He chuckled. 'Is there anything you're not entitled to?'

'Men,' I said bluntly. 'We must not think about them, talk about them or feel for them. If we do, we're dead.'

IX
DISCEPTATIO ET DECRETUM
-A Debate and a Decision-

Servitude had never been an issue within the House of the Vestals. The priestesses served the goddess while the slaves and guards served us. Everyone knew their place. Everything moved in perfect sequence every day.

At mealtimes, the slaves' task was to serve and taste everything for us. In my first days here, Val had risen from her couch and glided over to me, kneeling and giggling, 'They are just philistines. How can they possibly know the difference between poisoned wine and any other kind?'

Tonight's dinner, however, was different. Aries disrupted the entire process. It was clear that he had never served before. He was terrible at it. He did not let any other slaves set food down on my table. Nearly every moment I leant forward to take a piece of meat or fruit, his hand appeared out of nowhere, fingers brushing off my arm, to snatch it out of my reach before offering it to me, himself, sometimes even on bended knee.

The other Vestals simply thought he was being overly attentive, amused by his displays yet impressed at his dedication; even Occia spared him a pleased sideways glance.

I knew, though, that he was just teasing me, making fun of the other slaves and daring me to scold him in front of everyone. By all the gods in existence, I swear I tried to control my blushes. These were not hot flattered flushes, but those of embarrassment. With everyone staring, the peace was filled with panic.

When we retired for the night, we walked down the corridor, and he rushed past me and opened the door to my bedchamber, with a mighty low-sweeping bow. I passed him and went inside, but when I turned around he was there, closing the door behind him.

'What in the name of Vesta are you doing?' I demanded, shocked that he had dared to enter my private space.

He blinked, expression unmoving. 'I thought you might need some help getting ready for bed.'

I didn't believe him for a second. He was just seizing an opportunity. *To hurt me? No. To get close to me? Maybe.* I had no reason to suspect his bad character, but I still didn't trust him.

Thankfully, to my good fortune, the door swung open and Metallia walked in. Aries' head flung around as he took a giant step back from me. They froze at the sight of each other before turning their eyes back on me.

'Domina?' Metallia asked, her voice quivering.

'No need,' I told Aries, offering him my most triumphant smile. 'Help had already been arranged long before you ever arrived.'

A startled glint shone in his eyes, but that smirk only grew.

Metallia moved towards me, clutching her utensil box in her hands. She looked Aries up and down. 'Forgive me, domina,' she said, dropping a curtsey. 'I should have knocked.'

I smiled at her. 'A mere mistake, Metallia. Do not fret.' I turned around and allowed her to reach up to undo my outfit.

She had begun to unwrap me before we both realised that Aries was still standing there. She scowled at him. 'Leave. It is no place for a male slave to see a Vestal unclothed.'

He tightened his jaw, scowling. 'Forgive me, but I only obey orders from my mistress, herself.'

'Go,' I told him. 'Metallia is right.'

'Nothing I haven't seen before,' he muttered with a clipped tone before bowing, giving me one last emotionless stare.

In shock, I watched him leave the room.

When he had closed the door behind him, Metallia turned to look at me, giggling nervously. 'What did that mean?'

Clenching my jaw, I turned around. 'Ignore him.'

Finally, in my nightdress, I climbed into bed after she had left the room and had drawn the veils over the large windows. When I was nearly ready to blow out my candle, the bedroom door opened, and Aries stepped inside again.

I gasped, lifting the blankets up to cover myself. 'What are you doing?' I demanded, outraged. 'Get out!'

He raised his hands in defence. 'With all due respect, domina, I noticed you have no guards outside or within your bedchamber. Anyone could burst through the door or even climb through the window to kidnap you, and without someone watching over you, no one would know.'

'How do I know you are not such a man to steal me away in the middle of the night?' I accused him.

He raised an eyebrow, amused. 'Domina, I am merely trying to carry out my duties to the best of my ability. I would never dream of abusing our professional relationship.'

'Really?' I bristled, getting up from the bed with a rush of agitated energy. 'You have abused it despite everything I have said to you. During dinner, you didn't stop touching me, flirting shamelessly in front of my friends. Not only was it inappropriate, but also highly invasive of my personal space. You took advantage of my good nature because I have let you get away with such things before, but I see now it only increases your boldness. Well, I will not stand for it anymore. If you truly wanted to serve me as best you could have, you would not have put me at risk.'

'How have I done that?' he asked, cutting in. 'I told you I would never mention what happened at the baths. I swore to it.'

'Then you have broken an oath!' I snapped. 'Just now, you practically announced to Metallia, to her face, that you have seen me, a Vestal Virgin, nearly naked,' I whispered harshly, not wishing to bring the whole house down on us.

He bit the insides of his cheeks. 'Domina -'

My mouth parted in shock. 'Don't you dare laugh at me,' I hissed, charging up to him. 'I am a priestess of Rome, but I see that means nothing to you.' I made up my mind. 'I will be going to Occia first thing in the morning to have you removed from this house, and if necessary from Rome, and, if at all possible, from the empire.'

He sighed, sounding exasperated. 'Domina -'

'You know what? I'll go to her right now,' I decided and pushed past him, reaching for the door.

In one swift motion he grabbed my wrist. 'Wait!'

I yanked my arm away. 'Don't you dare touch me!'

He stood back and put his hands together in front of him, in a prayer. 'Domina, I beseech you to reconsider.'

I shook my head and began to turn away. 'You have made these worthless apologies before.'

Reaching forward, he took my hand. 'Please, do not send me back to the arena. It could be my death.'

I grew still, glaring at him.

He sighed and shook his head. 'Everything you have said is true. I have laughed at you and taken advantage of you. I have also broken a promise which I know in this place can mean death.'

I slowly exhaled. 'You may not take your duties seriously, but I do.'

He nodded. 'I know and I will take them seriously from now. I will also take you seriously, not just as my mistress, but also as the kind and forgiving soul to whom I owe my life.'

I frowned. *What?*

He saw my confusion and explained. 'At the baths, you asked for me to be spared and denied being alone with me, even though I had embarrassed you, injured you and invaded your privacy. You have not told anyone about how I behaved in my cell or how I have acted since coming here. There, again, you have been protecting me. You have been saving me from the moment I met you. I haven't earned it, but I intend to. Please give me another chance to try.' His voice had grown exceedingly quiet. Desperation was evident in his eyes. 'Just one more,' he begged. 'My life depends on it.'

I considered his words. *I could go to Occia right now.*

His eyes were big and brown, making my heart melt.

I sighed, defeated. 'Very well. One more. That is all. I refuse to be a pushover, Aries.'

'Call me Marcus,' he invited, smiling. Relief replaced the pain in his gaze. There was a glimmer of a genuine smile on his lips.

My chest felt lighter yet fuller at the same time. 'Marcus?'

He nodded.

It was a great deal less extravagant than 'the Glorious Ram of Jupiter'. 'Well, Marcus, since you plan on taking your position more seriously from now on and since you insist on guarding me at night, you may sit in that chair over there.' I pointed to the turquoise Egyptian seat next to the window.

'Thank you.' He made his way over to it.

Guilt began to rise within me as my mind flew over the argument that had just taken place. 'Goodnight, Marcus,' I said, climbing into the bed.

He sat down, sending me a smile. 'Goodnight, domina.'

It was difficult to sleep with him watching me. I felt nervous and also maybe, just a little bit, excited.

X
VIRIQUE VIRGINES
-Men and Maidens-

The dim light of the blushing dawn was beaming in through the window. My tired eyes landed on Marcus slumped in the Egyptian chair. At some point in the night, he had moved it right up next to my bed. With arms crossed, he was fast asleep, his curly brown hair falling over his closed eyes and his lips plump with sighing. With his head falling down, he looked endearing and vulnerable. I couldn't help but smile at the sight.

I looked around. Dazed and dozy, I sat up on my elbows and blinked a few times, trying to fathom the world. There was a bitter-tasting thirst in my mouth. Frowning, I lapped my tongue for moisture.

Water. Or wine? a small suggestive voice entertained.

I smiled. *Wine is nice.*

I pulled the blankets off my body and rose from the bed. I reached the door and opened it quietly, managing to not wake Marcus. Stumbling out into the corridor, I looked to see if anyone was there. Luckily, there were only a few sleeping guards on duty; no one else. I tiptoed past them, rubbing my eyes and yawning.

I got to the top of the stairs and, looking down at the atrium, I saw two figures standing face to face. The first was Rufina, wearing an intense frown, and the second was a lean figure, concealed by the hood of his toga pulled down over his face. He was accompanied by a man, lurking in the shadows, dressed in black and with a sword hanging from his waist.

To conceal my presence, I edged back against the wall. My muddled mind thought through the confusing sight. I craned my neck to try and see them, and hear their words. *What was Rufina doing?*

'Sir, I don't understand your reasons,' Rufina said.

'You don't need to. It is not your place.' The hooded man turned to leave, the hem of his toga brushing off the atrium floor.

I scowled. *The audacity!*

'But why me?' she called after him. 'Why not ask the Vestalis Maxima? Surely, she should be made aware of - '

The cloaked man whirled around, his hood slipping to reveal a head of short dart hair and a face familiar to me. Tiberius, heir to the empire, seized Rufina by the neck.

She choked on her words.

His bodyguard drew his sword. The sound of the blade scratching off its scabbard sent shivers down my spine.

'If you ever dream of being something greater than you are now, you will do this one thing for me, and not tell a living soul,' Tiberius hissed.

'The gods will know,' she croaked. 'They are all-seeing.'

'The gods are on my side,' he growled. 'They are watching to see that you obey, if you want a future at all.'

As he let go, she stumbled backwards, clutching her neck and wheezing, doubling over.

He covered his head with his hood once more and gestured to his man for them both to leave. The sound of their footsteps scuffing off the tiles grew softer as they walked out of the house.

As I watched, I resisted the urge to run to her side, my claws digging into the wall.

She let out a sob, before promptly straightening, brushing down her skirts and heading for the staircase.

Jumping to life, I hurried back to my bedchamber, deciding that it was better to find out the gravity of the situation before becoming involved. Until then, she could not know I had been eavesdropping. The wine would have to wait.

*

I woke up for a second time with brighter light flooding in through the veiled window. I looked to the right and saw a familiar curly head knelt on the bedsheets beside mine, where he had fallen forward in his slumber. I couldn't resist gently combing his curly locks with my fingers. I smiled as they bounced out of my clasp. I lay like that for a while.

His head moved as he raised it. There were dark circles under his brown eyes.

I cast a look over the stubble on his jaw. 'Good morning,' I whispered, smiling at his dishevelled appearance.

'Indeed,' he muttered in reply, his dimples appearing as he grinned. 'When do we have breakfast?' he asked, stifling a yawn.

I shrugged. 'Metallia usually comes in to tell me when it's ready. I think the slaves have their food in the kitchens.'

He nodded and slumped back in the chair. 'I should go down soon,' he mumbled, rubbing his eyes.

'Do you find it easy to speak with the other slaves?' I asked, suddenly curious, sitting up and leaning on an elbow.

He shook his head. 'Not really.'

'I suppose we have a mixture of different tongues downstairs.'

'That's not the only reason. It's hard because their mannerisms are so different to mine.'

I was confused. 'How can you find the ways of your own kind difficult?'

His dark eyebrows furrowed in a scowl. 'They are not my kind.'

I pulled back and looked at him properly. 'How so?'

'I was not born a slave, domina.'

I blinked. 'You're weren't?'

He shook his head and looked down, blushing. 'I was sent into exile a few years ago. When I tried to return to

Rome, I became caught up in the slave trade and was selected to be a gladiator.'

'Oh, I see,' I breathed in realisation. 'Why were you exiled?'

He sighed, fiddling with his fingers.

'Sorry,' I apologised. 'You do not have to answer that. I understand if you don't want to talk about it.'

With an intense glare, he looked up at me. 'What could the highest-ranking girl in the world possibly know about the life of an exile or a slave?'

I swallowed. 'Absolutely nothing,' I confessed in an honest whisper. Something made me reach forward and touch his hand. 'But I wish to understand as best I can.'

He seemed surprised, but smiled sadly as I tightened my hold around his hand. He squeezed it in return.

My chest warmed. It was an odd feeling, but not a bad one.

'I was accused of being insolent, stubborn and brutish. Some people even called me violent, but I was wrongly accused,' he stressed with apparent sincerity. 'I have always had my wits about me and I have always been considered a good enough person by most people I meet, I assure you. My grandfather is the head of our family. He has many virtues, but he considers it his greatest failure to have only ever had a daughter. She was my mother.'

'Was?'

'She too was exiled, but for adultery. My grandfather takes sin very seriously. I know not if she lives.'

'Marcus, I am so sorry,' I said quietly.

He glanced up at me. 'Don't be. She loved every man in the city except her husband and sons, but I still wasn't glad to see her taken away in chains,' he sighed. 'I am her third son and last child from her second marriage. My father was also called Marcus, but he died before my birth. My other brothers died a couple of years ago. So my grandfather decided, as I was his only living grandson, that

I would be his heir; I would inherit his land and wealth. I spent a few years believing that my future was made.'

I frowned. 'What changed?'

'Three years ago, there was an uprising in Illyricum. He was obliged to send a member of his family to help quell the revolt. I was not sent as I might have been, being the only young swordsman in the family, because he was advised that I was unpredictable and not to be trusted with the responsibility of such a mission. His opinion of me was brought so low that I was disowned and subsequently exiled.'

So much to take in! He seemed more straightforward to me now. Not only had he been a free man with the right to express his opinions, but, if his family could help quash an entire rebellion, it would have been a powerful one. *No wonder he had such cheek and confidence!* He was used to giving orders, not following them.

I asked, 'Where did they send you?'

'Planasia. It is an island in the Mare Nostrum,' he answered. 'It was very lonely there.'

'But you escaped,' I said, trying to lighten the mood.

'Oh, yes. My usual talents saw me through. I broke out about a fortnight ago.'

I smiled. 'So you came to Rome quite recently?'

He nodded.

'If you were exiled only three years ago,' I wondered aloud, 'how old are you now?'

'Twenty,' he answered, smiling.

I blinked, pleasantly surprised that he was only two years my senior. 'Did they have any proof of your bad character?'

'What bad character?' he asked, chuckling.

I grinned too.

Then he returned to being serious. 'I do not think so. I expect someone intentionally poisoned my grandfather against me.'

My face fell in horror.

'I was always a good fighter, but so is nearly every male citizen. Can one accuse all Roman men of being violent, based on that?'

I shook my head. 'No, of course not.'

He sighed. 'Whatever they thought was wrong with me, it was enough to take away my freedom, my fortune and my future.'

My heart was heavy with grief for him. He had lost everything. 'There is nothing wrong with you,' I told him. 'You're perfect.' The compliment slipped out before I could stop it.

Glancing up at me in surprise, he smiled. 'Thank you, domina.'

I quickly asked him another question: 'So, why did you return?'

'To see if I could salvage the life that I was promised,' he said. 'Exile had shown me a lot about the world, about people, about how one is treated when one is suddenly a nobody and has nothing to his name. People are manipulative and uncaring, not to mention cruel, if they have the upper hand. My guards, for instance, they were cruel.' He fell silent for a moment. 'But the worst thing about it was the feeling that I was wasting my life, purposeless. It was soul-destroying.

'However, enslavement taught me much more about cruelty - that everyone is capable of it. I have just been a slave for a few months, but I've met other men and women, learnt their stories, how they've been beaten by previous masters or sold into slavery by their own family. I've had to tolerate slimy traders who whipped their slaves into silence before putting them on show, torturing them at night, especially the girls, and laughing over their cries.' His throat bobbed. 'There was one elderly woman who was beaten to death, just because she spoke up. She passed away on a floor covered in everyone's shit. I saw slave-owners in the Forum, men I had known once, looking to buy. Once they had settled on a slave, they beat him into motion. It was disgusting. I met prostitutes, broken by men who raped them just because they were there for the taking; just because they could, and then not even pay the poor girls for their pain.'

Although I was speechless at his tale, one word stood out to me: rape. It was an ugly word, blurry in my head, but still ugly.

He continued. 'So I waited. I waited for the day that I would be bought. It was the only time the merchants would unchain us. I was purchased by a man who owned a gladiatorial school. He felt me up and down to check my physique, even places he didn't need to, before deciding that he wanted to throw me into the arena that day. The moment I was let out of my shackles, I bolted. He yelled for the guards to arrest me.

'So is true that I was running away, but not because of cowardice. I knew I could handle a few wild cats. The games were simply not part of my plan. I want to find my family and get my redemption as fast as possible. I did not come to Rome to be thrown into a death pit and die there.' He bit his lower lip, frowning and staring off into space. 'However, I will admit that I am afraid to go back, afraid of the welcome I'd receive. Maybe I will just let myself be sidetracked.'

'What do you mean?'

He smiled. 'Well, perhaps I've found some treasure here that will bring me good fortune, staring right back at me.'

I burst into surprised laughter. I glowed, although I couldn't possibly believe that he was sincere. However, I did not get to bask in his praise for long as the door swung open.

We broke apart.

My heart leapt into my throat.

Val stepped into the room. A strange expression of narrowed eyes with a tilted smile came onto her face when she saw us. 'I thought I heard voices, so I figured you were awake.' She glanced at Marcus. 'Although I am not sure why you would be conversing with a slave, Aemilia, or why he is sitting in your chair?'

Marcus remembered himself and shot up from the seat, bowing briefly to her before stepping to the side and gazing straight ahead at the space between us. 'Forgive me, domina.'

She frowned, unimpressed, approaching me. 'How are you?'

'I didn't sleep too well,' I confessed, giving her a sad smile.

'Why not?' she asked, sitting down in the Egyptian chair.

'The summer heat,' I said, smiling shakily through the lie.

'Well, if you did not sleep well - ' she muttered, pursing her lips thoughtfully, but leaving the rest unsaid. She turned around in the chair to face Marcus. 'Tell the other slaves to bring food and wine for your mistress.'

'I am not hungry,' I protested.

'She needs strength,' Val continued.

Marcus nodded, bowing and sparing a glance at me before turning towards the door. However, he did not have the chance even to touch the handle. It swung open and Prefect Gnaeus strode in.

Val shot up to face him, her body shielding mine.

I grabbed the blanket and covered myself, panicking silently. Out of the corner of my eye, I saw Marcus' hand go for a sword at his side, but it was not there.

Gnaeus grunted, 'I am here to see Aemilia on a very important matter.'

I choked on air.

'How dare you!' Val sputtered.

I saw her hands in fists, even if I could not see her face.

'Trespassing into the private quarters of a Vestal Virgin. It is highly inappropriate, Prefect!'

'I am paying a visit to my future wife,' he retaliated, voice gruff. 'Or at least, that's my hope.'

Val and Marcus both looked at me in bewilderment.

I would rather have died.

I pulled back the covers and stood up. 'Prefect Gnaeus.'

Val stood aside for me.

His eyes widened as they soaked up the sight of me in my nightdress.

I felt disgusting under his gaze, but I carried on. 'If you had any respect for your betters, you would never presume to intrude upon the privacy of any lady, married or unmarried, important or lowly. May I remind you that I am no further to becoming any relation of yours as I have not yet accepted your proposal. Moreover, it would be best if you never assumed it permissible to address a Vestal by her personal name when she has not granted you that privilege either. Every action of yours so far in entering this room has been a grave offence, not only to my feelings but also to the state which is far more serious.'

He shuffled his feet, searching the air for a reply.

'If you do not wish for me to tell the world about the disappointing magnitude of hubris that Rome's Prefect of the Praetorian Guard possesses, that he acts in such an appalling and insulting manner, I would greatly appreciate an apology here and now, but perhaps you think that is also beneath you?'

The middle-aged, war-toughened brute coughed nervously but did not meet my eyes. 'Sorry, domina.'

I raised an eyebrow. 'Is no one in this room worthy enough for you to bother bowing to?'

Purple and red rose in his neck as he swept a low bow. Then he straightened and, without looking at any of us, moved towards the door.

'Prefect?' I called.

He stopped dead in his tracks and glanced back over his shoulder.

'Tell slaves to bring food and wine. I simply must get my strength up for the day.' I clasped my hands and smiled pleasantly.

He nodded and slunk away.

When the door was fully closed, Val snorted in laughter, 'That was more entertaining than the games we went to see for your birthday, Aemilia.'

I giggled, pleased with myself. Then I remembered Marcus, who had remained quiet in the corner. I gestured to him. 'You remember Marcus was the one who fought that day?'

She looked at him in realisation. 'So it was,' she breathed. 'Then he was the one who ...,' she trailed off, looking warily between us, her smile vanishing.

I swore at myself ten times over. The Vestals had not recognised him when he had come here because he was just another slave. To most citizens, the pavement was more interesting. I had just given her something that no one else had figured out yet. I could see the mounting concern in her eyes.

'Yes,' I said, trying to rescue the problem. 'He has proven his virtue by killing the Emperor's assailant and serves us loyally. All is forgiven.'

She nodded.

I could tell she was biting her tongue.

'Very well, I shall leave you. I must tend to my duties,' she muttered, quickly exiting the room.

'Piss!' I exclaimed, my hands going to my hair.

Marcus laughed. 'Is that how noble ladies swear these days?'

I barely heard him, throwing myself back onto the bed. 'I can't believe myself,' I whispered, heart thumping madly.

'What's the matter?' he asked, stepping forward.

I sat up and looked at him. 'Nothing yet, but now she knows who you are: the spy in the baths and the gladiator with whom I sought a private audience. Everyone is already suspicious of me, a Vestal who willingly put herself alone in a room with a male slave she barely knew.'

He took my wrists gently, removing my hands from my face and holding them in his. 'You don't know what Vestal Valeriana will say. She may do nothing. Even if she does tell someone, no matter what people think, the gods know the truth. You are still entirely worthy of the position you hold,' he whispered. 'If you want me to be the quiet, obedient slave for the sake of your safety, I will.' He gave me a sad smile.

'Thank you.'

*

The rest of the day passed. After I had finished my lessons in the late afternoon, Marcus and I hovered by the windowsill in my bedroom. We were peering down on the others below in the courtyard of the house. They were gathered together in prayer in front of the outdoor altar of Vesta. Only Occia was absent, tending the Flame.

'So,' he began. 'Who is who?'

I supposed it was important that he knew whom he served. I pointed to my tallest friend. 'That is Rufina, the eldest daughter of one of Augustus' augurs. Her father wished her to become a Vestal Virgin and possibly even the future Vestalis Maxima after Occia.'

He gave a hum in agreement. 'Is that why she is so tense?'

I frowned. 'She is a strong believer, that's all. She grew up in a very religious family. Hardly a bad thing for the Order.'

'Only for her,' he mumbled under his breath. Then he gestured to the girl kneeling beside her on the grass. 'And that one is Vestal Valeriana, right?'

'Yes. Her father is a very influential business mogul who has done many deals with the Emperor. He became a senator just about a decade ago,' I said, smiling proudly for her.

'Before or after his daughter became a Vestal?'

'Excuse me?'

He didn't answer, instead pointing to Picia. 'The little one?'

I continued, nevertheless confused. 'Picia. Hers is a sad story. She lived with her family in the provinces. Her father was a governor there. Unfortunately, a fire killed off the entire household, including the slaves. Only she survived. She was put under the guardianship of her uncle who immediately put her forward for the Vestal candidacy.'

'Well, it was either that or marriage, I assume. What about that one?' He nodded towards Lavidia.

'That's Lavidia. Her father is a general in the Middle East. Her mother was reportedly as beautiful as Venus herself.'

'Was?' he said, looking at me.

I nodded. 'She was a very licentious woman and had many affairs. When the husband found out, he sold her into slavery straight away. It is not known whether she is still alive.'

'Brute.'

I scoffed. 'Well, Lavidia is not much different.'

He gave me a pointed look. 'No one betrays their partner repeatedly unless they are truly unhappy in the relationship. As for the daughter, I would say anyone growing up with such a father would quickly learn how to be just as nasty.'

'She abuses her authority and bullies everyone,' I argued. 'You don't know her.'

'And you do?' he asked. 'Perhaps she has suffered in her own way.'

'It is not your place to wonder about your masters. Anyway, why are you being so nosy?'

He gave me a grin. 'I just want to know what makes you so different.'

'It's not your place to wonder about that either,' I replied, smiling despite myself.

At last, night-time settled on the empire's capital and those people who had not slept half the day away required their slumber, Marcus included. By midnight, his eyes were closing of their own accord. As he sat on my bed, conversing with me, he stretched and yawned every so often before letting himself fall back.

I frowned at first. *No slave would dare sleep in their master's bed, never mind that of a Vestal.*

Heavy sighs seeped into the air; his soft lips parted slightly, with chest heaving. His face relaxed without his smirk. His dark, messy locks laid on my pillow. There was no tension, just a man who needed his rest.

It occurred to me that this might have been the best night's sleep he had in a long time, so I bent down and took off his sandals, resisting the urge to tickle the undersides of his feet.

Deciding to give him some peace, I took up a candle, opened the door and stepped out into the corridor to stretch my legs, walking barefoot down the hall. In the light of the glowing candelabra on the landing before the stairs was a sight I never imagined I would see.

A girl was held by a shadowy figure up against the wall. One of her bare legs was raised as the skirt of her stola rode up her thigh. The silhouette of her hair was tousled and messy, like a mane of a lioness. Her back arched like a feline as a high-pitched moan broke from her open mouth. That was when I saw a man, his waist enveloped by her long legs. Her face turned in the candlelight.

I stood there, dumbfounded. 'Lavidia?' I gasped.

XI
MYSTERIA
-Secrets-

Her eyes flew open and fixed on me. One of her elegant hands thwacked the shoulder of the man whose face was buried in her neck.

He grunted and pulled back.

She pushed him away viciously as he dropped her. She landed like a cat on the floor before straightening and fixing her skirts hastily.

In horror, I stumbled back, watching stupefied as the man glanced over his shoulder, his face still in the shadows, and as he legged it down the staircase. I picked up my skirts and began to run after him.

A hand landing on my shoulder forced me back against the wall.

Lavidia was right in front of me, with her nightdress ripped above her breast and her chest heaving. Her lips were swollen and she had a few bruises decorating her neck. 'Now, now,' she whispered, her eyes glaring straight into mine. 'That would be unwise.'

'You -' I began.

'What about me?' she asked, her eyes widening innocently. She smiled, baring her teeth. 'Whatever it is, who would believe you, a barbarian's bastard, over me?'

I blushed. 'You will not get away with this.'

She tutted, shaking her head. 'Oh, Aemilia. Don't you see?'

'See what? I've seen a lot tonight,' I seethed.

Her hand moved from my shoulder to my neck, leaving goosebumps in its wake. Her grip closed around my throat.

I winced. I did not put strangulation past my worst enemy.

'Now, now, let's be civilised ladies. That's what you were brought to Rome to be, was it not?'

I spluttered.

She kept whispering her poison. 'Take my advice: don't embarrass yourself by reporting this. Nothing would come of it and you, my dear, would be seen as an unstable girl who was probably just dreaming.' Then she smirked, removing her claws from my neck. 'Now, go back to bed and have a long think. Consider hypocrisy, for example.'

'Excuse me?'

She rolled her eyes. 'Go and cuddle up to that dreamy gladiator you have in there.'

My mouth dropped open in shock.

She smiled smugly and sauntered away with her hips swaying.

I turned back towards my room. When I was inside, I put the candle on the table and sat down on the edge of the bed. Sparing a glance at Marcus, sleeping soundly beside me, I focused my attention on the twilight outside and, just like she had suggested, I thought. Hard.

*

I stirred awake. Opening my eyes, I could make out the hazy image of Marcus next to me on the bed. Vision adjusting underneath the morning light, my chest grew warm at the sight of him sleeping soundly.

Then I realised how close he was. That was when my gaze flickered down to see his arm wrapped around me. Immediately, I was alert. Whatever the reason for his embrace, it had to end – affection was dangerous. I gingerly adjusted myself, rolling away.

His arm flopped down next to him.

That's better, I thought. Then I felt the cold air cling to my skin and couldn't help but regret what I had just done.

He slowly opened his eyes. 'Good night's sleep?' he mumbled.

My smile withered as memories of the previous night flooded back to me. 'Not exactly.'

'Why not?' he asked, frowning.

I propped myself up on my elbows. 'Something happened which I found rather disturbing.'

'What? Like in a nightmare?'

I shook my head. 'No, I wish it had been, though.' I sat up properly and looked at him sideways. 'Last night, I saw Lavidia with a man.'

His eyebrows furrowed. 'Who?'

'I didn't see his face, but he had her up against a wall and her legs were wrapped around his waist.'

Marcus glanced down.

'What is it?' I asked.

'Sounds like your little friend was breaking her vows.'

My mouth dropped open. 'Are you serious?' I gasped. 'You didn't even see it. How would you know?'

'A lucky guess,' he said, looking up at me through his eyelashes.

I thought aloud to myself. 'How would she?'

'What?'

'How would she know how to break her vows?'

'What do you mean?'

'How could she have broken her vows?' I repeated to him, exasperated. *What didn't he understand?* 'She wouldn't know how. None of us does.'

He stared at me for a few moments in perplexed silence before his expression turned dark. 'Aemilia,' he began, voice hoarse. He cleared his throat. 'Do you mean to say that no Vestal Virgin knows what it takes to no longer be a virgin?'

I nodded. 'It is a question I have been asking since the beginning of my servitude. No one knows, but the others don't seem to be as bothered by it. Occia says we will be told in time.'

He sucked in a breath, putting his head in his hands and ruffling his hair. 'So the Vestal who is supposed to teach you doesn't teach you?'

I shook my head.

He clenched his jaw. 'Ignorance is a dangerous thing, Aemilia. Many men would take advantage of what you have just said.'

'What do you mean?'

He stood up and paced around the room. 'This priesthood is simply a cult. This house, these walls,' he muttered, shaking his head while glancing out of the window, 'are a prison. That Occia is the guard, keeping you from outside knowledge.'

'Marcus, what are you talking about?'

'Sex! Rape!' he exclaimed, whirling around to face me.

I started from his intensity.

He sighed, his shoulders shuddering. 'Don't you realise that you're not allowed to know the one thing that you must if you are to survive as a Vestal? Doesn't that seem backward to you?'

I got out of bed calmly. 'Marcus, we are not even supposed to think about men. That is how we survive here. We don't even know what sex means or at least I don't,' I said quietly. 'If I was to find out, I would be ruined because being chaste is a state of mind, as well as of body. All I know is that if a Vestal Virgin makes even one mention of it, she is immediately suspected of having done it. If she is found guilty of sin, she will perish.'

He glowered.

'So, I am prepared,' I continued, 'to live in ignorance as long as I have someone to protect me from the danger of it. I have guards and loyal slaves. I have you, right?'

He exhaled heavily and nodded. 'Of course.'

'Good.' I smiled. 'Never say those words again.'

*

As was often the case, I spent the day in relative relaxation, going to my lessons, walking around the house and strolling in the garden, Marcus always a few feet away. Unfortunately, as I was pacing the atrium, I had the misfortune to encounter my greatest nemesis.

'Lavidia,' I greeted with a forced smile.

She glided towards me and linked her hands. 'Aemilia, darling, how did you sleep?'

'Well. I had plenty of time to think.'

With those words, she couldn't keep up the facade any longer. She glanced at the guards and slaves lining the atrium walls and at other Vestals going about their business. 'May we discuss this somewhere else?' she asked, lowering her voice.

'Why?' I asked, shrugging. 'I can talk about this here since I have done no wrong. Surely you can, too, if you are also guiltless?'

She clenched her jaw. 'Indeed.'

I stepped closer and dropped my voice, looking into her eyes. 'It seems to me that your activities last night consisted of a private meeting with a man in close quarters and no onlookers. Only that's not true - you had a witness.'

A pink rouge crept up her neck. Her knuckles turned white.

'What a mistake! I remember that you once went to Occia, accusing me of the same thing. Need I remind you that your effort failed miserably? You did not even have your own testimony to support it, whereas I do. I have more than mere speculation. I have details of what I saw.'

'You have a story, nothing more.' She glared at me as if there were knives in her eyes.

'It is enough,' I spat, my voice in a harsh whisper.

She clenched her jaw and raised her chin. 'So, will you tell Occia?'

I pursed my lips and hummed thoughtfully. 'I don't know yet. I might.'

'I will claim ignorance of any accusation you make.'

'But you wouldn't be innocent. It wouldn't be an unfounded charge.'

She opened her mouth to retaliate, but her words caught in her throat.

I took advantage of it. 'However, I might not go to Occia if you give me no more trouble about anything or anyone.'

She glanced at Marcus who stood behind me. Her face darkened. 'Fine,' she snapped. 'You have my word.'

I snorted. 'That is hardly good enough when I have just seen you break your vow. Or will you deny that you have done so?'

She gulped, eyes widening, but did not reply for the simple reason that I was right - Lavidia was no virgin.

'Your word is of no value. I will simply rely on your better judgement.'

I moved past her, feeling the best I had in days. I heard Marcus' steps trailing behind me.

'You're good at telling people off,' he praised, coming up beside me. 'First me. Then the Prefect. Now her.'

'Thank you for the compliment,' I replied as we approached the door to the records' room.

When I opened the door, I saw a girl bent over a chest, scrolls scattered around her, digging greedily through it, her hands like a wolf's claws. 'Rufina?' I realised aloud.

Her head shot up, her headdress tilted to the side with some of her hair falling out. 'Aemilia?' she asked, seeming to freeze, her eyes wide and scared.

I came further into the room towards her, dodging the mess of scrolls on the floor. 'What in Jupiter's good kingdom are you doing?' I asked warily.

'Nothing,' she answered quickly, standing up and brushing down her skirts. She seemed out of breath. Her chest was rising and falling rapidly.

'You can tell me,' I offered.

Her eyes went to Marcus, who was standing behind me. 'Get rid of the slave.' She looked around at the trashed room, tucking a dark lock of hair behind her ear.

Marcus didn't wait to be told anymore and gave us both a short bow. Sending an uncertain look in my direction, he left, closing the door after him.

I turned to her. 'What's wrong?'

She sighed deeply and rubbed her eyes with her palms. 'Nothing's wrong. Just not everything is right.'

'I see.' I wasn't sure what to make of that answer.

She groaned and looked at me again, dropping her hands. There was evident distress in her eyes. 'Aemilia, I have to tell you something. I have to tell someone.'

I nodded, guessing what it would be.

She took a deep breath. 'I had a visitor this morning: the Emperor's stepson and heir, Tiberius.'

'I see,' I replied, trying to appear surprised. 'For what purpose?'

'It was a surprise to me,' she confessed, exhaling heavily. 'I am to find the Emperor's will, which you know we keep here somewhere. Apparently Augustus wants to change a part of it. He said that I would be rewarded if I brought it directly to him. Tiberius, I mean.'

I frowned. *Was that what I had heard them talking about?* 'Surely he would have taken such a matter to Occia?'

Rufina sighed. 'I thought so too, but he mentioned that Occia has been a Vestal for forty-seven years and she may not live to see another decade pass; so, as the Vestalis Maxima, she is soon likely to name a successor with the Emperor's approval. As you know, that is a position I've always wanted. '

I groaned at her words, anticipating what she would say. 'And he promised you the position once he becomes Emperor?'

She nodded, panic in her eyes. 'Yes. He will vouch for me if Occia retires before Augustus dies.'

'So, you are to find his will, without telling Occia?'

'No one is to know anything, especially Occia. I'm only telling you because I'm desperate.' She gestured to the mess around her. 'I've been searching all day. It's not here.'

I raised an eyebrow. 'Rufina, you're a smart girl. Think. Would Augustus leave his own will, the most important document in the world which holds the future of the empire, in a room full of the papers belonging to thousands of others?'

She hung her head. 'No, of course not.'

'Right,' I said, crossing my arms. 'So, who do you think he would entrust it to?'

She didn't even blink. 'Occia.'

I nodded.

Suddenly, she seized my stola and yanked me close to her face, her eyes shining desperately. 'Will you help me?' she demanded, breath fanning my face.

I winced and hushed her. 'What do you mean?' I pushed her away. 'Have you not considered the risk?' I hissed, annoyed since she usually did.

Tears began to well up in her eyes and her lower lip trembled.

I realised I had probably been harsh. 'Rufina,' I began again, calmly. 'I know you are asking me to help you achieve your greatest dream, something which I would never wish to deny you.' I rubbed her arms reassuringly. 'But you are also asking me to help you steal the Emperor's will. This endangers both of us. '

Her head drooped, and she sniffled. 'I know.'

'I am truly astonished that Tiberius set you such a task. You do know that if you are caught -?'

'Aemilia, I know!' she interrupted. It was her turn to bat my hands away, tears streaming down her swollen cheeks from those dark eyes, the whites now red.

'It is criminal,' I whispered.

She nodded and her voice quivered. 'Do I have a choice?' She gave a dry laugh, wiping her cheeks with the palms of her hands. 'Oh Vesta, what have I walked into?'

'Nothing,' I denied firmly. 'This was forced upon you. You could have hardly refused.'

'Exactly,' she whimpered. 'What do I do?'

I thought for a moment. There was only one real solution in my mind. 'Tell Occia.'

Her face went slack. 'What? Are you mad? And let her know that I was going to conspire against her? I will not do that. I cannot!'

'You have already conspired against her, Rufina,' I said, gesturing wildly to the chaos surrounding us. 'However, it is not too late to stop.'

She gulped, gazing fearfully around the room. 'But I wouldn't have her trust anymore. I couldn't ever be sure of her desire to have me as her replacement.' Her brimming eyes returned to mine.

I took a step forward, desperate to help her see sense. 'What you seek could be years away. As old as Occia is, she is not yet weak or frail. There is plenty of time to regain her trust.'

She shook her head, refusing to be persuaded. 'She would never forget the betrayal.'

'No, but you could prove you have changed your ways,' I explained. 'You can still show her what honesty and truth mean to you by telling her that you were unable to go through with this plan, that you would disobey imperial instruction out of loyalty to her instead. She might trust you even more than she already did, but trust means truth.'

Her eyes closed and she put her head back, breathing out slowly. 'I would then betray Tiberius. He could poison Augustus against me and then, if Occia dies before him, I would never become Chief Vestal.'

'So you must choose between your two judges. Whose trust do you want more, Tiberius or Occia's?'

'I do not know.' Her face crumpled.

I rushed towards her and embraced her tightly, with her crying loudly onto the top of my head. I stroked her back with my hand and hushed her. 'There is only one way to have both, Rufina. We must tell Occia and trust that she gives you the will to take to Tiberius and remains quiet about the matter for the rest of her days,' I muttered. 'It is not exactly a failproof plan. She could very well think it improper and inappropriate.'

'I know she will!' Rufina sobbed.

'But we need to have faith in her. I think she will see how you've been put into a difficult situation and are following imperial orders.'

Rufina nodded, pursing her lips and considering my words carefully. 'Very well. Let me tell her about this in my own time,' she pleaded.

I nodded.

'This has been a minor hiccup, something which I can remedy,' she continued, talking to herself more than me, 'before I am too late.' She gave me a hopeful smile.

*

I walked through the gardens, picking colourful flowers along the way. Some slaves accompanying me helped, including Marcus who stooped to collect floral decorations for the House of the Vestals. Even with those brown curls, highlighted gold, that fell over his face, I could still see his eyes frowning at the ground. The sun was soaking his skin in its warm, golden light.

He straightened up and raised an eyebrow at me, a small smile playing on his lips.

Blushing for some reason, I turned away.

Once we had gathered as many as we could, I instructed the slaves to adorn the house with them, and they scurried off to do my bidding. I turned to follow.

'Wait, Aemilia,' Marcus said.

I spun around to face him, scowling. *'Domina', at least when in company, you fool!* Yet as I glanced at our surroundings, I saw that here in a garden enclosed by a tall hedge and flower beds, dotted by trees of every colour, and with the other slaves gone, we were alone. Only the birds and the gods were our witnesses.

He approached me slowly, holding his bouquet, a twinkle of mischief in his eyes or perhaps it was the glare of the sun. He was standing directly in front of me. He glanced down at the flowers in his hands. 'I wish to give you these. They are just for you,' he muttered. When I didn't immediately take them, he stepped back. 'But I understand if you do not like flowers.'

I stared at him, stunned. The warmth of the gesture invaded my heart. Unable to stop the beam spreading across my face, I surged forward and grabbed them, my fingers brushing off his. 'That is so sweet, Marcus!'

He looked at me in surprise.

I realised the sudden outburst might have been alarming. 'I mean,' I said, blushing, 'I care a great deal for flowers. I have never received them before, at least not in this way. Thank you.' I gently pried them out of his hand. I brought them up to my nose and the air was filled with the scents of lavender and rose.

'Has no one given you flowers before?' he asked.

I giggled. 'I've had them thrown at me from a crowd. Does that count?'

He frowned. 'Well, that's not right, at all. Everyone deserves to know precisely who cherishes them.'

I smiled. 'Thank you.'

He shrugged and scratched the back of his neck. 'They are beautiful flowers for a beautiful lady.'

I looked down, my face only growing hotter. 'Flatterer.'

'Truther,' he corrected me.

I could hear the delight in his voice.

Then, out of nowhere, his hand was on my face, lifting it up to his, and his lips were on mine.

XII
BASIAQUE BELLA
-Kisses and Wars-

I froze. I was rigid, but Marcus' lips were soft. His hand gently cupped my face and I could feel his breath, the perfume of a vineyard, dancing across my face. His lips fitted neatly over mine, pressing tenderly, and his warm thumb brushed my cheek. The ice in my veins strained in defiance, but when his fingertips touched my neck, it melted.

I kissed him back.

Perhaps it was the strange, yet appealing, knowledge of a man wanting me in this way; maybe it was the saddening realisation that the only kisses I would ever receive would be the sisterly pecks from the other Vestals and then possibly the repulsive ones of Prefect Gnaeus; or probably this simple show of affection released the knot of nerves that had been inside of me ever since I had met Marcus, that made me give in.

I tasted him shyly. *Grapes.* While I didn't know where he could have possibly found wine since slaves weren't allowed to drink it, I didn't care. I leaned into the kiss greedily, finding it addictive. His arm wrapped around my waist and pulled me closer to him until I was pressed against his chest. On my tiptoes, aching to savour everything I could, I barely felt the bouquet leave my grasp as I snaked my arms up around his neck, breathing him in and burying my fingers in those soft brown curls. Then I ran them over his face, tracing the arches and grooves. His hand caressed me up and down my back. There was pressure on my mouth. What had once been soft and gentle was now fast and nearly feral. My world was filled with hot and humid wine.

Then I felt something on my behind and I gasped, breaking the kiss in surprise, my eyes flying open and meeting his wide gaze. 'Was that your hand?' I asked, panting slightly.

'Yes,' he replied hoarsely, pink colouring his cheeks. His chest was rising and falling, too.

I smiled. 'I was unaware people did that.'

'That and more,' he said, smirking.

'I've never kissed anyone before,' I whispered, slow panic creeping up on me. I broke out of his grasp.

He frowned. 'Is everything alright, Aemilia?'

'I just -' I began. Then I caught sight of his swollen lips and messy hair. I touched my numb mouth.

'Did you not like it?' he suddenly asked.

I realised I was hardly having the best reaction. 'Oh, forgive me. Of course I did. I really enjoyed it,' I replied, nerves evident in my voice.

'Do you regret it?'

I opened my mouth to reassure him that I did not, but I could not lie to him. I would not.

At my hesitation, the sparkle died in his eyes. 'I see.'

'As a Vestal Virgin, I have to,' I explained.

'I understand,' he growled.

His sudden temper surprised me. A moment ago, he was all adoring, but now he had a face like thunder. He turned sharply on his heel to leave.

'Marcus! Please don't hate me,' I begged, following him.

Suddenly, he whirled around, his fists clenched by his sides. He was trembling all over.

I halted.

'How could I possibly hate you?' he hissed. His brown eyes were filled with pain. He looked down and shook his head, shoulders slumping. 'I know you are forbidden from lying with a man, but it's cruel that you don't give me any reason to hope.'

'Hope?' I interjected. 'Hope for what?'

His temper flared. 'I don't know. Happiness? With you?'

I was stunned. No one had ever spoken like this to me before. When I saw him scoffing and turning to leave again, finally a sound burst out of my mouth. 'You give me every emotion under the sun! You make me excited, annoyed, overjoyed and a wreck of nerves all at once.'

He stopped, turning around, disbelief written all over his features.

'And that kiss was one of the best moments of my life.'

At that, the tension began to drop off him like a waterfall.

'I'm sorry if you think I have been cruel, but can you please respect my promise to the gods and to the people of Rome, and what might happen if I break that promise?'

He sighed and looked down, nodding.

'If anyone found out, we would both be dead and damned,' I finished.

Not saying anything, he bent down and picked up one of the flowers from the bouquet I had dropped. Straightening up, he stepped forward and kissed me on the forehead, slipping in the flower behind my ear. He stepped back, looking at it and then at me, directly. 'Dead maybe,' he said, 'but after that, I consider myself eternally blessed.' Then he smiled sadly at me and strolled out of the garden.

Standing there with a flower in my hair and goosebumps on my arms, I saw a flash of light disappearing over the hedge. *Probably a sunray reflecting off some yellow rose or dandelion.* The giddy smile on my face was impossible to conceal.

*

Although Marcus couldn't avoid doing what other Vestals ordered, I could constantly instruct him to do things for me; that way, we were able to be with each other as much as possible. Of course, when we were alone, I did not make him fetch and carry, although sometimes he was pleased to do so anyway.

He would hold doors open for me, rub my feet, as well as take any chance to hold my hand, wink or smirk at me. He collected flowers during his free time and left them on my bed. He didn't kiss me again like he did in the garden, but he would peck my hand flirtatiously whenever he had the chance.

I enjoyed his attention and his desire to give it. I didn't have a problem with it, as long as it was all in private. There was no more fear or panic, so my heart only raced out of excitement.

I got to know him properly in the days that followed. He told me about his childhood, having the best education and the most luxurious possessions, but whenever I asked about his actual family, he changed the subject or simply shrugged. I supposed it hurt too much to talk about.

Once, as I was praying at the altar of Vesta, he asked me, with curiosity in his eyes, 'Is it true that Vestals have magic powers?'

Brought out of my solemn silence by the ludicrous question, I snorted. 'What? Of course not. That is ridiculous! Where did you hear that?'

His face fell and he shrugged, looking down at his feet. 'It's just what many people think. Vestals are a bridge between the heavens and Earth, so many believe you have godly powers and know the secrets of the divine.'

I shook my head. 'Well, I am sorry to disappoint, but I have no magical skills that I am aware of and,' I said, glancing at the altar, 'I know no godly secrets.' I looked back at him. 'Occia reassures us that we will know much more when we move into the second decade of our servitude, so ask me again in two years.'

He grinned.

We left the altar room and went up the staircase towards the corridor of bedchambers.

I heard hushed voices coming from nearby. Frowning, I slowed down my steps. One voice was relatively high pitched and stressed, the other quieter and hissing.

The first, Picia's, begged, 'Please leave me alone.'

'Or what? You'll do nothing,' Lavidia's voice snorted. 'But I could report you for breaking your vow.'

XIII
RIXA
-Strife-

I froze.

'That is not true! You know it is not!' Picia replied. I heard her burst into tears.

'It is so easy to get someone inspected,' Lavidia threatened. 'I've already told you what you have to do to avoid it.'

'I will not!'

I rounded the corner and placed myself in the doorway, enraged.

My fellow initiate was standing there, eyes red with tears streaming down her blotchy cheeks. Her head flung to the side to see me and, instead of hope and relief on her expression, fear dawned.

Lavidia's jaw clenched and lips pursed when she saw me.

Picia wiped her cheeks quickly and let out a nervous laugh. 'Aemilia, this is nothing.'

I raised an eyebrow and approached them. 'Oh? So you're not being threatened by this bitch here?'

Lavidia, veins bulging in her red and purple neck, slapped my cheek furiously. 'How dare you!' she spat.

I gasped as my head was thrown to the side. Feeling the sting across my skin, I met eyes with her, shocked and trying not to cry.

Marcus grabbed my arm and pulled me away from her, but I yanked myself out of his grip.

Lavidia voice lowered to a hiss. 'You have become rather bold, Aemilia. Dangerous, vicious and violent,' she fumed.

'Oh, I'm the violent one?' I scoffed, touching my cheek where she had smacked it. 'Remember that I saw what you did that night and, so far, I have not reported a thing. Look, I can put up with your constant bullying and belittling of me. I can even cope with your baseless threats, like reporting me to Occia, but I will not tolerate you showing the same disgusting treatment towards my friends.'

'Who says my accusations against you to Occia were without foundation?' she whispered, raising a smug eyebrow.

My heartbeat, which had been on a quick rise, now faltered. 'What - ' my voice caught. I coughed weakly.

'Girls, please - ' Picia begged.

'I, too, have an eye witness,' Lavidia said, with a smirk. 'Who saw you and him' - she glanced sideways at Marcus - 'together.' She looked back at me. 'I have more than just my suspicions now, more than what you have on me. I have the testimony of another which cannot be refuted. However, even without it,' she continued, raising an eyebrow, 'who would believe you, a barbarian's bastard instead of a Roman elite?' Her voice was like serpentine silk.

My blood raged in my ears and my throat ran dry at her words. Suddenly, all I saw was her neck.

'Aemilia?' Marcus asked in the distance. His voice sounded uncertain, even scared. *No wonder. I knew his past, but he never knew mine.* He didn't know what she was talking about or where the argument was going.

'Oh, we are informal today!' Lavidia gasped, staring at him as if he was a treasure hoard.

My heart tightened. If ever before Lavidia had not any evidence of our affection for each other, now she did: a slave familiar enough with his mistress to address her by her personal name.

'What is going on?' Rufina's voice echoed.

Our heads swivelled to see her standing in the doorway, accompanied by Val. They both entered, looking equally concerned.

'Ah!' Lavidia clasped her hands. 'Join the celebrations, girls. I am about to host festivities!' She looked back at me. 'Because our darling Aemilia, here, was just about to confess.'

Rufina placed herself between us. 'To what?'

'Breaking her vow,' Lavidia hissed at me.

Val sucked in a shocked breath.

'I have done nothing of the sort,' I retorted, eyes stinging. I couldn't help the tears anymore. It was all too much. 'I am a virgin.' My vision began to blur. I wiped my eyes with the back of my hands. *Stupid, weak tears.*

Val moved forward to stand beside me. 'This is ridiculous. Aemilia has never stepped out of line before. Why now?'

'Maybe because of a young and dashing gladiator by her side morning, noon and night?' Lavidia snapped back, raising her chin higher and casting an accusing look at Marcus.

'Each of us is surrounded by slaves all the time, yourself included,' Val pointed out. 'Aemilia would never risk her life for a slave.'

Lavidia clenched her jaw. 'But they have been spending more time in each other's company than anyone else,' she protested. 'Am I the only one who finds it odd?'

'Is this jealousy?' Rufina asked, sounding genuinely interested.

Lavidia scoffed. 'I have never been jealous of Aemilia, with her low birth and questionable ancestry. I would rather die.'

I laughed dryly. 'I insult you with my existence, do I?'

She didn't grace me with an answer.

'On the contrary,' Rufina said, perfectly calm as she stared Lavidia down. 'You are utterly envious because you fancy a slave who spends much more time with the girl you hate. If she finds him loyal and trusts him more than other slaves, that is not wrong. It is wise. So you are right,

Lavidia, you are the only one who finds it odd because you are the only one jealous enough to care.'

Lavidia's throat bobbed, staring up with fearful eyes at the taller girl. A blush crept up her cheeks.

'It is the only logical explanation,' Rufina concluded. 'She, low-born in your view, can secure the love and loyalty of so many, high and low, which you are not able to do, despite your noble birth. Is it all becoming too much to bear?'

'Don't be stupid!' she seethed.

'What in Jupiter's good kingdom is going on here?' Occia bellowed.

We turned to see her standing in the doorway with her arms folded in front of her.

She looked horrified. 'Shouting and screaming like children!' She stormed towards us. 'Not at all like Vestals or even proper ladies,' she scolded, lips thin and visibly trembling in anger. 'Your noise was reported to me and now I am neglecting the Flame. How dare you!'

I glanced around at everyone, staring guiltily at the Chief Vestal. There were too many people, too many questions and too much suspicion between us all.

'Domina, please,' Rufina stepped forward. 'Let me explain.'

The Chief Vestal's hand shot up in front of her face. 'Enough!'

Rufina looked as if she was about to implode.

'Besides,' Lavidia's voice sounded.

We all turned to look at her.

'Rufina is not to be trusted, domina. Not after ransacking the records' room to try and steal the Emperor's will.'

It was as if Saturn, the Lord of Time, had stopped the world. Faces turned in slow shock towards Rufina, who was now frozen in her place; her chin trembling as she opened her mouth to speak.

My heart sank for her.

Occia, her idol and everything she aspired to be, looked at Rufina, in horror and betrayal. 'You did what?' she breathed.

'That is a twisted report, domina,' I interrupted, rushing to Rufina's defence. 'Tiberius ordered Rufina to bring it to him, specifically without your knowledge.'

Her eyes widened, glancing warily between Rufina and me.

I took advantage of the silent shock. 'However, knowing it was a betrayal, guilt was eating her alive. So, she confided in me. She was planning to tell you as soon as possible. Truly, domina, she never meant to - '

'Enough, Aemilia!' Occia stopped me harshly.

I swallowed my words.

Rufina let out a sigh, tears streaming from her eyes. Other than that, she was composed and stood completely still.

Occia clasped her hands. 'Anything else?'

'Aemilia's sleeping with her slave,' Lavidia commented, sounding as if she didn't care.

I spun around to her, furious. 'That is not true! You have no proof.' I looked to Occia. 'Whereas I have evidence of Lavidia's own vow-breaking!'

'Domina Occia, Aemilia is right when she says that she is innocent,' Val intervened. 'If anything, that slave has been pestering her.' She gestured to Marcus, who was standing in the corner of the room.

Oh, gods! She did not just say that.

Val turned to me. 'Remember you asked me what I would do if unwelcome advances were made towards me?'

My mouth dropped open. 'That is not what I meant.'

'You sure? That is what it sounded like,' she argued gently.

'That is enough!' Occia shouted, her voice bouncing off the walls and ringing in my ears.

We fell completely silent.

'In fact, more than enough,' Occia said through gritted teeth. She glared at us all with disgust and fury. 'What a shame to this nation you are. Shrieking at each other like foul strumpets in a catfight! An utter disgrace to the noble titles you bear.'

I lowered my gaze, face heating up.

'I am so sorry, Occia,' Rufina muttered, hanging her head in shame.

I saw an unfamiliar coldness behind Occia's eyes.

She shook her head. 'I do not want to hear anything from any of you for the next while. None of you deserves a thing. Rufina, get to the Flame this instant. I will deal with you later. This silly squabble has caused us to forget our duty. However, a more important matter presses me now: the security of this empire. Therefore, tomorrow morning both Aemilia and Lavidia will be sent to the Emperor for inspections.'

Lavidia and I locked eyes in mutually shared horror.

*

'Aemilia,' a familiar voice said.

I exhaled shakily, turning around in my chair.

A blurry Marcus stood in the middle of my bedchamber.

I wiped my eyes with the backs of my hands, unable to stop a sniffle. 'Yes?' I asked. My voice was hoarse from sobbing.

He shuffled on his feet, staring at his sandals. 'I think it would be best if I leave.'

I frowned. 'Excuse me?'

He looked up at the ceiling. 'I don't believe it is wise for me to stay here any longer.' He finally looked at me. His face held no emotion, only the expression of a statue.

I barely got the words out, I was in such shock. 'You're quitting? You cannot quit. You're a slave. You can never quit that.'

He didn't reply, only raising his chin higher.

'Do you know what happens to runaway slaves?' I demanded angrily, standing up from the chair. 'They are branded as fugitives. They will send hunters after you. If you are caught, they will kill you!'

'A slave can be killed at any time for anything, even just for existing.'

I clenched my jaw. 'Very few masters take a slave's life for no reason.'

'What about in the games? If I had died, then, wouldn't that have been for no reason?'

'It would have been for sport. Yes, it's disgusting, but it is the custom.' I sighed, trying to calm down. I pleaded with him, now, to see sense. 'You are safest here.'

'My life here, as a slave, is barely a life at all,' he muttered, looking at me with a disappointed gaze. 'That was why I liked you. You recognise slaves as people too, as equals. I hoped you would have let me have my own life.'

He seemed determined, but I didn't want him to leave. 'Why do you want to go?'

He snorted, shaking his head. 'My presence here now endangers us both, and our relationship is no longer appropriate.'

I frowned. *The way he was staring at me - no, glaring - he seemed to be accusing me of something.* 'Is that my fault?' I asked, going on the defensive.

'Don't ignore your own part in this,' he advised with a warning in his voice. 'You viewed me as an annoyance. Honestly, I would have been less insulted had you slapped me.'

I gawped, shocked at his tirade. 'At the time, I did find it annoying. I worried you were playing games with my life, but when I realised that your affection was true, I liked it because I liked you. Yet, I was also terrified because I never had such emotions before. As for Val, I told her nothing.'

He scoffed. 'I got the impression you did.'

I shook my head frantically. 'I needed advice, but I specifically told her that it was Prefect Gnaeus who was unwanted, not you.'

'That bastard?' He sucked in a breath. Suddenly, with manic energy, his anger burst as he gestured wildly to the walls around us. 'This entire monstrous building is infected with the schemes of entitled brats!'

My mouth dropped open in shock.

'It's toxic, Aemilia! This was not what I came to Rome to do,' he said, pinching the bridge of his nose. 'I have been greatly distracted.'

'By what?'

'By you!' he retaliated, arms flying out and fingers curled as if he wanted to wrap them around my neck.

I felt my own anger rising. He had gone too far and this was the last thing I needed. *If he wanted to leave, who was I to stop him?* 'Well, that's not my fault. I never wanted you here in the first place.' I clenched my jaw. 'You know what? You're dead right. Get out. Now! Reunite with your precious family or perish in exile. Whatever you do, wherever you go, don't you dare insult this house, the girls in it or me any further with your presence.'

His lips curled, eyes flickering over me in disgust. 'Why would I want to stay? I hate this place.'

'Then what are you still doing here? Go!'

He nodded curtly, spun on his heel and left.

My eyes fixed on the door. The fury in my chest screamed at him to get lost and to never return. I sat down shakily in the chair and looked back out to the view of Rome. I later realised that it could very well be the last I ever saw of Marcus. My heart clenched, and fresh, hot tears stung my eyes before falling out again.

XIV
VIA AD VITIUM
-The Road to Sin-

Trying to keep the movements of the Vestal Virgins a secret from the public was like trying to hide pollen from a bee. As our sedan chairs left the gates, the people flocked towards us in eager curiosity and hungry desperation, as always. Thankfully, there was a linen wall between them and me. I took the opportunity of privacy to close my tired eyes. The god of slumber had not visited me last night. Restlessness and frustration accompanied by regret and guilt had plagued me in my bedchamber. The candlelight had been cold and unkind when it revealed to me how alone I was after becoming accustomed to Marcus sitting on that Egyptian chair.

I had tried everything to get to sleep. I paced until my feet ached. I rubbed my head until the joints in my fingers creaked. I recited Virgil until the words became blurred. Still, I couldn't do anything to quell my nerves. The thought of an inspection made my limbs tremble, but the absence of Marcus hurt my eyes and pierced my chest. Eventually, crying in the corner of the room made me weary enough to fall asleep.

I had woken up with new determination. There would be plenty of time to get headaches about Marcus. There was not as much time to deal with my next obstacle: the inspection. That had to be my priority now, not him. My only consolation was that Lavidia, who would never have imagined she would be questioned about her flawless perfection, was going through this as well.

It was late midday when we set off. The journey seemed to take forever; perhaps it was nervous anticipation that made time slow down or maybe it was the frustratingly restrained march of the slaves carrying us and the guards regulating them through the mob. A Vestal should never blame the people, I remembered. 'It only gives the masses leave to dislike her in return,' Occia had once taught me.

As for the inspection, all I knew was that it was a relatively private affair between the Vestal and the Emperor to avoid any rumours developing, I supposed - all scandals would be released to the public in the right way and at the right time.

After years of wondering what the inspection could involve, I had concluded that although it was a small affair, it was probably still very formal and official, with the Emperor questioning witnesses and gathering the accounts. We might have solicitors to defend us. Then he would consult advisors for his final decision.

I had spent the morning thinking through my defence. I would have to explain what I saw Lavidia do that night with that strange man. Although I had not seen his face, unless she whipped out her mysterious witness from beneath her stola, she had even less proof of my guilt. I would need to explain that she had constantly shamed me for my background and that this was no exception. She would most likely claim I was jealous of her nobility and wished to see her family name destroyed, but I would rely on the fact that Augustus had chosen me to be a Vestal Virgin, just like her, and that his fondness for me would help my case. Once the charges were dismissed, we would both be sent home, free of suspicion. Of course, I detested Lavidia, but I would never want her to undergo the fatal penalties for losing her virtue. At least, this was how it played out in my mind.

When I felt the slaves halt and heard a guard announce our arrival, my heart began to pound dramatically and my hands began to sweat. In reality, I had no idea what to expect.

As I was stepping out, my legs began to shake, and a guard quickly dived forward, offering his hand. I grabbed it and he helped me until I was steady. Glancing over, I saw Lavidia, standing tall and strong, smirking as Occia narrowed her eyes at me. Out of the two of us, I was innocent. *So, why was I the one panicking?* Realising my nervousness could be seen as guilt, I swallowed my fear. I let go of the guard, thanking him and clasping my hands together, standing up as tall as I could, trying to seem calm and confident.

We were approached by a second guard who bowed slightly to us. I spotted Occia's frown of disapproval. Even I had to admit that such a curt welcome was not customary for Vestal Virgins. *Were we not the highest in the land?*

Then I laid eyes on the creation behind him: the great, rising steps to the monstrously magnificent mansion which glowed golden under the midday sun. It beamed brightly, letting off a heavenly aura, like it was beating life into the empire just as the heart of humanity should. The House of the Vestals was a grubby hut by comparison.

Glancing back at the guard, I realised that any slave, soldier or senator here would have a life revolving around someone much higher than us - the revered one.

'Vestalis Maxima Occia,' the guard said, stonily. 'The Emperor invites you to have a luncheon with his wife while the inspections take place.'

A glittering smile danced across Occia's face as my heart plummeted. I had hoped she would be there to vouch for my good character, but now she would not be able provide such assistance.

'I would be delighted!' she said, clasping her hands.

He gestured to another guard who would escort her to Livia.

Occia smiled at us and turned away to enter the House of Augustus through the main entrance.

He reverted his attention to Lavidia and me. 'The Emperor will see you both separately,' he declared, even more monotonous and indifferent than before. 'This way.'

He turned on his heel and began to march up the steps, his armour reflecting the sunlight.

I exchanged a look with Lavidia. While she smirked and strutted after him, I followed hesitantly.

The House of Augustus was like none that I had ever seen. Columns lined the hallways and beautifully coloured Pompeian frescoes adorned the walls, with marble blocks and stoas. The windows looked down upon great green gardens and courtyards.

We followed the guard, passing through grand rooms and halls, past senators and slaves, all of whom bowed at the sight of our white figures. Soon we seemed to reach the back sections of the house with narrow corridors off which were small, dusty rooms.

I swallowed my confusion and the temptation to question him.

Lavidia, however, did not. 'Excuse me? Where are we going?'

He did not reply. Instead, he took a key from his belt and, turning another corner, opened a door. He held it open and gestured only to me. 'Please, in here.'

I blinked in surprise and peered inside. It was a tiny room, not even big enough for five strides. With no furniture, not even a torch, it was barely a room at all. Any previous feelings of cooperation I had felt did not extend any further to this soldier. Even if he worked with more aristocratic people, we were still his superiors. I looked back at him. 'You cannot be serious?'

He put his hands behind his back. 'Emperor's orders.'

'How dare you!' Lavidia screeched in my ear. 'These are cells and I will not be incarcerated like a slave!'

'You will be,' he stated in a deep growl. 'Or you'll face a different fate.'

'Just do as he says,' I snapped over my shoulder to Lavidia.

She squawked in response.

It took all of my willpower to walk into the room and stand there as I watched the guard struggle and wrestle to put Lavidia into the neighbouring one. She screamed, kicked and bit him. Fed up with it, he grabbed her hair and she cried out in pain.

Although I had every reason to enjoy the sight, I did not and, despite never thinking I would ever come to her rescue, I now bellowed, 'Guard, any harm you bring to a Vestal will only invite your death! Unhand her at once or she will have every right to execute you.'

His head shot up and he glared at me. Heeding my advice, he released her and stood back.

'Savage!' she hissed at him. Hate covered her face; hate for this whole situation, for the place she was in and the people she was with.

At least we had found something to agree upon.

'Lavidia!' I scolded her. 'Be dignified.'

She huffed, brushed down her skirt and fixed her headdress before he shoved her inside.

Wiping his brow, he gave me a swipe, pushing me further into the room, even though I was already on the other side of the door.

I squeaked in alarm.

He closed the door with a bang and locked me into the cold.

Trying to calm down and remember my strategy, I paced the cell. It was all so disarming, imprisoning us here like criminals. It was not as if there was any proof of our guilt yet.

Soon the door opened and the Emperor stepped inside.

I turned around, bobbing my most profound curtsey. 'Caesar.'

He gave me a pleasant smile and closed the door behind him, locking it with a set of keys. 'Dearest Aemilia, my child,' he greeted, clasping his hands together and looking at me with holy serenity.

I smiled as sweetly as I could. *Time to charm.*

'Shall we begin?'

I nodded, happy to obey.

'Good.' He gestured lazily to my dress. 'Now, take off your clothes.'

XV
VIOLARE
-To Violate-

Everything halted. All my plans. All the speeches I had prepared. 'Ex -' my voice caught. 'Excuse me?'

'This is a physical inspection, my dear,' he said, smiling.

I shook my head. 'I don't understand. No one mentioned that it was.'

'Well, to truly investigate if a man has contaminated your body,' he explained, eyes wide and sincere, 'the gods must see the pollution or hopefully the lack thereof, which will show from the bareness of your body.'

I gulped and glanced down, my heart starting to beat quite fast. 'I see.' My voice was small.

Chuckling, he took a step forward. 'My child, this is a private space, a safe space. It's just you and me. We will not be intruded upon. I have done this many times before.'

I looked up, too aware of every movement he was making, and nodded, despite feeling panic rising in my chest.

He placed his hands on my shoulders, rubbing them soothingly. 'There is no need to tremble or be alarmed, my child. I understand it is unusual for a Vestal or any respectable young woman to make herself bare before a man who is not her husband or her father, but consider yourself married to your beliefs and think of me as a father to you.' He gestured to himself. His gaze was kind, his tone gentle. It was comforting. 'Will you be a true, virtuous and obedient daughter?' He spread his hands, looking expectantly at me.

I swallowed. I supposed the reasoning was sound. *And if that was how the Emperor did things, who was I to argue?* I nodded.

Pleased, he clasped his hands, waiting for me to start.

My clammy hands touched my dress, uncertainly. *What would I even begin take off? Was there an order required?*

'Remove your palla and headdress, then the stola,' he said, answering my questions. 'Also, you should undo your hair and take all materials off - complete and honest nudity before the gods.'

I nodded. My shaky hands undid my palla, letting it fall to the floor. My throat was dry. Still, I offered him a small smile - I didn't want him to think I was nervous. Lavidia had been so confident that I figured I should be too. *Besides, there was nothing to be afraid of, right? My body wasn't contaminated; I was still a virgin.* Finding the strength to relax a little, I reached up and undid my headdress, avoiding the Emperor's eyes. With my hair loosening down over my shoulders, I let the ribbons fall too.

'Good, you're doing very well, child.' He gazed at me intently.

Flinching at the sound of his voice, I rubbed my hands together to stop the trembling. *Why was I nervous? There was no need to be.* Turning away from him, I slipped out of my sandals and kneeled to grip the hem of the stola, beginning to take it off.

'What are you doing?' his voice cut in, suddenly sharp.

Letting go of my dress, I anxiously turned around. My eyes met his disapproving ones. 'Caesar?'

'When you are praying to the gods, would you ever turn your back on them?' he asked. His tone wasn't angry. It even sounded concerned, but also like he was scolding me. It was the same inflection that Occia used when she was correcting me in class.

I gulped, realising my mistake, and gave him an awkward smile. 'Of course not. Forgive me, Caesar.'

'Please continue. Just face me,' he advised in a stern voice.

Nodding, I leaned down and, clasping the hem again with my sweating hands, pulled my stola and the underlying tunic up over my head. I dropped them on the floor, glancing at him.

Heart beating fast, I shakily removed my breast-cloth and loincloth. Goosebumps appeared on my skin, on every surface where his eyes landed, seeming to suck up every part of me.

Suddenly, I felt his cold, dry hands on my bare waist. I jumped, but resisted a protest as his gaze carefully took in my neck and chest.

'Try to stop shaking,' he murmured, leaning down until his nose was on my shoulder. He inhaled deeply.

I could hear his breath in my ear. *What was he smelling for?* I felt his lips brush off my skin as he sniffed my neck and my hair. I stood frozen still.

Then he spun me around, twisting me at the waist, without warning.

I yelped, my arms flying out to stop myself from hitting the wall. My fingernails dug into the cold, wet stone as his hands tossed my hair to one side, over my shoulder.

Those wrinkled hands slithered around my body and grabbed onto my chest from behind, pulling and squeezing harshly.

I whimpered, despite myself.

'Virtue can sometimes be painful,' was all he said, before pushing on the back of my neck.

I stumbled and was flattened against the wall.

'Just stay still for a moment.'

My cheek rubbed off the hard stone, but it was not colder than the moist, intrusive hand grabbing my behind and then spreading my legs apart. I inhaled sharply.

Suddenly, he touched something. I didn't know what, but it was so surprising that I jumped in shock. Meanwhile, his hand, still on the back of my neck, kept me pinned against the wall. 'Stay still,' he repeated, more firmly this time.

'Sorry, Caesar.' I felt tears prick my eyes.

Then there was pain, like a burning sensation, low and internal. I could feel something shoving repeatedly into me, jabbing at my insides. I winced. It felt like it was ripping me apart. 'Um, dominus, that hurts,' I protested, trying not to displease him.

'That's a good sign,' he advised. 'Just a few moments longer, Aemilia.'

I stood there, letting him move his fingers in and out of me. How he was doing it, I did not know. My insides felt on fire and my legs were shaking as the tears spilled down my face. I hadn't expected there to be so much pain.

Eventually it was over. He released my neck. 'There we go,' he said in a finalising tone.

I turned around, sniffling, in time to see him wipe his fingers, covered in blood – *my blood?* - on his toga. I covered my body with my arms, now that we were done.

He smiled and said, 'You were a virgin, Aemilia. You can get dressed now. After I examine Lavidia, you are both free to leave.'

You were a virgin. What did that mean? Before I could ask, he had unlocked the door, left the room and was gone.

A searing pain knifed my insides and I stumbled, doubling over. Legs trembling, I fell down onto the cold floor, surrounded by a messy pile of fabrics and ribbons. Pressing my back against the wall, I tried to gather my thoughts, my breathing uneven and throat tight. I burst into sobs. I didn't even know why I was crying in the first place. I reached forward and pulled up my stola to my chest for some warmth, hugging my knees.

I sat there for the next while; I did not know how long. I was not wholly aware of the tears falling down my face or the sobs escaping my mouth. As everything dried up, the area between my legs and my lower abdomen still felt sensitive and sore, although no longer in as much pain. I thought of both nothing and everything at once.

Moans and grunts filled the air, coming from the neighbouring cell. I could make out Lavidia's voice among them. I blocked my ears from the sounds until my fingers ached.

The shadows grew with the looming darkness of the evening. Figuring we would be going home soon, I stood up shakily and began to get dressed without a slave or looking glass. I couldn't do my hair the same as Metallia, so I just tied it in the ribbons and covered it with the headdress, but however much I tried to wrap myself up no amount of layers could keep out the memories of his hands groping my chest and moving up between my legs. Everything was branded into my flesh. Then I sat back down on the floor, staring into the dark grey stone.

Finally, that insolent guard let me out. I didn't care that he didn't hold the door open for me. I didn't care that he didn't bow. I moved faster than I had intended to, wanting to leave as quickly as possible.

'Couldn't handle a little lust, Aemilia?' Lavidia giggled in my ear, skipping confidently past me down the corridors towards Occia who was waiting outside the front doors of Augustus' house.

That was lust? I thought, watching her fast-floating figure.

'All well?' Occia greeted, smiling.

'Yes, domina!' Lavidia chirped.

'Good,' she said, letting out a deep breath. 'Well, let us be off.'

I barely heard the crowds on the journey back. My whole mind was focused on Augustus' grabbing hands and his voice in my ear, telling me that I did well and that I had been a virgin. *Had been.* Behind the white linen curtains of the sedan chair, I broke down. Luckily, the roar of the rabble outside was enough to drown out my sobs.

When we arrived at the House of the Vestals, I ignored Val and Picia who came running up to greet me. Deaf to their questions and concerns, I pushed past them, just barely holding myself together. I headed straight for my bedchamber. Closing the door behind me, I placed a trembling hand on the wall to steady myself as I slipped out of my sandals. I stumbled barefoot across the room and collapsed onto the bed, my lower lip quivering.

Tears tumbling down my face, I relived it all in my head. The memories overwhelmed me. I sobbed aloud and clamped a hand over my mouth, glancing wildly to the blurry door. My hair stuck to my hot skin and I felt vomit in my throat. I turned my face into the bedsheets and wept.

At one point, I managed to call a slave to tell Occia I was tired and wished to retire early. I did not have the strength to hold myself together in front of everyone and I wouldn't be able to bear a beaming Lavidia who seemed to have had the time of her life with the Emperor.

Metallia knew something was amiss when she undressed me that night. She saw my clothes, stained with dirt from the dungeon floor, and my hair, an unspeakable mess. She noticed my blotchy skin, bruises on my upper legs, waist and chest. 'Domina,' she breathed, confused horror coming over her face.

I stared at her through the looking glass. 'Yes?' My voice was hoarse and hopeful. Some inner part of me which had not yet perished hoped she would guess correctly what had happened and would help me.

She looked down at the dirty clothes in her arms, biting her lip. 'I will wash these for you tonight,' she whispered. 'They will not be dry enough in the morning, but there are other clothes and I will lay out a clean nightdress on your bed now.'

My tiny hope died. 'Thank you,' I whispered slowly.

She curtseyed, laid out the nightdress, and quietly left the room.

I stared back at myself in the looking glass, feeling lifeless. Unable to look any longer, I dropped the mirror on the floor, not caring that it broke, unconsciously putting on the nightdress, and I climbed into bed.

I lay there, unable to sleep. The obsidian night was filled with tears and agony. As for my faith, it too was shattered.

XVI
POSTEA
-Afterwards-

Over the following days, I barely noticed the world around me – the inspection was all I could think about. Augustus' breath filled my ears, his lips brushing off them, making me shiver in disgust. Every moment was filled with his gaze on my chest, his fingers pulling on me and then shoving into me. I couldn't sit comfortably with the nightmarish memories. When I opened my mouth, all that came out was a weak, shaking voice, and I hated it. I didn't eat much either. Sometimes, slaves managed to encourage me take some fruit or bread, but my stomach was filled with bile at the thought of his wrinkled hands climbing all over me.

Whenever Metallia attended me, I couldn't look at her. I even began watching her movements so carefully that maybe one day I might be able to dress myself and not have to stand naked in front of her. She might have been a familiar face, but all I could imagine was Augustus walking around me and touching me. Whenever she left, I burst into tears.

I couldn't sleep, but I didn't want to get out of bed. I didn't want to move because every time I did, those daggers were between my legs again. I couldn't stop thinking about his hands, his voice, his breath; how he had spoken to me so softly; how he had made me strip and how he had touched me afterwards. I didn't understand why, but I couldn't bear the thought. It made me sick.

My friends became concerned. Picia noticed it first - she had always been the observant type. One day, she pulled me aside as we were on our way back into the house from the garden. 'Are you okay, Aemilia?' she asked. 'You seem very far off, in another land.' There was clear concern in her eyes.

I said I was simply tired, and thanked her for asking. I did that whenever anybody asked because soon all my friends did the same.

Occia even said to me after classes, 'You don't engage in the lessons anymore, Aemilia. Is something wrong?'

I remember Val asking me, 'Aemilia, do you feel alright? You are quite pale. Did you not sleep well?'

I understood they were worried, that they cared. At first, I appreciated it, but the constant interrogation did nothing to stop those thoughts of Augustus, of what he did. If anything, it just made it worse. It wasn't going away and there was no sign of anything going back to normal. Soon, the questions were everywhere.

'Are you ill?'

'Have you eaten yet?'

'Have you even drunk anything?'

'Shall I send for a physician?'

'Is it because of him?'

Who? Augustus? I opened my eyes and looked up.

It was Val, standing in front of me before the window of my bedchamber, her arms crossed, with her back to the city.

I was sitting in the Egyptian chair, looking out. I frowned. 'Excuse me?' I said, my voice hoarse.

She raised an eyebrow and repeated the question. 'Is it because of that slave? I haven't seen much of him recently.'

Oh. I stared at her. 'No, I was not even thinking about him.'

Suddenly, I was. *Marcus. Where was he? Was he safe? Was he imprisoned? In exile? Had he been branded as a fugitive and killed? Or had he been raised from slavery? Most importantly, was he thinking of me?*

'Then, what have you been thinking about?' Val asked, getting down on her knees, peering up at me.

I hesitated, wondering how I should answer. I wanted her to know everything, but I was so sick of reliving it. All I wished for was to have anything else fill my mind. 'The inspection,' I sighed.

She nodded slowly. 'What happened?'

'I have no idea,' I answered, shaking my head.

'What do you mean?' She looked confused.

I sighed. 'I don't know what the Emperor did.'

A frown appeared on her beautiful face. 'I see.' She bit her bottom lip. 'Aemilia, you need to be careful of what you say about Augustus. He's the most powerful man in Rome. What is more, he is your boss and is responsible for everything in your life.'

I nodded. 'I know that. Believe me.'

She exhaled slowly. 'It is clear that you have changed recently, arguably since that day.' She reached up and slowly took my hand in hers. 'I want to be of any help that I can and if speaking against the Emperor will help you, I will not tell a soul, mortal or immortal,' she swore.

The intensity in her eyes was such that my lips trembled. 'You are a good friend, Val. I am very fortunate to have you.'

She smiled sadly. 'Then will you tell me?'

I shook my head. 'Not yet. I can't talk about it now.' My voice was shaky. 'Some other day, perhaps.'

She nodded.

'He had his reasons for what he did. But,' I choked, trying to hold back tears, 'there was so much pain.' I looked down for a moment, the waterfall beginning to tumble down my face. 'I feel disgusting and worthless. I feel dead. I do not know what he did or how, but, at the end of it all, he concluded that I was chaste, still a virgin. '

Her eyes widened. 'Well, that's something, is it not?' she asked, trying to reassure me. 'For that result, perhaps the pain was worth it.'

'Maybe, but he said to me, 'You were a virgin,' as if, after what he did, I somehow wasn't, anymore.' I sighed and shrugged. 'I don't understand it.'

She seemed to brush it off. 'It was probably just a poor choice of words, Aemilia. Even the Emperor can be guilty of that.'

I nodded, frowning. *Perhaps.*

We were both quiet for a few moments.

She sighed and stood up, looking out the window at the city of Rome. 'The empire moves on, Aemilia.' She sounded positive. 'It breathes life into the world because you are chaste. Our virginity represents the health and safety of all that is worthwhile. To the masses, we are like the heroes of old.'

I looked out on the city. 'I'm not a heroine, Val. I am no Achilles.'

'I bet, at times, he didn't feel much like a hero either,' she said. 'Certainly not when he threw that big strop at Troy and refused to fight.'

'It lasted years,' I noted.

'A hero of hysterics,' she agreed, and we both giggled.

The strange familiarity of laughter sent warmth through me that I had not felt in what seemed like a lifetime. My head and chest felt lighter.

Then she looked at me seriously. 'There are people here who love you. There are people out there who worship you. Both are always here for you.' She leant down and kissed my cheek.

I smiled at her. 'Thank you.'

She turned away, pleased that her work was done, that she had successfully comforted me. Perhaps that was true to a certain degree, although the problem was by no means solved. To be honest, I didn't even know what the problem was yet. However, my chest felt lighter and my headache had ebbed slightly. Augustus' hands retracted from my memory just a little bit.

That night, Metallia undressed me.

As usual, I hated the process.

Finally, when we were finished, she walked towards the door and I went to bed. However, as she was turning around to close it behind her, she let out an alarmed shriek as she looked past me to the windowsill.

My head shot up to see Marcus sitting there.

Blood ran down his forehead from his hair. His face was bruised around the temples and cheeks. His right eye was black and swollen. Some kind of blade had sliced through the skin of his left cheekbone. His lip was cut and stained with dark dried blood. There were rope burns around his wrists. He was barefoot, and all he wore was a ragged grimy tunic.

He slid down off the window ledge.

Metallia and I started in shock.

'Let me explain,' he began, holding up his shaky hands in defence, 'because I've thought about this moment all day.'

'You cannot be here,' I replied, my voice quiet, my heart loud.

'Please, Aemilia,' he implored. Tears were filling his eyes. 'Let me talk. Then you can do what you want with me.'

After a moment's thought, I turned to Metallia, who was still standing at the door. 'Fetch some spare clothes for him and bring me a bowl of water and a rag.'

He, hearing no protestation from me, dropped his hands, and his lower lip trembled. 'I have given up all hope,' he whispered. His shining eyes searched the ceiling, desperately.

'Tell me what happened,' I persuaded him, softly.

The tears began to spill from his eyes. 'I - ' he choked, 'went to my grandfather's.' He wiped his eyes, his words coming out in breathy gasps. 'But he ... was not there. My grandmother was.' He sniffled and looked back at me. 'She had me locked up and beaten, interrogating me about how I got there.' His eyes were full of pain. 'In the end, I had to escape. She would have had me killed. She said my grandfather would never know of my return.' He hung his head, crying into his hands. 'They do not want me back. They will never want me back. If I try again, they will surely kill me without any hesitation.'

I took a step forward, my heart breaking to see him like this, but something stopped me from going any further; I just couldn't touch him. 'Oh, Marcus,' I sighed. 'I am so sorry.'

He took a step towards me, looking for an embrace probably.

My hands shot out. 'No, please don't!' I begged, alarm coiling itself around my heart.

The exclamation stopped him in his tracks. His gaze bore into mine. All the pain in his expression died and was replaced with nothing. 'Of course. You don't want me either,' he mumbled.

Suddenly, I felt like a monster. 'What?' I asked, incredulous. 'No, you don't understand - '

'No, I do,' he interrupted, a slow anger building in his eyes. 'You told me never to insult you or this house with my presence again. I remember precisely what you said, but after being hammered and hated by my own family, I had hoped those words were not sincere. I came back for hope, comfort, safety - for you. I realised that I … ,' his voice faded. Then he spoke softly: 'I love you.'

My stomach dropped. *Or was it that my heart stopped?* Either way, those words were world-changing.

'What a colossal fool I've been!' He chuckled drily, shaking his head at the ground.

'I never meant what I said,' I objected. 'I regretted them immediately, and wanted you to come back straight away, but Occia sent me to Augustus for an inspection and - ' The words caught in my throat and I took a moment to reconsider them. I closed my eyes. They were stinging. 'And…' I opened them and found him frowning back at me. In anger, stress or concern, I did not know. My mind raced.

Would he understand? Could he help? If I wanted him to stay, I knew I would have to tell him, no matter how painful it would be to recollect. I licked my lips. 'Please let me explain, as I let you.'

He clenched his jaw, shoulders relaxing forcibly. Then he nodded.

At that moment, Metallia opened the door, hurrying in with a pile of fresh men's garments under one arm and a small ceramic bowl with a cloth draped over the rim in her other hand. She laid the items down on the bed and bobbed a curtsey before leaving again.

'You'll have to bear with me,' I continued, my voice shaking. My hands were sweating. 'I hardly know what I'm talking about.'

Throughout my account of the inspection, full of long pauses and tears, he listened earnestly, sitting on the edge of my bed, freshly changed and dabbing away at his wounds with a wet rag.

I, sitting on the other end, was trembling, telling him everything.

Although he wasn't some scrutinising teacher who would punish me, I still felt like a stupid pupil in a classroom, trying to explain the answer to a question on a test for which I had not studied.

Marcus squeezed the wet rag in his fist before throwing it down into the water-filled bowl. It created a small splash and spilled water onto the floor. Fingers linked tightly together, his knuckles were white. 'That bastard,' he muttered. 'And to think that …' He didn't finish his sentence.

'Excuse me?' I asked.

He looked back at me.

I could see from his eyes that he was feeling everything I was.

'Aemilia, there is an easy way to say what happened to you, but not half as easy to hear or understand. You will be confused, far more than you are already, because you have been left utterly in the dark by that hag of a Chief Vestal.' He stood up and shook his head. 'He took advantage of your ignorance and abused his power.'

'I don't understand.'

'In other words, he sexually assaulted you.'

My throat ran dry. 'What?'

He sighed. 'It's when someone, typically a man, gets to know a woman in the way that only her husband should, but without her permission.'

My forehead grew tense, and my heartbeat swift. 'I still don't understand.'

He ran his hands through his hair. 'There are certain parts of the male and female bodies, private parts, that create new life when they work together. That is what carnal knowledge is. However, to be naked in front of somebody is no small matter - there is great vulnerability. There should be trust, love and mutual respect, but in the eyes of the law marriage is sufficient. They are called 'private parts' for a reason, so any person who even attempts to see, touch or use another person's private parts without their consent is committing a sexual offence. Sexual misconduct is a huge breach of personal space. What he did to you was an evil, painful and violent crime.'

My lips parted in horror. His words had brought my world to a halt.

He was quick to try and make me feel better. 'However, you are still chaste. He would have had to use his own private parts,' he swallowed hard in disgust, 'for you not to be.'

'He said he represented the gods.' I sucked in a breath, recalling the event with a very clear memory. It wasn't hard to remember – it was all I ever thought about.

'That was manipulation.'

'He said that I should think of him as a father,' I breathed out quickly.

'That would be incest,' he sneered.

'Oh, Vesta,' I whispered in panic. I struggled to control myself, beginning to hyperventilate.

Moving to sit beside me, he asked, 'Aemilia, surely you know that a woman should not be seen naked by her father?'

I shook my head. 'How could I? What do I know of family?' I whispered, hot tears slipping down my cheeks. I gulped down a sob, trying to calm myself. 'The clearest memory I have of my father was being carried on his shoulders through Rome for the first time. I remember seeing the sunrise on the Palatine Hill.'

'What age were you?'

'Ten.'

'You would have had memories of him beforehand, surely?'

I let out a dry laugh. 'Marcus, throughout my childhood, my father went away for years at a time. Whenever he returned, he would have gifts for me and money for the people I lived with. He would play with me and love me as any father would. He never raised his voice at me and was nothing except kind. We spent all day every day together and I relished every moment. I cannot recall what we did or talked about, but I remember feeling so happy.'

I smiled sadly at the memory. My eyes stung, but I refused to cry anymore - I did not want Marcus thinking I was utterly weak. 'He never stayed longer than a week. He always departed in the night when I was asleep, so I never saw him leave. I understand that farewells can be painful and he might have wished to spare me that, but what was more heart-breaking was waking up the following morning to find him gone. I never got to ask him when he would be back and I never got to say goodbye. I woke up every morning in the hope that he would come back that day.' My voice cracked as a tear slipped out, despite my determination not to weep. 'I would have never even known what parents were had no one told me about their own or that he was mine. I have few memories of my childhood, but the strongest was the persistent feeling of missing him.'

Marcus had drawn closer, listening intently, with his brows furrowed. 'What about your mother?'

Sighing, I answered. 'I have no recollection of her. There was a woman where I lived, a nurse of sorts, who cared for me, but one day, my father took me from wherever she lived. We spent a few days travelling. I thought that he was finally taking me with him this time, that we would finally be a proper family. We talked and laughed so much together. I hoped the journey would never end.'

I sniffed. 'But it did. When we arrived in Rome, I was brought into the Order of the Vestals almost straight away. Augustus, himself, chose me. As you know, when a Vestal retires after thirty years, her place must be taken by a newcomer, an initiate. The selection ceremony is called The Seizure, and the girl is chosen by lot. My name was drawn. The Emperor took me away from my father with the words,' I gulped, 'which will stay with me forever: 'I take you, Loved One, to be a Vestal priestess, who will carry out the sacred rites which is the law for a Vestal priestess to perform for the Roman people, with all the entitlements of a Vestal Virgin.' Then he walked me into the Temple of Vesta and,' I took a deep breath, 'I quickly discovered that I was never to see my father again. Once more, I hadn't been able to say goodbye. Now, I cannot even remember his face.

'I had to take my vows. I was ten, with not the faintest idea what I was promising to protect. I understood that I had duties to perform, but the words chastity, virginity, rape and sex were all unexplained to me. I understood that they had meaning and importance, but I was never told why.'

Marcus sighed. 'Aemilia, I am so sorry that I abandoned you. Had I known what would happen, I would have gone with you to protect you.'

I frowned. 'I don't blame you. We fought and I told you to go.' My lip trembled. 'But please never do it again.'

He nodded. 'Of course not. I have nowhere else to be except right here.' He was trying to seem happy, but his smile turned sad.

That night I lay awake in bed, and he sat in the chair, also awake. We were looking at each other. It was not awkward. It had been all we wanted to do for several days.

Eventually, my eyes grew tired and I fell asleep.

When I awoke the next morning, Marcus leaned forward and rubbed my hand soothingly. 'Aemilia, what if I may not be welcomed back since I am still a fugitive in the eyes of the law?'

I reassured him that no one but Metallia and I knew he had returned. 'I'm not sure if your absence has been noticed, there are so many slaves here.'

Even so, we agreed on a plan to be sure he would be safe. When Metallia arrived to prepare me for the day, I asked her to spread the word amongst the slaves that Marcus had been dangerously ill the last few days so that his absence could be explained. There wasn't much we could do about his bruises and cuts, but time would heal those. I also kept him busy to ensure the other Vestals saw him as little as possible. It worked. No one wondered aloud why they hadn't seen him around recently, not even Occia. If Val noticed, she didn't say anything.

It seemed that life had returned to normal, and all the slaves had faded into the background once more, Marcus included. The question of my virginity was also forgotten. I even wondered, if Marcus had stayed through the whole thing, would it have subsided. I felt so much safer, now that he was back in my life, and no one seemed to care about us anymore. All they saw was a slave and his mistress.

*

Val and I were sitting on the steps outside the House of the Vestals in the late afternoon.

'He watches you,' she remarked. 'No. It's more than that. He watches out for you.' She smiled. 'Such loyalty in a slave is a blessing.' She gave me a sideways glance and caught my frown. Then she giggled. 'Aemilia, relax. I think that since you have been proven innocent, it would be highly unfair to suspect you or him of anything sinister. You two make a good example of what a slave and his mistress should be.'

I smiled gratefully at her. 'And what is that?'

She hummed, thinking. 'On your part, fairness and patience. On his, attentiveness, anticipation and loyalty.'

'Anticipation?' I asked, giggling.

'To know what you want before you do.'

She was right.

Marcus could phrase my thoughts and feelings better and faster than I could. He seemed to have learnt off by heart all my reactions to everything. He already knew what I was thinking before I opened my mouth. He also knew that too much intimacy might remind me of the inspection. Sometimes it did and I would panic, break down and want to be left alone, so he kept his distance, where possible, and learnt what affection was comfortable for me. For now, it was just hand-holding, but eventually I improved to being able to enjoy the odd unintentional brush of his skin off mine. Soon, he was stroking my hair and caressing my face. With every touch, I became used to him again. I enjoyed it. I had missed it, awfully. I started to desire his embrace, even his kisses. Sometimes we tried, but thoughts of Augustus invaded my mind. Marcus was so good when that happened: he was patient and knew just the right thing to say to help me calm down and remember that I was loved, at least with him.

His attention wasn't always romantic, but it was always caring. He would help me gather water from the spring, fetch scrolls for me off high shelves and hold the door open for me. When after the inspection I had believed I wouldn't be able to stand any man, his presence had become entirely necessary for me to feel safe.

One afternoon, on our way to the records' room, I stopped in my tracks.

Marcus paused behind me.

Turning around, I nodded at him to proceed without me. 'I'll follow shortly,' I reassured him.

With him going on ahead, there was no one else in the corridor except Rufina. She was sitting at the bottom of the staircase leading up to the first floor. She raised her head and looked at me.

It occurred to me that we had not spoken one word to each other since the day before the inspection. We seemed strangers now.

Silence passed, and while I was struggling for something to say, she only blinked her dark eyes at me, no emotion passing over her angular face.

'Rufina,' I began, shuffling my feet awkwardly.

She closed her eyes and sighed. 'Yes?' She already sounded tired of the conversation. She opened her eyes.

I decided to face her square on. 'If you feel that I betrayed you by explaining your dealings with Tiberius to Occia then I completely understand.'

She clenched her jaw and scowled at me.

I carried on. 'I know being the Chief Vestal has always been your biggest dream, something you always tried to prove you could be, and I understand that I might have ruined it.'

She nodded, hanging her head.

'I don't expect you to forgive me,' I continued, 'but I want you to know that it was never my intention to betray you or jeopardise our friendship. I don't blame you for avoiding me. You have probably been hating me. Anyway, that's all I wanted to say. I'm truly sorry.'

As I turned to leave, she suddenly stood up from the step and walked towards me, her face looking stern. 'When

Occia found out about the will, I was devastated. So, you are right - I did hate you. I believed that an inspection was the least you deserved - '

I was taken aback by her bluntness. Her words hurt me more than I could say, but I reminded myself that she and many others knew nothing of what happened in the inspection.

' - and I'm sorry for that. We all know the fear of an inspection, and of what could happen should it go horribly wrong. I shouldn't have wished that upon you. I also know that it was Lavidia who first betrayed my secret, not you. You were trying to save the situation, not worsen it. I understand that now.' She raised an eyebrow. 'Even if you failed catastrophically.'

I nodded, but my heart was still sore.

'To be the Chief Vestal was my greatest aspiration in life, but an aspiration is one of the many things I can have,' she said, looking at me with resignation. 'Most cannot even afford their dreams. I have so many privileges that come with this position. One of them is your friendship.' She wore a genuine smile on her face. 'Anyhow, being Chief Vestal involves so many responsibilities, I don't know if I would be cut out for them!'

After her words, my chest felt lighter and fuller.

With relieved giggles and a few hot tears, we hugged away any animosity that had been between us.

XVII
MINAEQUE POENA
-Threats and Punishment-

It was coming close to twilight. After cena, I was walking towards my bedchamber, and Lavidia was coming from the other direction. We passed each other.

Then her silvery voice travelled towards my ear. 'Where's your favourite slave?' she inquired.

I looked over my shoulder at her. 'Excuse me?'

She shrugged. 'I only ask as he's usually sniffing around you.'

I stopped and turned to face her, hands going behind my back so I wouldn't scratch her eyes out. 'I thought you were the expert in that.'

She laughed. 'My dear Aemilia, you astonish me!'

'Do I? I wouldn't have thought so. Choosing to lie with all the men you come across is hardly an unconscious decision, is it?'

Her smile vanished. She glanced behind us both, then bared her white teeth. 'How dare you suggest such a thing!'

'Men of all classes, I believe,' I continued. 'Do you want to know how I figured it out? There are no noblemen permanently in this house; so I figured, unless you're smuggling your lover in, the best you could do would be a guard or a slave.'

Her face was growing purple.

I grinned, knowing I was right. 'I must admit I am impressed. What a varied diet you must have.'

She clenched her jaw and fists. 'How dare you!' she growled.

'No, Lavidia,' I answered, stepping closer to her. 'How dare you. The finest hypocrite I have ever met.'

She raised an eyebrow. 'I was still proven innocent by the Emperor.'

I rolled my eyes. 'You were claimed to be innocent. We both know that the reason Augustus denied your sins was that he enjoyed them so much himself.' I paused and then added, 'But maybe it was a proper inspection, after all. Girls who are not used to such sensations are far less likely to enjoy them. You, however, were moaning, and I certainly heard you. The whole palace must have.'

She blushed deeply. 'Be clear, Aemilia. Are you accusing me of breaking my vow?'

'No,' I replied. 'Because you would only accuse me back. And frankly, I won't be inspected again, if I can help it.'

She did not reply.

'If, however, you should accuse me first, I would just do the same to you. I have twice the proof you have and far more support from those here.'

She scowled.

'People hate you. I might have taken your threats and bullying far more seriously if you were not so alone in this world,' I said.

Then I turned on my heel and left her behind me.

*

Occia had called me to her presence.

When the slave told me, I was certain Lavidia had accused me of losing my chastity. Fear coursed through me, as well as anger and determination. I prepared myself to charge her.

Marcus knew all about my frustrations with Lavidia, but he implored me not to accuse her in return. 'What good will it achieve?' he asked, standing behind me as I fixed my headdress in the looking glass. 'It will only create more controversy. The previous inspections barely escaped public questioning. Do you think anyone is going to ignore the same Vestal Virgins being called to the House of Augustus for a second time in the space of just a few days? Do you want to go back there?'

'Of course not!' I snapped. 'But me accusing Lavidia won't change whether I go or not. I have to stand up for myself. She has tossed me around like an abused puppy for years, and I have tolerated it. Well, not anymore.'

He nodded, looking down. 'Just be careful.'

I smiled and turned around to look at him properly. 'You know you're my strength.'

He shook his head. 'You were strong before I met you.' Then he reached up and tucked a strand of hair into my headdress.

I descended the stairs into the atrium, approaching the tablinum where the slave had told me to meet Occia. When I knocked on the closed door, she called from the other side for me to enter. I went inside and saw her scribbling away on some scrolls at the desk. I curtseyed before her, not standing until she said so.

'Rise,' she said, still writing. I did so, and she raised her head. 'Ah, Aemilia, my dear.'

'You wanted to see me, domina?'

'Yes,' she said, dropping her pen and clasping her hands, relaxing back in her chair. 'It is no secret that you have been out of sorts lately, Aemilia. As of now you still refuse to say what is going on. While I respect your privacy, I must demand better from you.'

I frowned. 'Domina?'

'You've been slacking. Day-dreaming. Sometimes, you are completely unable to carry out your chores or even make it to class,' she said, sounding quite annoyed.

Although I was relieved I hadn't been summoned on account of Lavidia's malice, this was the first time I had heard her grievances about me in this way. 'My apologies, domina. I will try to do better,' I muttered, lowering my gaze.

'You have said that before, Aemilia. I fear the time has come for more drastic measures.'

I glanced up at her, surprised.

She stood up from her chair, walking around the table, towering over me. 'I have determined that for you to learn to take your tasks seriously, you should tackle the most demanding duty there is for a Vestal Virgin.'

I swallowed, racking my brain. 'And that is?'

'Tonight, while the rest of the Vestals attend a feast at the Emperor's house, you will watch over the Flame of Vesta.'

My mouth dropped open. 'Domina?'

'Aemilia?' she mimicked, raising her eyebrows.

I stuttered and struggled for the right words. 'But I - ' I coughed and cleared my throat. 'I'm only an initiate. You don't think that one of the older Vestals who is more experienced would do this better? Valeriana or Rufina? Even Lavidia?'

She shook her head. 'No,' she replied. 'It might surprise you to know that I believe in learning on the job.'

'Might I know why you have chosen this particular task?' I asked, trying to come to terms with the situation.

She smiled. 'It is the perfect punishment. It deprives you of a night of frivolity with your friends, of meeting the imperial family and the rest of the aristocracy, while simultaneously guarding the Flame which, if it were to go out, could jeopardise civilisation as we know it.' She sighed to herself. 'I am quite proud of the idea. I came up with it myself.'

I didn't doubt it.

XVIII
FLAMMAE
-The Flames-

Standing alone in the doorway, the first thing I saw was the twenty commanding Corinthian columns, and behind them danced saffron flames - the Flame of Vesta. Above it, the ornate domed roof let the smoke climb out into the evening through a gap. The walls and pillars glowed golden. The tall circular walls protected the heart of the empire.

The Temple of Vesta was deserted. Although Occia had taught us that Vesta was constantly present in her earthly home, the place felt utterly abandoned by any divine being. The sacred water and the sacred cake used for sacrifices now seemed inedible among the sanctified items upon the pedestals. The Palladium, a wooden statue of the goddess Minerva in battle dress with her spear and shield, which the prince Aeneas had rescued from burning Troy, seemed cold and distant like the spirit inside her had vanished.

This was not the first time that I had seen the Flame. On days of sacrifice and festivity, I had witnessed this building come to life with people. On those days, Vesta's Flame seemed far more glorious. Now, it just seemed dangerous, like a raging force alone in the world.

Sitting down in front of the monstrous hearth with its loud fire crackling, roaring and spitting, I was afraid to get too close. I crossed my legs and leant back against a pillar, with two sticks beside me to rub together in case the fire ever went out. I tried to imagine that Vesta herself was sitting beside me so not I would not feel so alone in this place.

Despite everything I held faith in, I felt more than ever like I was doing nothing. Previously, watching over the

Flame had always seemed to me to be a spiritual and holy act, but now I just felt useless and bored. For a moment, I knew that if Saturn froze time and came to this temple, with me inside it, the fire would seem to have more life in it than I.

After some time, I heard footsteps. I turned around to see Marcus entering. He was carrying a bundle in his arms. As he came in, he kicked the door shut behind him, sending the temple into darkness, save for the space around the vast, glowing beacon.

'Good gods,' he breathed, approaching me, but his attention was on his surroundings. A smile played on his face. 'I haven't been here in years. I had forgotten what it looked like.'

For a moment, I was confused, but then I remembered he had grown up in Rome. 'You got my message, did you not? The slave I sent? I will be here for the night while the others are at the House of Augustus. There is no need to be on duty.'

He shook his head and tutted. 'A suitor is always on duty.' He winked.

'Suitor?' I smiled.

He shrugged, laying down the bundle, which seemed to be a bunch of items wrapped in a blanket. 'Sweetheart, lover, partner. You name it.' He uncovered the food, which I then pawed as I inspected it.

'We're not lovers,' I reminded him, trying to sound stern.

'Yes, I know,' he muttered. He then spread out the blanket and, sitting down, snatched back the bread I had taken. 'You'll have the chance to eat that soon!'

'Bread, cheese, grapes and honey-cakes. You are spoiling me.' I looked up at him, impressed.

'I took them from the house kitchens,' he admitted, scratching the back of his head.

I sent him a disapproving look.

He just grinned in return.

I smiled. 'You seem happy.'

'Of course, I am.' He reached over, wrapping his arms around my waist and pulling me next to him. 'I get to spend time with you.'

I rested my head on his shoulder. 'You spend all your time with me.'

He gestured to the empty temple. 'Yet we're never completely alone, with no one or nothing else to worry about.' He looked at me, his smile dying, but still some light of enjoyment in his eyes. 'We can really talk.'

'We talk.'

He shook his head. 'Not about serious things. Not about us.'

'Us?' My eyebrows shot up. 'Alright, what did you wish to discuss?'

'Since we have been together again, you have not once reminded me of your vows.' He looked at me inquisitively. 'Why not?'

I glanced away. 'I don't know exactly.'

'Because I was hoping,' he began, taking my hand in his, 'that this is something that you actually want, and you have accepted that.'

Perhaps it was the pull of his eyes that persuaded me to nod. 'I suppose I have,' I admitted, realising it as I spoke. 'Of course, I want this. I am happiest when I'm with you.'

A smile began to grow on his face.

A sudden urge made me lean forward and place a light kiss on his cheek. When I pulled back, he was wide-eyed and grinning. I looked away as there was a moment of silence. I wasn't sure if it was awkward or not. *Should I have kissed him?* My heart beat faster. Then I felt his lips on the top of my head and his arm wrapped around my shoulders. My chest warmed, and I tried not to smile too much.

His other hand gestured to the food he had brought. 'Now, this is not for decoration, my dear. Tonight, we shall dine like the kings of old!' he proclaimed.

I laughed. 'If we lived in the time of the kings of old, I would have a very different life. I wouldn't be a Vestal for a start. There were only two in the beginning. Rhea Silvia was the first.'

He nodded. 'Not to mention, she was the mother of Rome's founders, Romulus and Remus.'

I shook my head sadly. 'Forced on both counts. She became a Vestal against her will and the god Mars raped her in her sleep, impregnating her.'

'Yes, indeed.'

'As soon her twins were born, they were taken from her. Then she was weighed down with chains and thrown into a dungeon as punishment for losing her chastity. She wasn't directly executed since it is illegal to spill the blood of a Vestal, as you probably know.

'Her twins were thrown into a river and, although they survived and founded our city, she didn't ever get to hold them. She was killed for something which wasn't her fault and they tried to kill her children for the same reason.' I scowled. 'But people seem to insist on forgetting that.'

'A cowardly thing.'

'Thank the gods, it is different nowadays.' I breathed a sigh of relief.

'Why? How is it done today?'

'A live burial.'

His head swivelled to look at me with wide eyes. 'What?' he whispered, utterly stunned.

I raised an eyebrow. 'It is not exactly a merciful, painless or swift death. There is a funeral procession through the city towards the cemetery of the Evil Field, near the Colline Gate. The impure Vestal descends into a tomb, with enough food and water to last her a few days.

The vault is closed. She sits there, alone in the dark until she starves to death or dies of thirst.'

'Jupiter's good kingdom.' He sucked in a breath.

I shrugged. 'I think there have been worse fates in the past. I wouldn't have wanted to be one of the Sabine Women, for example, stolen from my friends and family, and forced to be with a complete stranger.'

He hummed in agreement. 'Romulus' worse moment as king, I think.'

'And Lucretia – she too had a bad end.'

'Yes,' he said. 'Out of all the wives of the friends of Sextus Tarquinius, the son of the king, she was considered the best. Did he not break into her house one night, when her husband was away, and said that if she didn't consent to lie with him, he would rape her anyway, kill her and put a dead slave in her bed, too?'

I nodded.

'And to avoid the shame of such an end, she let him have his way? From what I remember, he confessed everything to her husband and family the following morning. Then she stabbed herself in front of them because she knew she had sinned.'

'Exactly. She had to end her life for a decision in which both options were adultery, rape and shame,' I said. 'Sextus was the one who forced her, yet there were no repercussions for him.'

Marcus frowned. 'But it showed the corruption of the royal family, which was then overthrown and the republic established. In a way, Sextus got his punishment.'

'But did it have to happen at all?' I asked. 'His lust resulted in the loss of her life.'

'It should have never happened. I agree.'

'And Virginia?' I asked. 'Do you remember her?'

He swallowed. 'I think so. A plebeian girl desired by a patrician and kidnapped, possibly raped. Upon her rescue, her father, a mere centurion, knew the only way to protect her was to kill her himself, which he did.'

'You see?' I said. 'History is full of men's lust destroying women's lives.'

'Indeed, Aemilia, but Rhea Silvia gave birth to the founders of Rome. The Sabine women became mothers of the next generation. Lucretia's death lead to democracy, and Virginia's end showed the lengths that the poor would go to for their rights, which they then received. Each incident created a better world.'

'For whom? Men?' I demanded, scoffing. 'That was already the case.'

'What are you talking about? Women have it better too,' he argued.

I scowled at him. 'If women had it so much better, had it equal, I would be able to take the Emperor himself to court and walk away satisfied.'

He looked down.

My voice grew quiet. 'Or do you think that what happened between him and me was my sin and I am to blame?'

His head shot up. 'Of course not.' He was perfectly serious.

'Then can you say the same for all those women in the past? Don't you see how we should be ashamed of our history?' I asked him, genuinely wanting an answer. I looked at the Flame of Vesta. 'This fire represents the glory of Rome, but it is glory built on pain and not that of those who profited.'

He stared at me, wide-eyed for a moment before sighing in resignation. 'You are right.'

Slightly surprised he gave in so easily, I blinked. Then I nodded, choosing to pardon his words. I didn't want to draw out the argument unnecessarily.

We were silent for a few moments, in slight awkwardness. Then I said, 'The more I think about it, the more I believe that by complying with the Emperor during the inspection, I might have saved myself from a worse fate.'

Confusion passed over his face.

I explained myself. 'He could have decided to condemn me to death if I had refused to cooperate.'

He shook his head, looking at the floor. 'I don't like that,' he said, curling his lip. 'He is not at all the man I thought he was.'

'You're not alone there,' I replied.

He grabbed my hand tightly. 'That will never happen to you again, Aemilia. I swear it on my life.'

I smiled sadly and kissed the top of his hand softly, bringing it up to my lips.

He regarded me with a sudden fascination. 'Was there not a previous Vestal Aemilia?'

I blinked. 'The Aemilia of myth? She performed a miracle, so the story goes. After praying to Vesta, she rekindled the fire by tossing a piece of her clothing onto the embers. She was legendary.'

'Yes, she most certainly is,' he replied softly, and kissed me.

Blushing, I giggled. Then I remembered something else. 'There was also another Vestal Aemilia, I think, who lived around a century ago. She was found to be unchaste and was reportedly trying to corrupt other Vestals. She was executed for it. So, you see, I have two namesakes.'

He looked back to the fire. 'And what happens if it does go out?' he asked. 'What is the punishment for that?'

'The Vestal responsible is flogged naked by the Pontifex Maximus in a dark room, with a curtain to protect her modesty.' I shivered.

'He whips you?'

I looked up and saw the anger in his eyes. I nodded.

'The bastard,' he growled. 'I could kill him.'

'Don't think like that.'

He threw his hands up into the air. 'I can. I could. I would get away with it too. Anyone who harms a Vestal deserves death.'

I rolled my eyes. 'Yes, anyone except the Emperor.'

He huffed, hesitating before saying, 'Well, anyone who hurts you deserves to die, no matter who they are.'

I snorted. 'As if!'

He looked at me seriously, eyebrows high.

I looked down. 'I keep trying to think of the logic behind it.'

He scowled. 'What logic?'

I sighed, unsure. 'Perhaps it is a valid method of testing whether or not a Vestal is used to being touched in that way. Do you understand what I'm trying to say?'

He clenched his jaw. 'Unfortunately, I do. But you're trying to justify a crime, Aemilia, a crime against you.'

'I don't know how Lavidia could have possibly enjoyed it,' I wondered aloud. 'All I felt was pain.'

He nodded. 'You have not experienced lust yet.'

'What do you mean?'

He paused, thinking of the right words. 'Well, if you had been feeling lustful at the moment, the chances are you would have enjoyed it more.'

'Really?'

'Really, but I have no idea what lust to a woman feels like.' Then he gave me a gentle smile. 'Don't feel like you're missing out, Aemilia. Most people make those decisions in their own time.' His smile died. 'Sometimes, in circumstances which should never happen, someone else decides for them.'

I gulped, closing my eyes. I could feel Augustus' hand between my legs.

'I'm sorry,' Marcus said. 'I shouldn't have said that.'

'It's alright.' I took a deep breath. 'I must seem like such an idiot.'

He shook his head. 'No, you're witty, kind, careful and considerate, Aemilia, not to mention very beautiful. It is an honour to even sit beside you.' He clasped my hand and brought it up to his lips. 'And a very great pleasure.'

We both burst into giggles, nervous, relieved and delighted. We feasted on bread and cheese with grapes, followed by honey-cakes and wine. When we had finished gorging ourselves, we sat back, me in his arms, resting my head on his shoulder with him holding me tightly at his side.

XIX
CUPIDITAS ET CONFESSIO
-Desire and Confession-

That night, Marcus held me in his arms tighter than ever before. We kissed in drowsy affection. Before the glowing, golden hearth, I fell asleep in the familiar safety of his embrace.

He roused me in the morning, gently rocking me awake.

My weary eyes opening, I frowned at him, disapprovingly.

He grinned at me and said, 'Good morning, domina.'

I smiled at the sound of his hoarse and sleepy voice, coupled with his tousled hair. 'Good morning.'

He chuckled, looking down at me. 'The other Vestals will be here soon to take over and they can't find us like this.'

Lazily, we tidied up the blankets and the remnants of our modest banquet. He tucked them under his arm, and turned to me.

I couldn't help but smile, reaching up to ruffle his hair. 'You look very handsome,' I giggled.

'Thank you, domina.' He leant against one of the Corinthian columns, yawned and eyed me up and down. 'And while I can say you look beautiful, I doubt your fellow Vestals would agree. In fact, I think they would describe you as somewhat of a mess.'

Suddenly, quite awake, I rushed to make myself look presentable. I fixed my hair under my headdress and correctly rearranged my skirts. Then I looked at the Flame, and to my relief, it was still burning brightly. 'Thank Vesta, it did not go out,' I breathed, finally able to relax.

'Thank me! You were awful. You even fell asleep on the job. Whatever will I tell the Chief Vestal?' He grinned.

I spluttered and laughed before pecking his cheek. 'You were asleep for the whole night too.'

'Not the whole night,' he muttered, pulling me in for a kiss.

I laughed against his lips.

We remained in the temple until Rufina came in to take over.

*

On our return to the house, the other girls were filled with stories about the imperial banquet and the people present. Still in their nightdresses, Val and Picia, in their glee, restaged some of the conversations for me and then whisked each other in a dance around the floor of Val's bedchamber.

'How was last night for you?' Picia asked me, sitting beside me on Val's bed.

Amid the excitement, I nearly forgot about my secret, bursting to share that I had spent the night with Marcus, in his arms, kissing his cheeks and hands and being kissed in return, but I bit my lip and quickly reconsidered. 'I found it tiring, but I managed,' I replied, adding a little yawn for effect.

Occia asked me the same question at breakfast. 'How did your night go, Aemilia? I trust the Flame of Vesta burned brightly.'

'Ah, yes!' Lavidia pitched in, smiling toothily at me. 'I'm afraid your absence quite escaped our notice last night, Aemilia. We were having such a ball.' She smirked. 'But how was the great punishment? Was it arduous? Do tell!'

With a bread roll halfway on its journey to my mouth, I smiled at her, but addressed Occia. 'Indeed, domina, it gave me much time to reflect.'

The Chief Vestal nodded her satisfaction. 'I'm glad to hear it.' She clasped her hands. 'Now, I think we can consider the whole matter closed.'

I bit into the bread roll, showing my teeth to Lavidia.

*

'Ah,' Gnaeus said, bowing deeply. 'Greetings, Vestal Aemilia.' He straightened up.

I forced a smile onto my face and clasped my hands. 'Perfect, I am glad you made time to come and see me.' I gestured to the recliners in front of us. 'Please, won't you have a seat?'

We made our way over and sat down opposite each other.

I spied Marcus standing in the corner of the room, after closing the door, watching us. If he hadn't been there, I might not have been able to do this.

The Perfect cleared his throat, officially beginning the conversation. 'Does this concern what I asked you a while ago?'

I compelled myself to keep smiling sweetly. 'Indeed. I feel I have come to a decision.'

He nodded pleasantly, patiently waiting to hear it.

For the first time, I felt warmth from him; undoubtedly friendly, but it was not enough to change my mind. 'I fear it is not the reply you are hoping for,' I warned him.

The positivity in his countenance died immediately. He nodded again, thoughtfully frowning down at the floor. 'I see,' he replied, voice quiet.

A sensation of guilt began to grow within me. Despite being a brute, I still did not wish to see him disappointed. 'I am sorry,' I continued. 'It is simply that I feel that you have chosen your Vestal rather poorly.' I laughed nervously.

He looked up at me in confusion, even offence.

'However, that is a reflection on me, not you.'

'Go on,' he said, placing a hand on his knee, bracing himself for my explanation.

'Please do not think me ungrateful or that I do not feel the compliment of your proposal,' I went on, smiling through the blatant lie. I spotted Marcus reflecting on your reasons for wanting to marry a Vestal and I believe you should choose a different one to me.'

'Oh?'

'If you feel you will not need more children, if you would rather a female companion, then might I suggest that you choose someone much more knowledgeable than I am with whom you can have deep and meaningful discussions?'

He blinked, seemingly surprised at this idea.

'Despite having the best education a girl can get, as inexperienced as I am, I do not think I would succeed in that.'

He frowned again, but also seemed to smile, as if amused. 'So you're rejecting me because you think I would not be satisfied with our conversation?' he asked, sounding baffled at the notion.

'Yes,' I chuckled nervously again. 'But I am also thinking of the children you already have. I am so young and without any wisdom. I never knew my own mother. I do not know how such a figure is to function in a child's life.'

'But by the time you are free from your duties, you would be more mature,' he argued. 'Besides, my children will be much older by then. They will not need a mother.'

'Perfect Gnaeus,' I said, seeing I would have to try a different approach. 'If what you desire is the wealth and status which would come from having a Vestal for a wife and if you do not care for fertility, why not choose one who is at the end of her servitude now, not one who is hardly halfway through?'

He shifted in his seat uncomfortably, now that I was getting down to the ugly facts, and opened his mouth to speak. Yet, no words came out. His eyes searched the air for an answer.

'Are you married now?' I asked suddenly, realising I did not know but had always just assumed he was widowed or divorced.

His gaze landed on me, wide-eyed. He gulped visibly.

Ah. 'Well then,' I concluded. 'Therein lies my first and foremost reason for declining your offer.' I shook my head. 'I will not entertain marriage prospects from one still wed. When you are no longer married, you may ask me again if you so desire.'

He nodded, accepting that. 'I think I will.'

Gods above, would I never be rid of this man? I realised I would have to appeal to his more practical nature.

'However, there is one more reason why I think you should choose a different Vestal,' I continued, dreading what I would have to say next.

He raised his eyebrows in anticipation.

'There are so many other girls here whose families are grander, older, wealthier and more powerful than mine ever was and ever will be,' I pointed out. 'In fact, all of them. You would gain far more by marrying any other Vestal than me, because to even compare to their families, I would first need to have one.' I glanced down at my hands, murmuring, 'Which I do not.'

As I looked up, I saw him appearing confused. 'What?'

'You have heard a great deal about the achievements of my father, Prefect,' I expanded. 'But as far as I know, he is dead and I have no other family. If you imagine I have two rich grandfathers and several successful cousins then you are terribly mistaken. I have no relatives of which I know. I consider myself entirely orphaned. My only family are the Vestals. There is no other fortune or social standing I possess, except what has been given to me by the Order. So by marrying me, you would be marrying nothing.'

His eyes widened in horror. His face revealed the shock at his mistake in pursuing me, a destitute girl with nothing to add to his world. He almost immediately looked away.

I tried for a chuckle. It came out as more of a wheeze. I stood up, clasping my hands. 'I am sorry to have had to tell you that, but there it is – my own little tragedy.'

He stood up slowly. Not even looking at me, his throat bobbed as he thought carefully. Then he finally spoke in a low and gruff voice. 'I am sorry to have taken up so much of your time, domina.' He bowed curtly, then turned on his heel and left.

My eyes began to sting and I looked away, facing the window.

Marcus was immediately in front of me. 'Aemilia,' he whispered gently, cupping my face. 'He is not worth your grief or shame. You don't have to care what he thinks of you.'

I looked up into his eyes, my vision slightly blurry. I sniffled and looked down, letting some tears slip out. 'It's not so much his reaction, but knowing that it would happen.' I breathed out shakily. 'It is always what happens. It is the truth, and it drives people away.'

He turned my face towards him, guiding my chin with his fingers. 'Don't you dare include me in that.' He wiped my tears away with his thumb.

I smiled at his words as he brought me into his arms.

XX
CLADES
-Carnage-

Val came bursting into my room. I had just swung my legs out from under the bedsheets. Alarmed, I drew the sheets up to my chest, but she seemed not to notice. Appearing demented, her hair was like the nest of a bird, and she was still in her nightdress.

Marcus, who had sat in the Egyptian chair last night, jumped up from his sleep as if ready to fight something, but upon seeing Val he relaxed and swiftly moved out of the way.

'Aemilia!' she cried, dashing towards my bedside. 'Dreadful news! Truly disastrous!'

I stared at her in shock as she knelt before me. 'Calm yourself! What is going on?'

Tears welled up in her eyes.

Rufina and Picia appeared at the door, also unprepared for the day. Picia was tear-stained and red-faced, while Rufina was paler than a corpse, and stared into space, unblinking.

Val bit back a sob and sniffled. 'Word has just reached Rome that three entire legions and all their auxiliaries were massacred at the frontier in Germania.'

My bones felt like ice.

'It was an ambush, they're saying,' she continued, tears overflowing from her eyes. 'Apparently, they were attacked and killed by some Gallic tribes. They say the Emperor has gone mad!'

'When did this happen?'

'The night before last,' she answered.

Rufina whispered from the doorway, 'They do not yet know how many were enslaved.'

I looked back at Val in horror. 'And how many killed?'

'At most?' she gulped. 'Twenty thousand men were slaughtered.'

My entire body felt numb and my hands went to my open mouth. My eyes stung. Perhaps Marcus swore from the corner of the room, but I hardly heard him.

'They're saying it is the greatest defeat of our army and the worst tragedy of the Roman Empire ever,' Picia said, wiping her nose with her sleeve and staring at me, wide-eyed and trembling.

I jumped from the bed and told Marcus to fetch Metallia. We rushed to get dressed and then the entire household - slaves, guards and Vestals - bolted to the atrium where Occia had summoned us all to officially deliver the devastating news.

Just like us, the rest of Rome could not understand. *It was inviolable, was it not?* Sure enough, there had been defeats, only small and insignificant skirmishes in the past, but nothing of note. However, there had never been a loss on this scale, of this grandeur and magnitude.

'Can you imagine it?' Picia whispered.

I peeked sideways and saw her eyes were open, staring at the ground and shining with tears.

'Marching in strange lands, cutting through knotted tree branches, only to be cut down yourself with the slow realisation that you will never see your homeland or your family again, as you're robbed of your life.'

No one answered her.

'It reminds me of the Spartans,' she murmured, staring into the sacrificial fire on the altar of Vesta in our atrium.

'What?' Rufina snapped.

Picia, for the first time ever, I believed, didn't seem to notice or care for Rufina's bad temper. 'Their power was more unstable and vulnerable than they had realised. Although they were thought to be invincible, the moment it was proved untrue, their reputation - their myth - was shattered, and they were no longer the masters of the world.'

Val scoffed. 'Oh Picia, do shut up,' she said, eyes closed in prayer.

The small girl fell quiet, flushing in shame.

I realised, despite her innocent childishness, often mistaken for stupidity, that in her sadness Picia was wiser than the rest of us.

Messengers came and went during the day. The reports that Emperor Augustus had gone mad were seemingly accurate. Apparently, he would not leave his garden and kept banging his head against the trees, shouting at the sky, at the dead soul of General Varus, who had led the expedition, to give him back his legions.

'This is a time of disaster, my dears,' Occia murmured during a melancholy midday lunch.

She was right. Once the shock had settled, despair ensued. The House of the Vestals was quiet, almost ghostly. Very few Vestals conversed unless they had to. The liveliness was sapped from the walls and its inhabitants, and everyone was affected. Even Marcus was far away in his mind and, like other slaves, was shaky and absent-minded in carrying out his tasks.

Occia sent a messenger to Augustus asking if there was anything the Vestals could do.

He replied after a while with the words: 'There is nothing that any mortal can do. Until the gods smile on us again, all that the Vestals can do is perform their duties with the same dedication as always. But this I require of everyone who holds a place for Rome and its people in their hearts.'

So, obediently we went about our day, but the air was heavy with woe and lamentation.

In the late afternoon, there was a knock on the main door of the house. Believing it was another messenger with an announcement from the Emperor or news from the front

– anything to prove there was still hope for Rome and signs of life out in the cold northern Gallic forests – we all crowded into the atrium, but it was no messenger.

At the door to the House of the Vestals was at least half the Praetorian Guard. We were alarmed at the sight of an armed host crowded at the entrance.

'What is the meaning of this, Prefect?' Occia demanded as Gnaeus marched through the doorway, entirely clad in armour, the clanging of his footsteps against the floor of the atrium echoing around the house.

'Vestal Occia,' he announced gruffly, his small mean eyes glaring at her and scanning the Vestals around her. 'As you know by now, Rome has been blown by grave misfortune.' He coughed, clearing his throat, and held up a scroll in his hand. 'But however strong mournful emotion may be, justice does not stop for it. It cannot.'

'Excuse me?'

He raised his chin higher. 'All reasons for this setback must be found and those responsible punished. I have it on imperial authority to arrest all Vestals guarding of the Flame of Vesta on that fateful night.'

My heart began to hammer.

Occia spluttered in shocked laughter, 'You believe that the blame falls on the Vestal Virgins?'

'I do not believe anything, nor does the Emperor,' he corrected her, spitting harshly, his neck turning red beneath his armour. 'But as I said, we must explore all possible reasons.'

'You mean scapegoats!' she spat back.

At that, he drew his sword with such swift prowess that the sound of it passing out of its sheath sliced the air, and I winced. Hands flew to mouths in shock and Picia let out a cry of protest. Occia, however, did not flinch, not even when he placed the tip of the blade beneath her white throat.

'Domina Occia,' he murmured, deathly calm. 'I hope what you are saying does not imply disrespect for justice, an offence for which all persons, including your great self, can be imprisoned. Take into consideration the twenty thousand lost souls.'

Her hands curled up by her sides and her knuckles turned white. 'I am, Prefect,' she hissed in reply. 'I wonder why you would call it a 'setback'.'

'I urge you to be compliant. I have to arrest the priestesses responsible for the Flame of Vesta the night the battle took place.'

'How should I know when it occurred?'

'Two nights ago, domina,' he answered smoothly, even going so far as to smirk. 'Cast your mind back. You and your ladies came to the House of Augustus for a banquet. But you must have left at least one behind.'

She seemed to freeze in realisation.

'If you tell me no one was looking after the Flame, I will arrest you instead,' he threatened with a growl.

She swallowed and lowered her eyes. 'There was just one: Vestal Aemilia.'

When all the eyes landed on me, I realised that I had known all along that this would happen from the moment I first met Marcus. I could hear nothing except my heartbeat in my chest and drumming blood in my ears. My throat and mouth were dry, my hands sweaty and there were flutters in my stomach. Somehow I knew not to object or resist, but to step forward and offer myself up to the Praetorian Guard with all my dignity. So I did.

The whole room was silent as I moved.

Gnaeus dropped his sword from Occia's neck, his eyes glaring into me like demons would from the depths of the Underworld, and he approached me. He bared his teeth at me in a bloodthirsty grin, raising the tip of his sword again and poking my chin with it. 'Vestal Aemilia, you are arrested on the charge of letting the Flame of Vesta go out, and whatever reason led to it.'

'I have done nothing wrong,' I managed to croak.

He chuckled. 'Don't bother trying to convince me. You'll have to answer to the whole country for your actions.'

I blushed, knowing he was right.

'Now, all I want to know is: were you alone?' He glanced at everyone around me.

I scowled at him. 'I was the only Vestal there. Spare the rest of them your bullying and arrest me. It's what you came to do. I wonder how the Emperor would feel if he knew you had wasted precious time,' I snapped.

He gritted his teeth at me, his knuckles growing white around the hilt of his sword.

I realised it had been wrong to challenge him from a position of weakness. I glanced behind him to Occia, who was looking defeated at me; there was nothing she could do now.

Suddenly, my vision was blocked by a head of chocolate brown curls, and my nose filled with his familiar scent.

'The lady has forgotten,' Marcus said, after coming between the Prefect and me, 'that I, her slave, was with her that night.'

Shock shook the room; the Vestals gasped.

Gnaeus stared at Marcus in bewilderment.

Marcus kept speaking while he could. 'I can also vouch that the Flame of Vesta burned all night.'

I shook my head, absolutely stupefied by his colossal idiocy. My heart told me he meant well while my head screamed at him. *What on Jupiter's good earth was he thinking?*

'Slaves are biased witnesses,' Gnaeus growled.

I saw Marcus' back become still in realisation.

'Whatever you vouch for means nothing.' He turned to his men. 'Arrest them both!'

Several soldiers ran forward before either of us had chance to react. They grabbed me by the arms and forced my wrists together, binding them in rope.

Marcus, I saw out of the corner of my eye, had also been arrested.

'Furthermore,' Gnaeus bellowed, 'seeing as you were alone with a man for an entire night' - my blood ran cold and my lips opened in horror, knowing what he would say next – 'I see it is only appropriate to charge you with the breakage of your vow of chastity. For such an action constitutes the dying of the Flame of Vesta and the subsequent obliteration of three whole Roman legions.' He then nodded to the guards restraining us. 'The imperial dungeons. Now.'

XXI
CARCER
-Prison-

It was the same cramped room as last time. I wondered if the Emperor knew and it was just a sick joke to him or maybe it was just a coincidence. One glance at the tight walls and the memories swept back of how he had invaded me. The only way I could distract myself from those nightmares was to remember Marcus; how he had cherished me and helped me understand it all. He tried to heal me, and for a time he had succeeded, but I, now, understood that wounds such as these would never fully recover.

Marcus. The gladiator. The hero. The slave. The fool who felt the need to protect me and give attitude to a man so much more powerful than he, getting himself arrested and gaoled too, when he could have stayed out of it and stayed alive.

I had known that this road of love led to death. I had known it all along and just trotted merrily down it, forgetting all my sensibility. I should have never let him into my heart in the first place. Now, we would both go to our doom because of each other.

Curling up in a ball once again on this floor, scolding myself, scolding him, cursing the Emperor and his Prefect, apologising to all the Vestals, to the world, to the gods, I cried. I wept for the loss of my dignity and reputation. I wept for the loss of Marcus and what we had. I mourned the passing of the most incredible time of my life. It was all gone now.

What could I do? I stared around the room, desperately trying to find some faith in my better fortunes. My hands found the floor and, with my tears wetting it further, I pressed my face against it. Sobbing into the stone floor, I struggled to pray. *Were the gods even listening to me anymore?*

I did not regret it. I had feelings for him, intense feelings. Furthermore, he, as far as I knew, returned them. The time I had with him, the emotions, the affection and what we did together were the most extraordinary things I have ever experienced. *Would I ever know anything better?*

*

Cornelius Bestus was the most average man I had ever come across. Normal height. Unremarkable build. He had a short haircut and a clean-shaven face like all the rest of them. In his late twenties, I assumed. Old enough to have been in the world of law for a few years, but not long enough to have made a name for himself. He certainly would after this.

I would make his career or break it before it had barely begun.

'I am sorry you have to do this,' I murmured, after he had stepped into the room and introduced himself. I quickly got over the initial terror of a strange man in such close quarters. I was still wary.

'Do not apologise, domina,' he said, smiling kindly. 'It is an honour to serve you in your time of need.'

It was not the countenance I would have expected from any Roman man, considering my current situation. I raised an eyebrow. 'I doubt you will be saying that when I am dead.'

He was not put off by my words, but smiled brightly and clapped his hands. 'Which it is my job to avoid. Shall we begin?'

He turned, knocked on the door and a soldier brought in two stools for us to sit down on. He looked at me expectantly.

'I suppose so,' I muttered, doubting what good it could do as we took our places.

He turned serious, leaning in, his light-grey eyes wide and genuine. 'Domina, if you are going to convince anyone, you must seem to be utterly convinced of it yourself. You have to appear confident. If you appear ashamed and already defeated, you will immediately lose.'

I sighed, understanding.

'There is no point in wallowing in self-pity. Harden your mind,' he encouraged. 'Sit up straight! Focus on survival.'

I obeyed, surprised at his positivity. Had he not studied law, I would have recommended him to the army.

'Now, are you ready to begin?'

I chose to believe in it. 'Yes,' I answered firmly.

'Brilliant!' he celebrated, grinning and throwing his hands up before clasping them again. 'Now, domina, there is only one person on earth you can trust with the truth: my good self. Why? Because I need to know exactly what to say and what not to say. I need to tell your story in such a way that you live through this.'

'I do not know where to begin,' I confessed. 'There is much to tell. I don't know if you will want to hear some of it.'

He smiled reassuringly. 'Domina, it doesn't matter whether I like it or not or if my good opinion of you deteriorates. If I successfully defend you, I get my name engraved on plaques all over the empire. That is all I care about.' He cleared his throat. 'Would it help if you simply answered some of my questions instead?'

Maybe it was foolish of me to blindly trust a complete stranger with the secrets of my past to safeguard my future, but, somehow, now that I understood our success depended on each other, I decided to trust him.

So I told him everything, from the time I first set eyes on Marcus to yesterday when I was arrested, including every last detail of our relationship. I told him about the teachings of the Vestals, about the Emperor's inspection, and about the night I guarded the Flame of Vesta. I even told him about Lavidia's affairs.

He remained so silent and still throughout it all that when I was finished, he didn't speak for some time and just stared at me, hands clasped in front of his mouth.

I almost regretted telling him as much as I did, but the relief from finally telling the whole, absolute, unobscured truth washed over me, and I relaxed, slouching in my chair.

'Well,' he croaked hoarsely. 'That was quite the narrative, domina.'

I blushed.

He coughed nervously. 'I will not tell most of that to the jury. I fear that, from this moment, only three people may ever know the whole truth: you, the slave and me.'

I nodded in agreement.

He sighed. 'Our best course of action is to say there was never anything between you both. You were simply a kind mistress and he a loyal slave. How does that sound?'

'That seems best.'

'We could also turn the blame around on Vestal Lavidia who, as you say, is definitely not chaste,' he suggested, raising an eyebrow. 'In fact, she could be the real reason behind this military disaster, not you.'

I frowned. 'I don't think I could do that.'

He licked his lips, clasping his hands on his lap. 'Domina, with all due respect, you are in no position to be kind. When one's life is on the line, the only course of action is to be ruthless to all, even friends.'

'I would hardly say she's my friend.'

He threw up his hands and grinned. 'Well then! Why would you protect her? It seems she would waste no time in blaming you. She has broken her vow, yet she goes free. You have remained true, but you are accused of causing the greatest catastrophe of our age and are facing execution. If you are dead, there is nothing to stop her bringing more disaster down on our heads. Think of the rest of us,' he implored.

I shook my head. 'We have nothing other than my witness testimony. Would it look plausible when the accused Vestal tries to shift the blame onto someone else, with no more substantial evidence?'

He nodded, sadly. 'Perhaps, it would not. Our case would be fragile. But still, we could try our best.'

I frowned. My heart was telling me it was wrong. 'No. If I die, should you feel a sense of duty to bring her sins to public attention, you may. As you say, if the roles had been reversed, she would have accused me without hesitation, but I will be a better person than her, even if everyone else thinks otherwise. I will not feel responsible for her death, nor will I leave any more carnage in my wake.'

Thus he moved on, discussing the charges with me and building up arguments. When he left, I felt a new sense of hope that I hadn't before. He had given me the courage to fight on a bit longer. Over the following days, I could not leave my little room. The only person I saw was Cornelius. Once, he brought me a list of the witnesses which both the defence and the prosecution would question.

I looked up at him. 'What can each of them possibly know?'

'Well,' he thought aloud. 'Your friends will vouch for your good character, I'm sure. Vestal Lavida will probably do her best to condemn you, which I will try my utmost to thwart. The Chief Vestal will hopefully discuss your virtues. The Emperor's inspection will most likely be mentioned - '

I sucked in a breath.

' - through which you must hold yourself together with every ounce of your being.' He took up my hand and squeezed it gently. 'This will take all your strength, domina, but you must, no matter what, stick to your story and stay confident.'

'Do you know if what they say is believable?' I croaked.

He nodded. 'As I am sure you know, the word of a Vestal is held in absolute esteem, trusted entirely as the truth.'

My lower lip wobbled, knowing he was right. I tried to swallow my nerves, despite trembling all over. Then I realised that Augustus was to oversee the trial. 'But one word from the Emperor and my fate will be sealed!' I cried shakily.

He frowned. 'Augustus will not recant his earlier decision from the inspection, that you were unspoiled. If he did, he would be only drawing negative attention to himself. But yes, the jury is only there to give a general consensus. The final decision lies with Augustus.'

I understood and dreaded it, asking, 'Will we mention the assault?'

Slow alarm crept up into his face. 'I would strongly advise against it, domina. To charge the Emperor with such a thing would be treason. An incredibly powerful senator might just be able to pull it off, but for a woman of any station it is unthinkable. No one would believe you. You would be signing your own death warrant. The Emperor is adored.'

I felt let down. *What could I have expected?* The power of men was evermore supreme.

'Remember, domina,' he whispered softly, 'you have done nothing wrong. What is most important is that you are still a virgin and, because of that, the Flame of Vesta didn't die. Germania is not on your head.'

I couldn't help but let a few tears spill. Finally, I broke away, wiping my cheeks. 'Sorry.'

He smiled gently. 'Don't apologise, domina. Sleep well tonight.'

'Why?'

'Well, the trial is in the morning.'

I froze in fear.

He must have seen the terror on my face because he rubbed my arms, reassuringly. 'Slaves will come first thing to dress you for court. I beg that you do not show any signs of exhaustion or tears.'

'Marcus, my slave,' I managed to say. 'What about him? Will he be there?'

Sadness fell upon his face. 'If he is, he will not testify - slaves are deemed biased. He will be kept alive until your trial ends, but if you are condemned, he will be too.'

I let out a strangled sob. 'Without his own trial?'

Cornelius winced. 'He is a slave. In the eyes of the law, he is not worthy of his own trial. His fate will be decided for him.'

'And how will he die?'

'The punishment for a Vestal's lover is death by public scourging,' came the dreaded words.

Flogging. I let out a strangled cry.

I couldn't stop shaking that night, and without a bed to lie on, I most certainly could not sleep. It was just me, my fears and the night.

*

A clamour of a key sounded all around me.

My eyes blinked open to see a white figure stepping through the doorway, wearing the veil of a Vestal. Frowning, I raised my head. I had thought I had been denied any visitors save for my advocate, but, apparently, that was not the case.

'How deplorable,' her voice echoed within the stone walls.

I groaned. *This was the last thing I needed.* 'What do you want, Lavidia?'

She threw her veil off her face and smirked down at me. 'I have come to secure my future.'

Now genuinely bewildered, I raised my head off the wall. 'Excuse me?'

The smug smile fell from her face and she linked her fingers in front of her, clearing her throat. 'We both know that you have certain knowledge about me, about things I have done.'

I nodded slowly, knowing where she was going with this. 'I do.' I gave her a pointed look.

'Well, do not attempt to make me the cow to be slaughtered.' She raised her chin, glaring at me. 'It would be unspeakably foolish.'

Although I had already told Cornelius that I would not blame her for anything, I wanted to see her quiver in fear. 'Dissuade me.'

She clenched her jaw. 'In accusing me, you would be bringing down the scrutiny of the entire aristocracy on your head. Every one of the nobility, including the Emperor, would support me. You would fail miserably and it would be humiliating for you, although entirely entertaining for me.' She smirked. 'I would advise you go to your death with the last little bit of pathetic dignity you have left. Save yourself further shame.'

I nodded. 'So, without putting up a single fight, I am to willingly place myself upon the sacrificial altar beneath your blade? Forgive me, but surely by now, Lavidia, you know I can see right through you. I make no promises to those who don't keep any themselves. You broke your vow and now twenty thousand lives have paid for it.'

Her gaze darkened.

I paused, looking her up and down in disgust. 'You are a whore, Lavidia.'

Her eyes widened at my bluntness.

I went on, uncaring. 'One day, the whole world will know. That day may or may not be tomorrow.'

A glint of disbelief appeared in her eyes. She spluttered, 'You would not dare. You're bluffing!'

'I don't gamble,' I replied.

'Then this is a threat!' she snapped, enraged. 'An empty threat!'

I shook my head and smiled at her. 'The Fates have their ways. This is a prophecy.'

Alarm flooded her face, and her mouth parted in shock. Although she was made of sin, she was not without her faith. She feared the wrath of the gods just like the rest of us. She took to her heels and fled the cell.

Although I had finally made her afraid of me, right now as I tried to go back to sleep, I realised how meaningless it was. I returned to my tears.

XXII
DIES IUDICII
-Judgement Day-

The slaves found me awake in my cell. Among them, I was overjoyed to see Metallia whom I embraced without hesitation.

She told the others to set up a bath for me. She gave the slaves my old clothes to be burned. She bathed me and rubbed oils over my skin, removing all the grime. She soaked my hair in lavender and cleaned my skin with rosewater. After applying my cosmetics, she beckoned me to stand so she could dress me in all the finery of a Vestal Virgin. We moved in silence. She said nothing, but I saw her lower lip quiver and the forlorn look on her face. She forced a pleasant smile at me through the looking glass, barely holding herself together. However, she had done an excellent job; while I had been clearly crying last night, the makeup covered the redness. When I was ready, she packed up her things to leave, but as she did I realised that every movement we made was one closer to my death. Trembling, I pulled her into a fierce embrace and she returned it just as tightly.

After some time, I stood back and asked her just one thing: 'What do they think of me?'

'Who, domina?' she asked, voice hoarse.

'The people. The public,' I clarified, my voice catching. I looked away quickly. *No more tears.*

She sighed and said, 'No one knows what to think. None know the details. Today they will, I hope. But, domina, whatever the verdict is, they will trust it is the truth.'

I nodded. *That was reasonable.*

She smiled and whispered, 'And I trust in you, domina. You have been nothing except good and kind to everyone.'

She left after a final embrace. I knew I would never see her again.

Cornelius came to escort me to the trial, which was to be held not in just any regular courtroom but in one of the many grand halls of the House of Augustus. He informed me the entire senate would be there. Augustus would act as the presiding supervisor. The prosecution and defence would make their speeches first and then they would both question witnesses.

When he held out his right arm in a gesture towards the cell door, every part of my body screamed at me not to obey, so I froze where I stood, needing to close my eyes. For the first time, I didn't want to leave this cell.

He must have seen me grow rigid. 'Look at me.'

I was met with an earnest expression.

'You carried out your duties perfectly. You are still chaste. That is the truth and whether or not they believe it, the gods know it.'

'Is there no task I can undertake to prove myself?' I begged him. 'I have heard that Vestals have been allowed the opportunity in the past. Did Vestal Tuccia not carry water in a sieve, a miracle which proved her innocence? Could I not try something similar?'

He shook his head. 'No, domina. Augustus has refused you such a chance. He wants a quick judgement passed, given the situation. But I will fight for your salvation which the heavenly ones will grant, I am sure.'

I felt weak at his words. I was exhausted. My back and limbs ached from the nights lying on the cold, hard, wet floor. I decided he was right: the gods would protect me; if I was going to get through this, at all, I would have to put my faith in them. 'Thank you for everything, Cornelius,' I murmured in reply.

He smiled sadly back at me. 'You are very welcome, domina,' he replied and, holding out his arm for me to take, he guided me from the room.

We were escorted to the trial by the Praetorian Guard. I ignored Gnaeus' glare as we went. *Grateful, no doubt, for his lucky escape*, I thought.

The imperial court had come to the House of Augustus for the trial. With every step, an armed guard was in place. Senators and gleaming generals stalked the halls. Among them were rows of mighty statues of ancient kings and war heroes from Rome's glorious past, all watching me as I passed by.

I was led through two huge golden doors into the very heart of the Roman Empire: the throne room.

This hall was crowded with more senators and lawyers. Those I had seen outside started to stream in. It seemed to me that every chair in the world had been set out for them. Mixed in the throng were battered soldiers. As we entered, they stared at me, faces turned, mostly emotionless, and the volume of the room fell considerably.

'Survivors of the Battle of the Teutoburg Forest,' Cornelius whispered to me as we walked down the aisle, created for us by the crowd.

Is that what they are calling it now?

'They have come to see who is responsible for their failure.'

My face grew hot beneath my veil. I saw the wariness written across the faces of them all, uncertain whether or not they should feel blessed by my presence or cursed.

'Fear not,' Cornelius reassured me. 'They just want someone to blame for this whole bloody mess. Someone other than themselves.'

I tried to put the mass slaughter out of my head. Then my sight was drawn to someone I could not ignore.

Aloft on his golden throne was Augustus – the revered one - Emperor of Rome, Pontifex Maximus, First

Citizen, glorified throughout the world, he who had transformed the political structure of civilisation and made himself its supreme head. He had always seemed invincible to me as a child. He still was, in a way. He was my nightmare.

I looked away from him, my throat feeling tight. I followed Cornelius who led me to my seat, a cathedra between the Emperor's platform and the rest of the audience. Directly across from me on the other side of the throne room was the jury, their members plucked from the rich and wealthy masses.

Cornelius sat down at a table in front of the platform where the prosecutor was also sitting. He was a tall and slender gentleman with a hooked nose and narrow, dark eyes, thin lips, and smoothed back hair.

Glancing over my shoulder, I saw the rest of the Vestal Virgins seated as witnesses along the front row of audience seats. Nearby, in chains, I glimpsed a prisoner standing. I did a double-take as I realised it was Marcus.

Good gods.

He looked broken, nearly destroyed, with his lacerated bottom lip, two black eyes and bloody scars all over his face and arms from blades had slashed at his flesh and whips had flogged him. He met my gaze.

I saw the raw rage in his eyes and the hurt in his heart. I could tell from the trembling shackles around his wrists that he was boiling with fury. I looked around. No one else seemed to notice his condition. The only acknowledgements sent his way were expressions of disgust, like he was a bad smell; his presence was an offence; nothing else.

I realised how selfish I had been over the past few days. As I had been weeping with self-pity about my own situation, had I ever spared one thought for him or how he was being treated? Had I listened for his screams and howls among my own? No, I had not. Blushing with shame, I had to look away from him. *Self-indulgent. Conceited.*

Augustus stood up, raising his hands and hushing the room, glowing with pride from his seat of glory.

In that moment, I was not so sure the gods were on my side.

'Senators!' he called out, calming the room with slow downward movements of his arms.

Hate churned in my gut at the sight of those hands.

'Generals, soldiers, jurors and lawyers,' he greeted before turning to the few women in the room. 'And our most honoured Vestal Virgins.'

I doubted that I was included in that esteem.

'We are gathered here to consider the cause of our defeat at the Battle of the Teutoburg Forest, which claimed the lives of too many undeserving young Roman men.' He paused sadly. 'Today, here in my home, we may discover the true reason behind this,' he added earnestly with an air of wonder, sweeping his arms out in a grand gesture to the walls around us. Then he frowned and jabbed a finger at us all. 'That world - our world - is at risk! It is under threat, and we must be rid of this danger,' he said. He brought his hands together and linked his fingers, nodding thoughtfully. 'Today, we may discover and exterminate it.' Then he gestured to the small square space of open floor, framed on all sides by the lawyers and the audience behind them, the jurors, the Emperor himself, and finally myself and the witnesses. 'I invite the trial to begin with the prosecution's speech. Publius Martius, please begin.' With that, he settled back into his throne with an imperial flourish.

I looked at the advocate's table where Publius stood.

'Caesar,' he began, speaking with a clear-cut voice. 'Before I begin, I would like to request that the slave, Aries Gloriosus Iovis, be removed.'

My heart clenched. *What?*

He waved his hand dismissively. 'He is not going to testify and has no place in an ordinary courtroom, never mind your holy house.'

Cornelius jumped to his feet, exclaiming, 'Caesar, the slave is instrumental to this trial.'

Augustus pacified them with his hands. 'Now, let us compromise. Let the slave be taken back to his dungeon. He will be sent for if necessary.'

'Of course, Caesar,' the defence consented in defeat.

As he sat down, he met my gaze with equal uneasiness. We both knew that Marcus would not be sent for. I might never even see him again.

It took all my self-control not to look back over my shoulder as they escorted him away through a side-passage to get him out as quickly as possible. I closed my eyes behind my veil to try to stop the tears. My last sight of him: battered, bloodied and bruised.

XXIII
PERSECUTIOQUE DEFENSIO
-Prosecution and Defence-

The prosecutor cleared his throat. 'Thank you, dominus,' he said, bowing before moving out from behind the advocate's desk and addressing the audience and jurors.

'Gentlemen and jurors!' he began, projecting his voice. 'There is little value in debating whether this Vestal before you is chaste or not until you understand the full picture.' He gestured lazily to me. 'For that to happen, I must delve deep into Vestal Aemilia's past to prove to you that she was not even born pure.'

The audience gasped and murmured. *It was quite an opening.*

I forced myself to look straight ahead at the opposite wall like Cornelius had instructed me - confident, poised and steadfast. I could not allow myself to be swayed by anything the prosecutor said as it could give me away. But my past? That was another matter entirely. It was something untouched, unknown to all except a few, but now that would change without my permission. Again.

The prosecutor paced, his voice building a story. 'She arrived in Rome with her father, Aemilius Valerius Faustus. By all, they were avoided and ignored, for none knew who they were. So, to ask the obvious question,' he said, 'who were they?'

Some audience members chuckled.

'Well, Aemilius had fought in the Battle of Actium forty years ago as a youth of eighteen years and a new recruit in the Roman army. He was described at the time, by the Emperor, as the noblest soul who had saved him. This man, Aemilius, seemed to be a lionheart.

'Afterwards, he continued to serve his full twenty-five years in the army. However, then he vanished off the face of the earth! Suddenly, eight years ago, out of nowhere, he appeared in Rome, a middle-aged man of nearly fifty years, with a daughter he claimed to be ten-years-old and, except for their clothes, there were no other possessions to his name. He was the last of his family line, but his house in Rome had been given away because he was presumed dead. He was destitute, and there was only one person in the city he knew: the Emperor.

'Aemilius arrived at the House of Augustus and reminded the Emperor that he would not be alive today without him. He requested that as a show of gratitude, his daughter, Aemilia, would be welcomed into the Order of the Vestals where she could become one of the most educated and influential women in the world.'

Publius paused before saying, 'Recognising the man, his poverty and past piety, Augustus, in his holy and humble heart, defied tradition and did just that. The protagonists of this tale are Aemilius, himself, who wanted the best for his daughter, and Augustus, who disregarded ancient rules for an old friend. And see how poorly both have been repaid?' The prosecutor gestured to me.

I looked away, my face hot.

'As we all know, there are several criteria to be filled for one's daughter to become a Vestal Virgin,' he continued. 'Aemilius was a Roman, but he was not a nobleman and he was not even married! A Vestal Virgin has to have two living parents, but there is no record of Aemilius' marriage. Of course, at the time, he would have promised that he had a wife who was both alive and Roman-born. Clearly, Aemilia was born of a woman, as are we all, but is it so hard to guess the obvious? Where would he have found a Roman woman whilst in the army? Would there be one training with him in the barracks?'

A chuckle rumbled through the audience.

My palms began to sweat. They were laughing at me.

'What is more, army soldiers are discouraged from marriage so they can devote themselves to their duty. They are only allowed to marry under exceptional circumstances. Thus, the child could not have been the product of a blessed union and even if he had married, unbeknownst to the state, it would have been at least two years before he completed his servitude in the army, to possibly have a child who was ten-years-old. Who is to say he was even her father? Gentlemen, the times do not fit. Neither do the people!'

'So the Order of the Vestals has been cursed,' he declared in conclusion, before adding slowly, 'for eight years by a girl born of some barbarian whore or prostitute. The virtuous Vestal has hoodwinked us all! For she is a bastard.'

My eyes stung. My only solace at that moment was that Marcus had been taken away.

'This brat was never meant to be a Vestal. Her father lied about her parentage and then about her age. She has continued these falsehoods every day since. And just like her harlot mother, she was destined to follow her in the art of seduction.

'The crime for a Vestal losing her chastity is incestum, as we all know. When those who are daughters of the empire, under the guardianship of the Emperor, choose to lie in sin, it is an abominable crime!' he spat, disgusted. 'Which Vestal Aemilia has committed.

'As for the slave, is it any wonder that a man would chase after a Vestal, who we consider to be heroines among us, a bridge between the gods and our lowly selves? No, nothing is shocking about that. However, what is surprising is that she was desirous in return, full of lust and pining for someone to satisfy her. A slave no less! But I guess there's no accounting for taste when it comes to the lower classes.'

Laughter rippled through the courtroom.

My face felt on fire.

Publius continued. 'They encountered each other in the Baths of Agrippa as he spied upon the Vestals' privacy.'

I froze. *How did he know about that?*

'But she was drawn to it, of course, in her twisted mind. A criminal and a barbarian - a match made in the depths of hellish Tartarus!

'As my witnesses will attest, when he began to serve in the House of the Vestals, the two were suspiciously familiar with each other in a way that none of the other Vestals and slaves were. He was incredibly attentive, and she unusually sweet. He followed her everywhere and even spent his nights in her bedchamber! What more proof do we need of her crimes?'

My heart hammered wildly. How he had discovered such secrets which I had tried so hard to contain, I didn't know.

'But he abandoned her when almost discovered. However, the tramp missed him sorely in her whoring heart. When he returned to her, they were closer than ever. How revolting!' He shot me a look of disdain.

'She timed her sins well. Yes, she schemed how she would ruin us all for her own sexual gratification. The Emperor proclaimed her innocence. Then their cursed union was consummated on that very night, the night of the Battle of the Teutoburg Forest. They were alone in the Temple of Vesta, right in front of the sacred hearth. The goddess herself was forced to watch the sin unfold in her own home. They offended her and they did a thorough job of it!'

By this point, the audience had been repeatedly shocked, letting out fresh gasps of horror with every sentence he had uttered.

Already, I was deafened by his shouting and their disgust.

'He had polluted, supposedly, the holiest of women, and she had let him. She broke her vow of chastity which embodies the health and safety of our empire. In the days they knew each other, her duties were grossly neglected, not just her chastity and the Flame of Vesta betrayed.'

He paused and looked directly at the jurors. 'It is no mystery that we were vanquished in Germania. Our security was compromised from the beginning. This entire military massacre lies on the head of this brat, and although she will have to pay the price, it will never be enough to relieve the sorrow felt nationwide at our loss. So jurors, dutiful to the gods and to the state, condemn this wicked wench and free us of her curse!'

As Publius' fists came down on the advocate's desk, the audience clapped and cheered, whooped and whistled at the end of his speech.

Complete and utter character assassination - the most outstanding achievement of the Roman law courts.

His invective tirade over, I licked my lips, uncurled my sweating fists, let out a sigh that billowed against the veil of my headdress, and tried to relax, ignoring the ache in my head.

As Publius took his seat, Cornelius stood, with his brow sweating. He had quite the task ahead of him: to convince this room and then the world that not only was I not what Publius had painted me to be, but the opposite.

Where Publius had thrown himself into the centre of the room, Cornelius slowly paced out in front of the Emperor, looking at him, then turning steadily and holding his gaze with the jurors, and then addressing the audience. He sighed, hanging his head and shaking it.

I watched him anxiously.

'It is a wretched day for Rome,' he began, 'when the world chooses to question the virtue of one in whom, beforehand, they had held so much faith.' He gestured to me. 'And all because of a military failure on the edge of our vast and expansive empire.' He defensively held up his hands as the people in the audience exchanged offended glances and murmurs. 'I do not belittle it nor diminish the importance of the lives lost.' He clasped his hands in front of him. 'But I am disappointed in everyone here before me today.'

I swallowed my nerves.

'Do you not realise that in questioning her good character, you question the Emperor's good judgement?' he bellowed, his voice reaching all corners of the room. 'Augustus never would have accepted her as for the Vestal candidacy if he was uncertain of her history. If you do not believe in her, you do not believe in him! Shame upon you all,' he scorned them.

The audience frowned and looked at each other.

I watched Augustus shift uncomfortably in his chair. Had I not been so scared, I might have laughed at the irony.

Cornelius gestured a hand to Publius. 'This sorry excuse of a man said she was born from a sinful rascal. Well, I ask you this: was it sinful to save the Emperor's life that day? Was Aemilius' bravery sinful?' he demanded angrily, spitting at them. He shook his head. 'I think not!'

Then he turned wildly and pointed at me. 'I would politely ask the prosecution and every man in here to place no shame on this girl that is not founded.' He approached the advocate's desk and slammed his hands down on the table. 'What evidence have you, Publius, that this young woman is a bastard?' he thundered, speaking directly to the prosecutor. 'What proof have you that her mother was unmarried, a prostitute or a barbarian?'

He turned and addressed the jurors. 'I can tell you all now: he has none. Publius spins a web of lies fit to undermine Minerva. Quite simply, Aemilius was not a sinful man - he was worthy enough in the eyes of the gods to successfully save the Emperor's life.

'And why would a virtuous Roman tell falsehoods about his daughter? Moreover, why would a righteous Roman lie with a barbarian? Why would any Roman, for that matter, want to? And why would he bother to procure such a future for an illegitimate, barbarian daughter who was not worthy of it? Why would he even bring her to Rome in the first place? No Roman would care about his bastard barbarian daughter. If anything, she would be disowned! And he was of true Roman blood, as we know. Therefore, it is only logical that any child of his, for whom he cared enough to make her a Vestal Virgin, must have been born of his Roman wife.

'Publius believes it impossible that Aemilius found such a woman out in the provinces. Other men have done so before him. He may very well have married in the two years before his retirement, while on leave. Their marriage record may have been lost in fire or water. It would not be the first time.'

He swung around and pointed at me. 'No, Publius. Speculation is not proof. I argue that this young lady is of a true and blessed union between two pure-blooded Romans, who were both alive when Aemilia entered the Order of the Vestals, as is a necessary requirement which the Emperor would have ensured. Why would Augustus endanger his own priesthood or his empire?'

He smiled at me. 'She is virtuous. As the Vestals will testify, she never caused any trouble. She was perfect in almost every regard: quiet, humble, helpful and caring. Is it any wonder that she was adored by her slave? She is the epitome of a virtuous woman!

'So often, and so recently, Vestal Aemilia has proved it. At the Baths of Agrippa, she found it in her heart to forgive a man who had been brought so low in this world. Prone to compassion, faith and sympathy, she decided to take it upon herself to ensure that this man knew he would not die by any offence to the Vestals, but by the will of the heavenly gods above with which she, the holiest of maidens, would never dare to interfere.

'If you question her virtue, not only do you question the Emperor, but also the other Vestals, those who taught her, such as Chief Vestal Occia, who we know is nothing except kind and good.' He gestured to the woman sitting behind me. 'You question the woman who nurtured Vestal Aemilia when her own dear mother was absent. All the

Vestals, including their mistress, will claim there is no kinder soul in their house than Vestal Aemilia. Emperor Augustus declared her innocent of being touched by a mortal man.

'As for the gladiator, Aries Gloriosus Iovis proved his own virtue when he, without hesitation, slew the Emperor's assailant just days beforehand, in the arena.

'There is no doubt that she was a kind and compassionate mistress to a hardworking, loyal slave. Gentlemen, this is the ideal we must strive for, not the base we should punish.'

He paused for effect, letting the jurors think on what they had just heard. Then he continued: 'No, my honourable countrymen. It is not Vestal Aemilia who is responsible for our loss. How can she be? She was not ready to undertake this task of guarding the Flame. It was unnecessary and careless. Only Vestals in their second decade of servitude are trained to protect the fire. She is but still in her first. How could she have hoped to carry out such a demanding task for which she had no training? Vesta knew it, became angry and sought her revenge by punishing our campaigners in Germania. If anyone other, than a Vestal at least in her second decade, had undertaken the task we would still be here today with twenty thousand lives lost. Gentlemen, that is the only reasonable cause for our defeat at the Battle of the Teutoburg Forest.

'All you see before you is a legitimate Roman daughter whose father saved the Emperor's life; a loving friend to her fellow Vestals; a perfect mistress to her slaves; and a kind, forgiving soul. When you come to your decision today, I ask you to consider her heroic father and the ridiculous lies of Publius. Consider the love her friends and slaves have for her, and the previous declaration of innocence made by the Emperor. Are you really prepared to sentence to death a young, kind-spirited girl who still has so much to prove and who was only following orders? She broke no vow. I ask you to acquit her and release her from this trial so she can return to her duties as a true, blessed and virtuous Vestal, protected by the best of slaves, friends and the heavenly ones, themselves.'

XXIV
TESTIS
-Witness-

My head was pounding as Cornelius sat down, my blood rushing in my ears, my palms sweating. Augustus shuffled in his seat, frowning. The jurors were murmuring amongst each other.

The speeches were over and the witnesses would be next, but the words from both men were still sinking in. Publius had lied. Cornelius had lied. *Already, the truth didn't have a chance.* Falsehoods, my panicked head tried to remind my guilt-ridden heart, might keep my life my own.

Publius' point: I was a barbarian's bastard, cursed, uncaring and sinful. Cornelius': I was a legitimate Roman, virtuous, loving, kind and chaste. These would be either be proved or disproved when the witnesses came to testify. Cornelius had explained to me what would happen. The prosecution and the defence could ask each of them questions that would help bolster their cases. He had told me not to look at any of them as they took to the stage in front of me. I hoped my friends would support me. I didn't expect Lavidia to do a thing to help; quite the reverse. Occia I couldn't account for, yet she was first. I couldn't help but watch her out of the corner of my eye, my heart racing.

'Vestalis Maxima Occia,' Publius began, standing up. 'You have been a part of the Order for forty-seven years now. Your judgement, by now, ought to be trusted. Why did you purchase Aries Gloriosus Iovis as a slave for the House of the Vestals when you had dozens already?'

Occia, her back straight with her towering figure, magnanimous before the court, appeared confident. 'I did not buy him. He was a gift to the Vestals from the Emperor, one of many slaves.'

'I see. Do you feel it was wise to let Vestal Aemilia become attached to one particular slave?'

She shook her head. 'I do not believe it unwise to surround oneself with those one believes are good-hearted and loyal. I think there is virtue to be seen here, in both parties: hers was the wisdom to keep him with her and his was that unique and special fidelity which too many slaves often lack.'

'But were you certain of her chastity?'

I heard her hesitate. 'In my position, I always have to have my suspicions with regards to my Vestals, not just when they are accused. It is my duty. But any doubts I had were dashed after she was declared innocent following the Emperor's inspection. My opinion was his.'

'And now?'

She was steadfast. 'I still doubt her guilt.'

'Aries Gloriosus Iovis was first an exile before he was a slave, banished from Rome for bad behaviour. Did you know this? If you did, what made you think her chastity would be safe in the presence of such a criminal?'

She flushed, with embarrassment or anger I could not say. 'I have raised her over the past eight years. I have taught her the values of the Vestals. I also know her sensible nature and I have always deemed her wise. Vestal Aemilia never does anything without meditating on it at great length. I do not believe that any good Roman girl would throw everything away for a common slave. The notion is ridiculous. As for his background, I am sure anyone would be disturbed by such tales. But do we all not have to cope with them when we decide to procure slaves? Do you not have slaves yourself?' Occia asked, head held high.

Publius seemed to blush, put in his place.

I tried to bite back a smile.

'I have one final question, Vestalis Maxima Occia.'

She raised an eyebrow in challenge.

'When the slave, whom you vouch so fiercely for, was accused of polluting Vestal Aemilia, he abandoned his post, did he not? Vanished!' He raised an eyebrow back.

She lowered hers in realisation and glanced at me quickly.

I looked away as Publius turned to the audience.

'Then, when the coast was clear, when Aemilia had been found chaste by the Emperor, he suddenly returned to his post.' He looked back at her. 'Now, wouldn't you call that guilty behaviour, and why did you welcome him back? Why did you not report him to the authorities?'

I cursed myself. Occia did not even know that Marcus had fled that day. *So, who told Publius?*

Occia's chest was heaving slightly as she searched for a response. 'The Emperor found Vestal Aemilia to be innocent. If she was, so was he. He was also originally a gift from the Emperor that I felt would be wrong to destroy or turn away. That is my answer. That is my opinion.'

He smirked and turned to the jury, while still addressing her. 'Forgive me, domina. I believe many here would agree that you had a duty to report your slave missing. In failing that duty, why should we trust you can fulfil any other responsibilities? Does your opinion really count for anything?'

He spun on his heel and swaggered over to his chair.

Cornelius popped up.

The glare from Occia lightened, and she gave him a welcoming smile.

Cornelius cleared his throat. 'Vestalis Maxima Occia, I only have a few questions for you. Do you regret putting Vestal Aemilia guarding the Flame, a task for which she had no experience?'

Her smile withered. She spared a guilty sideways glance at me. 'Admittedly, I regret the decision now,' she said, blushing, 'if it did, indeed, anger Vesta and cause those thousands of deaths in Germania.'

He frowned. 'But why did you instruct her to do it?'

She avoided his gaze and focused her eyes on the floor. 'Duties are taken very seriously in the House of the Vestals. Everything we do affects the empire on a minuscule scale. I felt she was neglecting her duties, and that had to be corrected.'

'Can you say that otherwise she has been a perfect and obedient priestess?'

'Yes.'

He nodded his head. 'Do you have anything further to add?'

She raised her chin in a final dignified stance. 'When I first gave her the task, she, herself, pointed out that she was not equipped to deal with it. Nevertheless, she obeyed and carried out my orders. I would like to say that this only adds to my opinion of her sensible character and wise judgement where mine was lacking.'

Cornelius seemed impressed.

Indeed, so was I. Occia was willing to bear much more responsibility for this issue than I had expected, considering the fatal punishment.

'That is all, Vestalis Maxima. Thank you for your cooperation.'

It took a great deal to wilt that woman. She was born with an impressive height. However, after all the questions, as she walked back to her seat, she seemed smaller.

After her, Val was called to testify. Publius asked her about our close friendship and whether or not she had suspected anything. He asked about the conversation we had in which she understood that Marcus was making unwanted advances towards me.

'The other Vestals can testify that you said this pre-inspection,' he said. 'Is it true?'

'Of course not! Aemilia never said that it was a slave who was making those advances towards her. She clearly stated that it was Prefect Gnaeus of the Praetorian Guard,' she answered with a confident smile.

A murmur rumbled through the audience, and looks were spared to the Prefect who sat somewhere amongst them.

Publius did not ask her anything further, but Cornelius did.

'Do you have evidence of such unwanted attention, domina?' the defence asked her.

She beamed. 'Yes indeed. Once, he dared to burst into her private bedchamber uninvited! He had not even given her the chance to change out of her nightdress.'

'Is there anyone else who witnessed this?'

'Myself and the slave, Aries Gloriosus Iovis.'

'Objection!' Publius declared, standing up from the advocate's table, addressing Augustus. 'Such evidence is void since it is given by a close friend and the other was a biased slave.'

However, Cornelius argued, 'Vestal Valeriana's word is a fact.' He turned to the jury. 'The keyword 'unwanted' is vital here. Vestal Aemilia welcomed no romantic advances from anyone. It is in this that we find her virtue, which is at the heart of this entire debate.'

Publius sat down, thoroughly displeased.

Third was Rufina.

Cornelius asked her about my character and if I had a relationship with the gladiator.

She shook her head confidently. 'I highly doubt it. As the Chief Vestal rightly said, Aemilia is thoughtful, sensible and wise. She would have never risked her life nor her reputation for some slave she had barely known for a few days.'

She then walked back to her seat, sparing me a sad smile, yet it was hopeful.

I thanked the veil for hiding my blushes.

However, it was then that Fortuna seemed to turn away from me and leave me to the cruel Fates; the fourth witness to testify was Lavidia and, judging from the grins mirroring each in hers and Publius' faces, I was doomed.

'Vestal Lavidia, did you ever suspect Vestal Aemilia of breaking her vow?' he began.

'Oh, from the beginning,' she replied smoothly. 'I heard that she had sought a private audience alone with the gladiator. She sought him out, not the other way around. I fear that it continued in this way from then on.'

'It is understandable that these events should infuriate any good Roman, yourself included. Did Vestal Aemilia ever anger you on a more personal level? Did she ever show signs of bad temperament or even violence?' he led her.

A triumphant light appeared in her eyes. 'I cannot speak for violence, but certainly the former. The day before her inspection, when we argued, she called me a foul name.' She nodded seriously.

My heart dropped, remembering precisely what I had said.

'Do you think any virtuous Roman woman knows this word?'

'Of course not. I blush to think of it myself, never mind use the term.'

'And what did she call you, domina?'

Lavidia paused before looking down at her lap and causing her lower lip to wobble. Actors and prostitutes could have taken lessons from her on how to put on a good show. Her voice came out crisply: 'A bitch.'

Gasps erupted around the room. There were shouts of outrage from the audience. Augustus raised his hands, biting the insides of his cheeks, trying to calm the court. Even Cornelius stared at me, astonished. Shocked numb like everyone else, he was unable to question her, but there was no point anyway. He, his head in his hands, and I, eyes closed, trying to imagine myself far away from here, both knew that no question on earth could show Lavidia's reasonable opinion of me, for it did not exist.

Of course, she ruined my character further, stating I had blackmailed her with gossip about crimes which, according to her, she had never committed, and how I had threatened to blacken her name with lies that she had broken her vow, too.

However, it was Publius' next question that was the most damning. 'The slave, as usual, was present during this row. Can you remember how he addressed his mistress?'

How in Jupiter's kingdom could he ask that? It was such a specific question. I narrowed my eyes at her. *Unless she had told him to.*

She thought for a moment, pursing her pretty lips. Then realisation and remembrance dawned on those features. 'Oh, Vesta! It was shocking.'

'Please answer the question, domina,' he pressed. 'Tell us, what did he call her?'

She batted her eyelashes at him, pouting. 'Aemilia.'

The room inhaled in shock.

My heart sank, remembering the moment. I understood the audience's reaction perfectly - the lack of respect from a slave to his mistress was abominable for many to hear. On Marcus' part, such impertinence would not be easily forgotten by the court. However, they would not readily forgive my allowing such informality.

'She did not even reprimand him. I had to. But what can one expect of vulgarians?' she said gloriously.

Publius asked one final question. 'Vestal Lavidia, you claimed that you had a witness to their affair, someone who saw them together in sin. Now, can you tell the court who it was?'

The corner of her mouth lifted. Venom filled her eyes. 'Advocate, call your next witness.'

He did.

Picia took the floor.

My heart stopped when I saw her. *She was Lavidia's witness?* My head struggled with the idea. *But how?* Dread filled me. Sweet, innocent and loving Picia, with her childlike spirit and curiosity, all this time had been an actress.

Publius asked her that question. 'In what way did you witness the affair?'

She squeaked something I could not hear, her wide eyes shining up at the prosecutor.

'Speak louder, domina,' he scorned her.

'I saw them in the gardens,' she repeated, voice shaking. 'I heard them talking.'

'But what did you see them do?'

Her lower lip trembled. 'I saw them kiss.'

The world sucked in a collective breath.

It felt like my heartbeat came to a screeching halt. Casting my mind back to the day of the kiss in the garden, I remembered the flash of yellow on the shrubbery. Now, I realised it had been hair. Her hair.

She had spoken the damning words. Her face crumpled, tears spilling over her cheeks.

Publius returned to his seat, beaming triumphantly.

Cornelius stood, frowning in thought. He slowly approached her before handing her a rag with which to wipe her eyes. 'Here, domina.'

Sniffling and staring at him wide-eyed, she took it gracefully. 'Thank you,' she mumbled.

He pursed his lips. 'It must be difficult for you to testify against your close friend.'

She nodded, sending me a guilty and embarrassed glance.

'Has Vestal Aemilia been a good friend to you?'

'Oh, yes. She has always been kind to me, like a loving sister.'

'Did you ever believe her capable of criminal activity?'

She frowned. 'Never.'

He nodded thoughtfully. 'You stated you saw Vestal Aemilia and the slave, Aries Gloriosus Iovis, kissing in the gardens of the House of the Vestals.'

She nodded.

'From what angle did you observe this happening?'

Frowning, she tilted her head, closing her eyes and re-imagining the scene. 'I was at the entrance to the garden. So, I saw the back of the slave's head,' she explained, sniffling.

'And the girl he was kissing? It was Vestal Aemilia?' he pressed.

She faltered. 'Well, who else could it have been?'

'Did you see her face?' he demanded, interrupting.

Her features relaxed in realisation. 'No.'

I breathed out a sigh of relief.

'So how do you know for certain it was Vestal Aemilia?' he asked.

'I don't,' she muttered in response.

'Jurors!' Cornelius called, whirling around. 'I put to you that the girl Aries Gloriosus Iovis was kissing could have been anyone. Indeed, she simply may have been another slave girl. There is no proof that it was Vestal Aemilia. None at all. The witness has recanted her earlier claim that it was her friend. Now, she admits it could have been anyone. Remember that.'

When Picia moved to sit down again, she whispered to me as she passed, 'I'm so sorry.'

I could not look at her. I was focusing on controlling my expressions, but my heartbeat was manic. It was all too much.

Augustus rose from his throne and spread his arms. 'Advocates, your speeches have been heard and your witnesses questioned. All that is left is for the jurors to make their decision.' He looked at them. 'Gentlemen, you will be given time to deliberate together in a separate chamber after which I will summon you back. Based on your verdict, I will deliver the final decree for Vestal Aemilia's fate.'

XXV
DAMNATIO
-Damnation-

It felt like Saturn was laughing in my face, dragging time slowly behind him. Sitting in my chair for what felt like forever, it was difficult to keep my worry from showing, to prevent my foot tapping the ground or my clammy hands rubbing together. Cornelius exchanged reassuring glances with me. My body ached to turn around and look at my friends, but he had specifically instructed me to act always as if everything was going my way.

Who had spoken in my favour? Val and Rufina, I remembered clearly. Lavidia had torn my good name apart and threw the tattered remains to Hades. Occia had noted my good character yet claimed impartiality. Then I closed my eyes, remembering Picia. *Oh, Picia.*

There was a veil of lies that surrounded nobles who were seen by all others as virtuous and blessed. Publius had transformed me into a barbarian whore and cursed sorceress, without proof. Even Cornelius had managed to dress me up and turn the truth on its head at various intervals. Val had suspected Marcus' advances were happening early on, but lied for me anyway. Picia had been convinced into lying, whether or not she was intelligent enough to figure out Cornelius' tricks. As for Lavidia, lying was second nature to her. Of course, all that was nothing compared to the lies I had told. However, Augustus: in the eyes of the people, he was the bearer of truth, their moral father, but only the gods knew how much he had lied, and how many women he had mistreated.

After a significant length of time or what seemed like it to me, the jurors returned to the courtroom. The audience, which had trickled out into the hallway to stretch their legs and discuss the whole affair among themselves, packed themselves inside once more.

My throat was tight, and all I could hear above the chattering was the pulsating rage of blood in my head. I fixated on the men who determined my fate. Now, they simply had to say it.

Eventually, the clamour died as Augustus hushed them with his holy hands. He gestured to the speaker for the jurors to stand and deliver the decision. 'Gentlemen, I hope you have all reached a verdict so that we may put this ghastly business behind us.'

I had to close my eyes to focus on trying to relax my body. My legs were shaking. My stomach was churning so much that I feared I might throw up everywhere if I didn't calm down. I averted my gaze, unable to look at them any longer. My head was hurting. It felt like some god somewhere was compressing it.

The speaker's voice sounded, croaky and scratchy. 'Caesar, it is the opinion of the jury that on the first charge of letting the Flame of Vesta die out, we find Vestal Aemilia guilty.'

My stomach lurched. I chomped down on my tongue and tightly pursed my lips to prevent any sounds or vomit from escaping. I clenched my eyes shut and my fists curled beneath the folds of my stola.

Augustus' voice rang in my head. 'Why?'

'We believe the Flame of Vesta died as a result of a lack of knowledge about the task, which would have angered the goddess Vesta.'

Wait, really? I looked up with mixed emotions: the relief that they knew it wasn't my fault, followed by the impending dread of the flogging to follow.

Augustus frowned. 'So, what is your verdict for the second charge - her loss of chastity?'

I held my breath.

'We have been unable to reach a unanimous decision on that,' the speaker continued.

I felt imaginary boulders lift off my shoulders. My world relaxed. Slumping, I released my breath. *There was a chance.*

'The prosecution's speech was strong, yet the witnesses strengthened the defence's case. Therefore, for the first charge, the jury suggests the traditional punishment should be carried out, followed by a second inspection to determine the current state of her chastity,' the speaker said.

A second inspection? My body went still, frozen with memories of the first. A flailing I could bear, but a second invasion by the hands of that awful man? Excruciating. Not just for my body, but also my soul.

I swallowed my fear. It would have to be done. I had no choice. *And surely any amount of torture would be bearable if the Emperor decided I was still a virgin?*

I glanced sideways at the Emperor, who was staring darkly at me in return. Whatever confidence I had perished immediately. Frozen under his glare, I could already feel my face against the cold wall and his fingers creeping around my upper thighs. With growing panic, I realised that all I had gained was another few moments of life, but not the chance to keep it. Moreover, the extra breaths I had been granted would be filled with pain. My innocence did not matter to the Emperor. He would kill me no matter what because, as Cornelius said, he needed his scapegoat. His gaze had me locked in a trance. I could sense these were my last moments. Breath seemed so valuable to me now, for my life had just been put in the hands of the man who most wanted me dead.

Then Augustus spoke, making the final decree. 'This advice will be followed. Vestal Aemilia will be punished for letting the Flame of Vesta die. It will be immediately followed by a second inspection, during which I will decide whether or not her virtue remains intact. Once I have done so, I will inform the world of my decision.'

*

I was marched back down to the small cell-like rooms by two soldiers of the Praetorian Guard. My only consolation was that Marcus had probably been put into one of them after being dragged from the courtroom. I also knew that this flogging could not go on forever. The Pontifex Maximus, himself, carried out the punishments, but the arm of an old man was not that of a mighty hero; I doubted he was even able to lift a sword. Then again, Augustus had done the unexpected before.

However, this time I didn't return to my familiar haunted space. They brought me to a different room, the walls coated in red.

I tried not to cry out as they ripped my headdress off, tears already flowing down my face. They threw my clothes across the room, before ordering me to kneel on the ground, my back to the door. I obeyed, shaking from the cold. It was not the first time I had been forced to be naked in company, but I was no less embarrassed and tried to cover myself. I supposed that was part of the humiliation.

As soon as my knees touched the cold, wet cobblestone, I heard the door open behind me. Looking over my shoulder, a fist met my face. I cried out. The force slammed into my cheek. Instantly unbalanced, I fell forward onto my hands.

'Face forward,' one of them growled.

Gulping the bile rising in my throat, I shakily returned to kneeling.

'Hands behind your back,' the other ordered.

I obeyed, and soon I felt the harsh burn of ropes around my wrists, binding them together.

'Thank you,' a familiar voice said.

Augustus.

'Caesar, shouldn't there be a curtain between you and her to protect her modesty?' one of the guards asked.

'Should there be anything to protect anyone who has wreaked such havoc upon Rome?' the Emperor replied. 'Recall how there are twenty thousand dead.'

'Yes, Caesar.'

'Leave us,' he ordered.

There was the scuffing of sandals on the stone floor. The door closed. Augustus and I were alone. Again.

'Vestal Aemilia,' he sighed as if disappointed.

I shivered at the sound of his voice filling the room, filling my ears and my mind.

'We must appease the gods, you understand?'

I gritted my teeth and nearly jumped at the touch of his wrinkled hand on my shoulder. I clamped my eyes shut, trembling.

He rubbed his thumb against my skin as if to reassure me. 'It is for the best.' His hand reached over my shoulder from behind and smoothed over my collar bone. 'And it will all be over soon.' It travelled down and brushed against my breast.

I bit back my tears.

Then his lips were against my ear. 'Thank the gods for their mercy. Thank me.'

I swallowed a sob. 'Thank you, Caesar,' I whispered, my shaky voice echoing off the stone walls.

His hand traced the grooves in my neck before he ran his fingers down the long-lined dip in my back. 'Such a beautiful body. Such a pity.'

I heard him take a few steps back. I braced myself for the first whiplash, sucking in a deep breath.

First, it was leather. Then it was the burning fire. A scream tore through my throat as the ropes of the flagellum hit my skin. Gasping out in pain, I writhed on my knees, toppling forward, and hit my face on the cobblestone. My back was in agony. Now, a bolt of pain shot through my head. I sobbed into the floor.

Then, yanking my hair, he made me cry out again as he pulled me back up onto my knees. 'Stay still!' he barked in my ear.

The whippings kept coming. I kept falling over. It was impossible to keep my balance, with the pain. Soon, I was stretched out on the floor, with my arms tied behind me, and him flailing my back over and over again. I felt my skin was alight. I was screaming, turning and twisting with each strike. I hoped Hades could hear me.

Finally, he ceased. 'Stop crying,' he spat. 'It is unbecoming.'

Choking on my sobs, I tried to silence myself and ignore the burning sensation in my back.

Suddenly, above my heavy gasping, I heard a blade being drawn. Desperation created a surge of energy within me, enough so I could push myself up with my arms and flip myself over to face Augustus, running me through with a sword or knife.

But it was Marcus, holding a dagger to the Emperor's neck, Augustus frozen in his grip.

'Touch her again,' Marcus growled in his ear, 'and I'll make sure you go to the pits of Tartarus.' He tightened his hold on the Emperor.

Both men met my eyes, one in alarm, the other in anger.

Augustus, surprisingly spritely for an elder, stamped down on Marcus' foot and elbowed him in his side. He let out a grunt as the Emperor leapt out of his grasp. Reaching down, Augustus grabbed my arm and hauled me to my feet, ignoring my whimpers. He restrained me, wrapping an arm around my neck.

Marcus straightened up, knife still in hand, and met eyes with the older man behind me.

The imperial grip suddenly became slack and still.

I tore myself away from the Emperor and ran to the other side of the room. Panting and turning to watch the two face each other, I saw the look of pale horror on the Emperor's face. Terror, even. Petrification.

'Hello, grandfather,' Marcus greeted, flashing the dagger skilfully in his hands.

I felt as if I had been hit straight in my stomach.

'Agrippa,' the old man breathed, staring at his grandson in astonishment.

Agrippa? My muddled head thought hard. *Why would he call him Agrippa?*

'How in the world - ' the Emperor wondered aloud.

'Quite easily,' Marcus snapped. 'After you banished me to that little shithole of an island, I did everything I could to come home to convince you that it was the wrong decision.'

'How did you get out?' the infuriated Emperor demanded.

Marcus laughed. 'With surprising ease, once the guards were asleep under the full force of the midday midsummer sun. All I needed to escape was the keys and Fortuna on my side.'

Of course! I realised the truth. He was named after his father, Marcus Vispanius Agrippa, the son of Julia who was Augustus' daughter by his previous wife. In other words, Marcus was indeed Augustus' grandson.

I stared at him in wonder. His luxurious upbringing and education made sense now. It explained his cheeky and brave personality. The power of his family was evident. Of course, he had never told me his full name - the name of the imperial family to which he had once belonged. *No wonder he had made such a terrible slave.*

'How is Livia? My loving grandmother was so kind as to lock me up and torture me when I stupidly set foot in this place a week ago. It must have been around the same time you assaulted her!' He gestured at me.

Augustus glanced at me with an expression, not guilt but not pride or defence either. It was as if he was just realising what he had done to me.

Marcus seethed with fury. 'Oh, yes. She told me all about your 'inspection'. Do not presume, old man, that when she didn't understand it and tried to justify the pain you brought her, that it would fool me too. At first, I could not believe that my own grandfather, who instructed piety in all matters, would do such a thing. But now I see there is every reason to detest you. If the Roman people heard how you abuse your power like this, I could guarantee a speedy return of the republic!'

He bared his teeth and for the first time I was nearly scared of him. 'I should have helped that Gothic gladiator who nearly took your head off, not killed him. You didn't even recognise me at the games or the trial. I, your blood, was invisible because I was labelled a slave!' He huffed, like all his emotions was coming out in one breath, and shook his head sadly. 'But maybe it was better you did not care. You might have had me killed. I suppose insignificance is both a blessing and a curse. As a slave, people don't bother wasting their life on you, and they don't care at all about wasting yours.'

He laughed dryly and pointed the dagger at his grandfather. 'Well, I am delighted I came back. I finally discovered the truth.' Then he glanced at me. 'And the love of my life.'

My face heated up.

Augustus looked at me in horror. The Emperor's voice was quiet in shock. 'Then it is true. You confess to the affair?'

My breath caught in my throat.

Marcus and I exchanged glances.

He replied, stiffly, 'No, grandfather. She is chaste.'

The Emperor scowled and jabbed a finger at him. 'That, boy, is for me to decide.'

'You won't trust the word of your own family?' Marcus demanded, spitting.

'I won't trust the word of a violent lunatic!' Augustus bellowed, red-faced.

'You're the violent lunatic here! I have always had my senses,' he yelled back. 'But you, you vile brute, put your faith in an ill-conceived border campaign and that hydra of a wife.'

The burning rage in Augustus' eyes was evident. Marcus had defamed the name of Livia, the woman Augustus, somehow, loved and trusted. 'You go too far, young man,' he growled.

Marcus shook his head. 'I can only assume it was she who convinced you that I should be exiled, something which you never investigated yourself. She wanted me gone so her precious Tiberius would inherit. You banished me without a word of goodbye. Don't you realise how much that hurt?'

Augustus scoffed. 'Your girlish sentiments revolt me. Be gone before I have you executed.'

'I am not letting you alone with her for a moment longer,' Marcus snarled. 'You might rape her for all I know. You should know that as her loyal servant, I take my job very seriously.'

'You would threaten the life of your Emperor? Your own grandfather?' Augustus hissed in rage.

'I would threaten the life of any villain such as you.'

Then the door opened, and a third man walked in, tall with small, narrow eyes just like his mother.

Tiberius. The last time I had laid eyes on him was when he had threatened Rufina in the atrium that morning, and sent her on her mission to misery.

When he caught sight of Marcus, wielding a dagger against the Emperor, his shoulders heaved and his eyes widened. The anxiety in his gaze was replaced by colossal relief. 'Agrippa,' he breathed, lips upturning.

'Stepfather,' Marcus growled in reply.

Tiberius didn't seem fazed by the cold greeting.

I stared at them in shock, momentarily forgetting the blood pouring from my back. Tiberius was the second husband of Marcus' mother, while Marcus' father had been her first.

'Tiberius, get out,' Augustus snapped. 'Forget that you ever saw him.'

'What do you mean?' he stepped further into the cell towards Marcus. 'This is brilliant.' He gestured to Marcus, a smile spreading across his face. 'He can resume his rightful place as heir. I don't have to inherit a thing!'

Augustus snorted. 'A slave in charge of the empire? Ridiculous.'

'Manumit him - free him - and then he won't be.'

'What makes you think I want that?' Both Augustus and Marcus snapped at the same time.

Tiberius frowned, looking between them. 'I don't understand.' He looked to Marcus. 'Agrippa, you will inherit the world and eternal glory beyond your comprehension.'

'Yes,' he nodded with a sad smile. 'But it is glory built on pain. This empire has grown on the suffering of others. We rape, torture and kill, throwing people to the lions and laughing while they fight for their lives. It is sick. It would be my greatest shame to rule over such a monstrosity.'

I glowed with pride.

Then he smirked. 'But I would never deny you the honour, stepfather. That is what you exiled me for - the chance to be overlord of everything.'

Shock covered Tiberius' face. 'I had no part in your banishment. Believe me. That was my mother's doing. Furthermore, I have tried everything to change my fate!'

'Like manipulating Rufina?' I said, my voice shaking with the realisation. 'Playing on her wildest dreams and her worst fears?'

The Emperor and Marcus looked at me in confusion.

'Shut up!' Tiberius hissed. 'I don't know what you are talking about.'

'I had been wondering why, if the Emperor required his will so urgently, he didn't just go to Occia? Or have her come to him?' I couldn't stop talking, now that it was all starting to make sense.

'What is the harlot babbling about?' Augustus snapped at his stepson.

202

'Why did you need it?' I begged, more tears flowing down my cheeks. 'Why did you ruin her life? Was it to scribble your name out as heir? It seems the most likely reason.'

Tiberius looked away, his eyes momentarily landing on Marcus, but it was enough of a moment for me to realise everything.

I followed his gaze and my heart fell. 'Was it to write his name in? So he would take your place?'

Tiberius scoffed. 'How could I? I didn't know he was in Rome.'

'Exiled or not,' I whispered, 'Marcus is the one person left alive who can take your place. You knew that. And you couldn't leave the will empty. It would never be credible that Augustus didn't choose any heir before his death.'

Tiberius' expression went slack and he glanced sheepishly at Marcus.

'Enough!' Augustus roared, screwing up his fists. 'Tiberius is the heir! That's the end of it. Praetorian!'

Nerves jumping, I stumbled back into the corner of the room. Marcus looked over his shoulder to see Perfect Gnaeus and the imperial guard already marching through the door.

The Perfect drew his sword. 'Caesar,' he greeted with a bow.

'Seize this man!' Augustus growled, gesturing to Marcus, and before anyone could react, two soldiers had caught him and forced him to let go of his dagger, yanking it out of his hand. 'He is an illegally returned exile, a lunatic who has interrupted my sanctified duties - '

'You bastard!' Marcus roared, writhing in their grip. 'Sanctified, my ass!'

'Augustus, please - ' Tiberius begged.

' - and threatened my life. Throw him in gaol. He shall be publicly scourged tomorrow,' Augustus ordered.

What? That meant only one thing.

'They're right about you!' Marcus bellowed at his grandfather. 'You have gone mad!'

'Augustus, please reconsider,' Tiberius pleaded, getting down on his knees before him and grabbing at his toga.

Fear gripped me, as well as courage. My back was numb, but my legs were not. I bolted towards Marcus, being dragged away, when the hilt of a sword knocked into my temple. My body stopped and I fell, barely feeling the impact. Suddenly, the world was lost to me or I to it.

XXVI
VALE
-Farewell-

I had woken up in my familiar holding room with a pounding headache in my temple. I sat up slowly, wincing in pain, and leant against the wall. The light from the crack underneath the door seeped into the room, along with the memories from what had happened. I sat there, eyes sore, the blood drawn by that infernal whip now dried. Where they had taken Marcus, I did not know. If they were passing the normal sentence given to a Vestal's lover, my heart raced at the thought of what was going to happen to me. I struggled to contain my breath. It was like my body was trying to suddenly live as fast as it could. My heart ached. My head thumped. My back was in searing pain. I had lost a great deal of blood, not that it mattered - I would be gone from this world soon.

I shook my head, trying to remind myself that Augustus was deaf to the gods now. I was a notorious whore on whom lay the blame for the annihilation of three Roman legions, but both he and they knew I had committed no crime. At least there was one little light on my horizon: if I was going to die soon, Marcus would too; we would go to the Underworld together and never be parted. However, my lower lip shook to think that maybe I would never see him again, not even in death.

As I sat reflecting in the darkness, I wondered why Marcus had never told me he was of imperial blood. I supposed he might not have wanted to intimidate me or he wouldn't have wanted me to associate him with Augustus. *As if I ever would.* He was all love and the Emperor was all evil.

Had I ever told Marcus that I loved him? No. But he had said I was the love of his life. Another tear fell out of my eye. *What a thing to say!* Did he know that I felt just as strongly about him? I hadn't even known it, but I did now. I loved him so much that his absence was maddening. I was bereft.

That morning, guards came in and hauled me to my feet. They had to hold me while I stood. I would have collapsed otherwise. I had no more energy, not even to cry. Slaves entered with water and oils. They cleaned my body of blood, and the imperial physician was called to attend to me. He rubbed some herbal remedies on my back wounds. My body was in agony and spending the night on the cold, stone floor hadn't helped.

I managed to gather the strength to ask the physician, 'I wonder why the Emperor cares so much as to send in cleaners and a healer, to waste their time and talents on one who is about to die?'

He did not reply. Perhaps he had been instructed not to speak to me. Besides, I had already worked out the answer for myself: appearances' sake.

Sometime later, I was dressed in the clothes the slaves had brought, which were not my usual garments but a simple white palla, with no footwear. My hair had been rinsed of blood and now it was hanging around my shoulders, still quite sodden and soaking the top of my stola. I was put in a chair they brought to the cell.

After a short while, Val walked into the room. When she saw me, her eyes began to shine and she visibly gulped, but she didn't say anything.

I smiled sadly, but it felt false. 'Come to say goodbye?'

She nodded, swallowing and clasping her hands in front of her. 'I have. The others are outside too.'

I frowned. She was not behaving as I had expected. 'What is it?' I asked her after a moment of awkward silence.

She closed her eyes and bent her head. Then she looked at me again. 'You lied to me, to all of us.'

I felt my stomach flip at the statement. I realised what she was feeling. Rushing forward, I grabbed her hands. 'I only lied about there being nothing between Marcus and me.'

She ripped her hands out of mine.

I continued desperately. 'I never lied about my chastity, Val.'

She shook her head. 'The Emperor - '

'Is lying,' I interrupted. 'He has lied about a lot.'

She crossed her arms, scowling at me. 'Such as?'

I sighed, knowing I would have to be completely honest. 'You once asked me what happened during the inspection, and I didn't tell you. Well, now I shall. The Emperor assaulted me. Sexually,' I stressed, hoping she would understand. 'The inspection is just his pretence. One day you'll find out for yourself.'

For a moment, she stared at me in confusion, then horror, disbelief and finally fury. 'Do not think I would ever let myself sink so low as to be inspected.' She glared at me as my heart plummeted. 'You cannot convince me of your innocence, so don't even try. It is base of you to accuse Augustus of such things,' she snapped. 'I trust him. Everyone does.'

I stepped back, feeling winded. 'You said I could trust you. You said you would support me.'

'Those words were for the girl I thought I knew,' she hissed, 'the girl who I didn't think would ever lie to my face, much less commit a crime. But best friends don't lie to each other.'

I turned to sit back down in my chair, still shocked. She didn't believe me. She didn't even seem to care. If she didn't, none of the others would either. My shock turned into pain, and the pain into anger. 'How could I have possibly told you I had feelings for my slave and that he returned them?' I whispered, unable to look at her. My vision blurred. 'If it had been you, you would have never dared tell anyone.'

'You should have trusted me. And you're wrong; I would have told you,' she replied.

'How do you know that?' I looked her up and down: a pampered princess, naive and brainwashed. 'When you know nothing.'

She sighed and drew herself up tall. 'Don't you dare put me down just because you're feeling sorry for yourself. There is no one else to blame but yourself,' she scorned me.

Then she swept from the room as grandly as an important young Roman lady would. It was the last time I would ever see her.

Next was Picia. She ran into the room, already in tears.

I stood up to greet her as she flung herself at me, wailing, 'I don't believe them, Aemilia. I never did. It must be a lie!'

Relief swept over me. Yesterday, I had cursed Picia. Now, I thanked the gods for her. She couldn't believe anything bad about anyone. Her soul was too kind and too pure.

I hushed her and patted her head, trying to soothe her. 'Everything will be alright.'

She mumbled into my shoulder, 'I am so sorry I didn't tell you about the kiss. I should have, but Lavidia blackmailed me about my own chastity, so I could not.'

I clenched my jaw, remembering how I had overheard her threatening Picia with ruin. 'That doesn't surprise me.' I shook my head. 'Do not worry. I forgive you.'

She giggled and pulled back. 'They are lying, aren't they? You are still a virgin, right?'

I hesitated before answering. 'Yes, I am, Picia, but the love I had for my slave was genuine.'

An expression surprise gradually came over her delicate features and then she nodded. 'I see. Well, I think that true love is beautiful and anyone who finds it is blessed.' She smiled at me.

I found myself beaming back at her. 'Thank you,' I heard myself whisper. I wiped her cheeks gently. 'But be careful what you say. You don't want to end up like me.'

Her presence was replaced by Occia who strode in and regarded me with a raised eyebrow.

Immediately, I prepared myself for the worst scolding imaginable. 'Vestalis Maxima Occia,' I began, unable to keep the hostility out of my voice, curtseying curtly.

She made a humming sound as she looked at me. 'You fit the description of a cadaver very well in that get-up.'

'So would you, domina,' I replied speedily. 'The costume creates the character, like a Vestal.'

Her eyes widened. 'I beg your pardon! The Vestal clothing is the uniform of a servant of the state. I taught you that.'

'You taught me much,' I conceded. 'But there were a great many more things you failed to teach me: how to protect myself against the one sin I was to avoid.'

She snorted. 'That would go against our principle of psychological virginity, our ancient and traditional ways.'

I shook my head. 'Knowledge enables a person. If the Vestals knew what to avoid, they would still do so as the punishment would be enough to deter them. However, if they remain ignorant then how will they know if they have sinned?'

She was silent for a moment. Then she said, 'They will be inspected and told.'

'Of course,' I muttered under my breath, rolling my eyes.

She didn't seem to hear me. 'Aemilia, if all the maidens in the land knew what was in store for them when they married, we would be giving them the tools to do away with purity. It is better that they remain in the dark about it, happy, away from risk, danger and suspicion.'

I shook my head. 'Ignorance does not lead to a lack of danger or happiness, domina. Assault, over which the ignorant have no control or knowledge, is dangerous and brings with it some of the worst pain and grief imaginable. Danger is not removed by ignorance, and the innocent are still suspected of sin. I was. You say we are not even to think about it, yet we are threatened daily with its punishment. How then can one not think about it?'

She was looked away, jaw clenched. She seemed unmoved but I could see the doubt in her eyes and, even with my last breaths, I would still try to make her see sense.

'Have you ever been inspected, Domina Occia?' I inquired.

She looked at me, alarmed. 'How dare you suggest such a thing!'

'Evidently not.' I got to my feet, approaching her. 'Well, imagine I am an innocent Vestal, untouched by a mortal man, but because of the malice of another, I am accused of sin and inspected by the Emperor. Imagine I return home. The Emperor has declared that I am still a virgin. I approach you, and I ask you, eyes filled with tears, why Augustus demanded that I strip naked before him and then why he forced me against a wall putting his fingers inside me?' I pointed wildly towards the wall where it had happened to me.

Her eyes widened, and she stumbled back in shock and horror.

I kept approaching her. 'And, domina, my teacher and protector against the violent ways of men, I ask you: why did it hurt so much?' My eyes were watering.

She stared at me wide-eyed.

Although I fully expected a reply, I got none. 'Of course, you have no answer because you have never been inspected,' I continued. 'What is worse is that I don't think you actually realise what you were doing, what you were sending me to the inspection. You act like you know everything, but I wonder,' I said, 'how much in the dark you really are?'

She glared down at me with contempt. 'You are a Vestal Virgin, Aemilia. You have no right to fall in love.'

I shot back. 'Venus gave us all the right! But it baffles me that some would choose against it and force others to do the same.'

She drew herself up to her full height, fuming down at me. 'You forget your place, Aemilia, questioning those wiser than you.'

I narrowed my eyes. 'But that's just it, domina. I don't believe you are.'

She huffed. 'The inspection is a faultless way of testing for virginity.'

'How?' I spat. 'Because a virgin isn't used to feeling those things?'

She shook her head. 'No. It's because of the blood.'

My mind was momentarily white. 'I don't understand,' I muttered.

'When a woman loses her virtue, blood comes out.'

I frowned for a few moments, blinking. 'I didn't - Augustus, he ...', I choked up, unable to speak, remembering how the Emperor had wiped his bloody fingers on his robes after inspecting me. I turned away, eyes stinging with tears. *No wonder he said afterwards that I had been a virgin.*

'Aemilia, don't try to understand things you're too young to comprehend. That's what I've always told you,' she said, sounding exasperated and disappointed.

Unable to reply, I watched as she turned to leave, the door shutting behind her. I instantly burst into quiet sobs, tears streaming down my face. I clamped a hand over my mouth, shaking my head. However, I barely had the time to gather myself when Lavidia's voice sounded from nearby.

'Oh, Aemilia!' she exclaimed, laughing in glee. 'I do believe this is the best you've ever looked.'

I wiped my face with my fingers and turned around to face her. At least now, if I was already on my worst behaviour, there was nothing to gain or lose by speaking to Lavidia as she deserved.

She raised an eyebrow. 'I wonder if the reason you liked that low-life so much was that you believed him to be a kindred spirit.'

My mind darkened. She knew nothing about him.

'For so long, you've been asking yourself where you belong,' she said, feigning a frown of concern, 'that you actually decided it was with him.' Then she snorted with laughter. 'How hilarious!'

Maybe she was right, I conceded. I came from outside Rome and had few memories of my father. I had always been searching for myself, but I refused to admit that to her. She had enough victory to bathe in already. Still, there were other reasons.

'I recognised that people are people, no matter who they are or where they come from. He was a man just like any other with his own feelings, misfortunes and struggles. Shockingly enough, Lavidia, low-lives have hearts and souls too,' I told her.

'He was a slave,' she remarked, shaking her head. 'Barely human.'

Mute, I watched as she moved into the centre of the room and gazed out the window, like a queen over her kingdom.

'So this is what it feels like to be the hated whore of Rome,' she said aloud, taking in her surroundings before looking at me again.

'I would have thought you already knew what that felt like.'

She scoffed. 'Oh, don't be like that, Aemilia!' she said, pouting. 'Why can we not end this as friends?'

'Because we never started it as friends and never have been friends,' I said and approached her. 'You always hated me for the mere possibility that I wasn't fully Roman.'

She glared at me, her face transforming into a snarl. 'You, Aemilia, are of impure blood, with no place among the Vestals. The first time I laid eyes on you I knew you were like a rat or some other vermin, something to be exterminated.'

I blinked. The hurt turned to stone within me. 'I always detested your bullying, too. Picia, poor girl, was the most recent victim of yours.'

She grinned. 'Her story did the trick though. It helped the prosecution. In case you haven't noticed, you're about to die. So, poor you, actually.'

I nodded and raised my chin. 'While the real harlot goes on whoring.'

Her grin vanished, and she pursed her lips, raising an eyebrow.

'Don't forget,' I hissed. 'I know what you've done, as do the gods. You will be found out eventually, even if it is before the judges of the Underworld. Then you'll be punished for eternity and not just because of your sins or your bullying, but for taking twenty-thousand lives.'

'Is that a threat?'

'I don't need to threaten you, Lavidia. You know very well it will happen,' I replied in a whisper. 'Now get out.'

Clenching her jaw, she bolted past me.

'Wait!' I called after her. 'I have one question for you.'

She stopped and turned back, huffing.

'How did you know Rufina had been searching for the Emperor's will?

A genuinely pleased grin spread across her face. 'Oh, Vesta! Aemilia, have you forgotten your principles already?' Her smile vanished as she deadpanned, 'Servitude doesn't just come in slaves. Think!' she snapped. 'Who else could have been there?'

The realisation washed over me. 'Guards.'

She nodded and gave me a slow sarcastic clap. 'Yes. They line the walls of every house in the empire. They, too, have eyes and ears and a mouth to tell me what goes on.'

'No doubt they were all underneath your skirts at some point,' I said.

She smirked. 'No doubt.' She went to leave, and over her shoulder, she called the words, 'I applaud you, Aemilia. So much for your morality.'

Then she left, leaving me disappointed in myself, for she was right. *So much for my morality.*

In my cold misery, I waited for Rufina to enter. If her thoughts were anything like Val's, possibly worse as her principles were less pliable, I expected her to scold me and happily send me to my death, but she never came. Darkness was already descending by the time I realised she wasn't coming to say goodbye. It pricked my eyes and my heart broke a little more. However, in a way, it was a relief that I didn't have to look upon her disgust and disappointment. I probably couldn't have withstood another conversation similar to Val's farewell to me.

Thus, I concluded one thing: my father was right to spare me from farewells all my life - they were too painful.

XXVII
SEPULTURA
-The Burial-

I was ready to die. I wanted to. I had said goodbye to those I loved. Admittedly, not all farewells had gone to plan, but I was ready to leave them all now, including the evil Emperor who despised me, and the city which was probably baying for my blood.

Many people awaiting execution would be dreading their death day, but not me; I was impatient, pacing around my little room. They said I was going to the Fields of Punishment for deceiving and endangering everyone, as well as condemning twenty thousand men, but I knew I was chaste, as did the gods. I was confident that I would be judged fairly in the afterlife where I hadn't been here, that I would go to Elysium, and that Marcus would be there with me soon. I only hoped with all my heart that they wouldn't hurt him too much during his flogging, that he would pass away quickly, and that they would bury him so his soul could cross the River Styx and join mine.

Lavidia would go to the Fields of Punishment and be tortured forever. Such was the fate for those who abused others.

Augustus Caesar, the man of my nightmares, was old and would die soon. That was for certain. I hoped he would fall to the lions in the arena and be eaten alive and then end up in Tartarus with all the other monsters. Perhaps Tiberius' rule would be different. Unfortunately, he scrutinised everything and suspected everyone. Since there was so much of that already in the Order of the Vestals, matters could be worse than before. Nevertheless I still had hope: he had once known love.

I prayed that Rufina would follow in Occia's footsteps and reform the teachings of the Order. She was a smart girl who could fix the flaws in the institution.

Remembering my advocate Cornelius, I prayed he would find success and that my trial had not killed his chances of popularity. While he might not have entirely convinced the jury of everything, he made them doubtful enough to hand over the ultimate decision to Augustus.

Lunchtime came. The slaves brought me my final meal, nothing compared the lavish feasts I was used to.

Afterwards, the Praetorian Guard arrived to escort me to my burial. Gnaeus, himself, opened the door, grinning down at me maliciously. As he shackled my hands and feet with heavy iron, I wondered which unlucky Vestal he would prey on next. I hoped it would not be Picia. She was far too sweet, but maybe she would rub off on him. I supposed he could find a perfect match in Lavidia.

As he marched out the door, I followed in solemn silence, the rest of the Praetorian Guard behind me. Their armour and my chains clanged against the floor, and the clamour signalled to the world our approach, and my exit.

I was led up through the House of Augustus, along the marble corridors and grand rooms with columns that reached the heavenly ones above. The walls were lined with senators and generals and the other most important men in Rome. No one spoke a word. The atmosphere was tense and still.

We neared the main entrance of the house where the giant golden doors opened out onto huge steps descending into the masses below, I heard the noise. The voices of thousands of Romans gathered together, shouting and roaring. Seeing the size of the crowd gathered, I was impressed. The masses extended onto the horizon, becoming blurred. I had known Augustus would have wanted to build this into a grand occasion where everyone could see the whore of Rome off to her death, but he had outdone himself.

Decorating the stairs, the other five Vestals stood in black pallae with veils over their faces, hands clasped in front of each other, facing straight ahead, seemingly deaf to the rabble around them, their skirts billowing in the wind. I saw Occia's silhouette leading them from the front, near the bottom of the steps. I spotted Rufina's and my eyes threatened my face with tears.

At the top of the stairs, behind those nightly shades, were two guards standing on either side of a closed litter on the ground. They looked at me expectantly, and I realised I had to get in.

I obeyed, carefully lying on the litter and letting them hoist me up, with an unsteady jolt, into the air.

Together, with the black Vestals around me keeping time, everyone descended the steps of the House of Augustus, marching in unison.

I found myself gripping the sides of the litter to keep myself on it. The last thing I wanted to do was to tip over the side as it rocked, falling face-first into the mud. Soon, as I found my balance on it, sailing over the heads of the masses, the screams of Roman men, slaves, women, and children filled my ears. There was no cry I could make out which sounded in my favour nor any other for my damnation.

A terrifying thought hit me that, somewhere among them, Marcus was being tortured, his body being beaten senseless by flails. I knew what it felt like. However, he had saved me then and I couldn't save him now. It was that realisation that caused my eyes to water and spill over with tears. *Soon*, I told myself, breathing heavily, *we would be together again.*

Thus I was carried towards the city's extremities, down a road cleared of people for the funeral procession to take place. Although the noise was deafening, it did not disturb me.

Finally, we reached the cemetery just inside Rome's walls by the Colline Gate where I would be buried: the Evil

Field. As the litter was placed on the ground, I turned my head and saw my tomb. Around an open grave, the black Vestal Virgins and other priests within the College of Ponitifics were gathered.

The earth had been dug into, exposed, and a stone vault had been placed inside, the capstone removed. A ladder led down into my place of death, drawing my attention to the recliner, the burning lamp on the table of food and drink which would last me a few days. In the corner was a small shrine to Vesta at which I could pray for mercy.

Upon seeing it, panic grew in my heart. It wasn't fear, not yet. I had nothing to be frightened of; I had done nothing wrong and had no reason to fear eternal punishment. However, the afterlife was something I did not know. *Was it not sensible to fear the unknown?*

As I sat up to get off the litter, I entertained saying something spiteful when entering my grave. It would be my only chance, but I knew that no one else would believe me if I made a final claim or accusation. Besides, there were a few people who truly knew what I had suffered. Maybe they would take the matter further, or perhaps one day, there would be a Vestal with the courage to tell the truth to the world. Justice would be served one day, I reassured myself, if the gods had any mercy.

Suddenly, a hand flashed in front of my face. I flinched and turned my head to see Emperor Augustus standing over me, his arm outstretched to help me out of the litter, decked out in all his holy robes and golden trinkets. The solemnity in his face did not match the ecstatic triumph in his eyes.

Ignoring his hand, I got to my feet. I stared up at him boldly. With a flash of annoyance on his face, he beckoned me towards the tomb and gestured grandly to the ladder by which means I would descend.

My heart felt still for a moment as I glanced uncertainly between the tomb and everyone else. They were staring at me waiting. Then it hit me: there would be no eulogy, no final words said by any one; no words of praise or affection for memory. Perhaps I should have expected it – so many despised me and couldn't wait to see me gone forever. Nevertheless, that was the final blow to my hope, and I abandoned all preconceptions of parting words. *If they did not feel the need for it, why should I?* I decided not to waste another breath on those who hated me so much that they wished me dead.

Within the dark tomb was a man I did not know, dressed in black. *The executioner*, I guessed. He, too, held up his hand to help me, which I also ignored.

I watched my steps carefully, despite my trembling limbs, not wanting to fall and make a fool of myself. Heartbeat in my ears, I forced myself down into the vault.

When I landed on the stone ground, the cold hit me. It didn't come from any familiar wind and it wasn't refreshing. It was an empty, earthy and sinister chill. Unable to hide a shiver, I went over to the recliner and sat down, shaking. The small lamp on the table nearby was my only source of heat.

The executioner took my place, ascending the ladder to join the world above.

Over me, the distant muffled voice of a priest, probably the Pontifex Maximus, said a prayer for my soul, but I ignored him. There was no need for his blessings. I didn't fear for my soul. I would be just fine.

Not wanting to look up at the world I was leaving, I lay back on the recliner, wincing at the sensation of it against my wounds, and squeezed my eyes shut, trying to block everything out. It was the first time in a week that I had something comfortable to lie on.

Suddenly, I heard a scraping sound. When I opened them, the capstone had been pulled over the top of the tomb. The candlelight was so low that I could only make out the most immediate parts of the recliner around me and the surface of the table.

My own breath was all I could hear now, along with my heartbeat. I could almost sense the Underworld beneath me, ready to receive me. I exhaled heavily, trying to calm down. *There is nothing to fear.*

Trying not to descend into terror, I picked up a roll of bread and began to nibble at it. Then I frowned. *Why was I savouring it? Why was I delaying death, delaying paradise and my reunion with Marcus?* I wolfed it down. Suddenly famished, I ate all the food on that table and downed all the wine. I thought to remove all the food so I would not be tempted when starving.

However, when I was finished eating my fill and as I was listening to the silence, I realised that I had one more thing to do. There was one person I had yet to address.

Getting up slowly off the recliner, I knelt before the altar. The candlelight did not reach this far, so I was mostly in shadows, with hard and rough stone beneath my knees. Breathing out slowly, I tried to calm my nerves and stop my hands and legs from trembling. The cold was biting away at my skin, but I would not succumb yet.

'Who …,' I began, my voice hoarse, 'hurt you? Did someone break your heart once? If not, why would you keep yourself or anyone else from love? Loving Marcus was the best thing I have ever felt. The care, affection and sense of security are incomparable. You are the goddess of the home and hearth. Surely, you must know that while shelter, food and fire can give the body the home it needs, love provides a haven for the heart. Is that sanctuary not a home of a different kind?'

I sighed. 'I am sorry if the lives of those legions really do lie upon my head. I apologise if I am an impure, barbarian bastard who cursed the Vestals with her presence, but I cannot help my birth. I cannot help that Augustus chose to do what he did to me. I cannot help if Venus enchanted me to fall in love and, even if she did not, I don't know if we can help who we are attracted to. Valeriana told me that we can't,' I recalled aloud.

'Unfortunately, I am so ignorant and in the dark that I don't know what I should know or whose teachings to follow.'

I took a moment to breathe before shaking my head and muttering, 'I hope that one day, Vesta, you will forgive me for any sin or offence I have committed against you, for this is the time to forgive. I forgive Occia. I forgive Lavidia. I forgive Rufina, Picia and Valeriana. I forgive,' I swallowed, bringing myself to say the dreaded name, 'Augustus.' I took a deep breath. 'For all offences they have committed against me.

'I hope that you will let Venus grant every Vestal the chance to discover a love of her own after her servitude has ended. Even the worst of them deserve it, for if they are happy, perhaps they will change for the better. I hope they will find peace in their hearts.'

My eyes stung and I let the tears fall. There was no one to see or criticise so I sighed. 'I don't know if this was always your plan for me or some other god meddled in your affairs. Maybe my legacy will be proof that even a Vestal can find love. More likely, my death will be an example to all future Vestals not to venture beyond the boundaries set for them or maybe I leave behind nothing at all - '

A tapping sound from the ceiling above intruded on my prayer.

My voice died as another, muffled, spoke from above. 'Aemilia?'

XXVIII
AMOR
-Love-

The earth around me was mute, yet my blood roared in my ears, heart pounding with excitement.

The voice spoke again. 'Aemilia?'

My chest filled with hope and terror. *A saviour? Death?* 'Yes?'

With my heartbeat drumming, I waited for a reply, but none came. I frowned. *Maybe I just imagined it.*

Suddenly, the scraping sound came again. I jumped, startled. The scratching sounds of stone against stone filled my ears. I winced.

Then the cool night air and a gleam of moonlight flooded into the tomb. I stared in shock at a gap in the ceiling above. The grave was filled with my name on the breath of a girl's voice, which I recognised.

I surged forward to stand beneath the crack in the capstone, where it had been pushed back from its closed position. I saw a familiar face by the edges of the tomb above me.

'Rufina!' I gasped.

She beamed down at me. 'Aemilia!' she whispered in return.

'What are you doing?' I hissed.

'My duty,' she replied with a smug look, and cocked an eyebrow. 'It is my professional opinion, as protector of the state, that this empire cannot possibly flourish without its very best Vestal alive and well.'

I burst out into laughter. 'Oh, you cannot be serious!'

A finger shot up to her lips, and I put a hand over my mouth. 'Indeed, I am,' she whispered, reaching down into the tomb. 'Do you need a hand?'

'Or two?' another voice sounded down into the underground chamber.

This one I knew by heart. My chest spasmed with pain and then filled with joy.

With a bounce of curls and a flash of dimples, Marcus' face appeared beside Rufina's.

My jaw dropped and my head reeled.

'Good evening, domina,' he flirted down at me with a wink.

I blinked to make sure that he was not a figment of my imagination as he reached his hand down into the grave. I stretched up to link my little finger with his, skin on skin. It could not be denied. He was real.

A cry sounded into the night - my cry - followed by a flurry of shushing. I choked a sob before my palm flew to my mouth.

'Hush, my dear. Everything will be alright.' Marcus hooked onto my little finger, shaking it reassuringly.

I nodded, but the tears still poured. I couldn't help it.

'My darling,' he whispered. 'Listen. Can you do something?'

I sniffed and nodded, wiping away my blurred vision.

'Rufina said there should be a table down there with you. Can you bring it over here and stand on it?'

The words were understood, but I couldn't obey them. 'No, I don't want to let go,' I cried, my face crumpling again.

'My love,' he rushed to reassure me. 'Just do this one last thing, and you will never have to let go again.'

It took the help of the gods, but I finally brought myself to release him. I forced myself to drag the table underneath the crack in the capstone, but I worked quickly, desperate to return to him. Shakily, I stood on the table and reached my arms up.

Rufina and Marcus grabbed a limb each, pulling me up from the tomb.

When I got to my feet, I launched myself at him.

We fell back through the darkness, lips together, onto the soft grass. Then he held me in his safe, warm embrace as we kissed. He gently smoothed away the tears from my face.

I breathed him in, touching his chest and digging my hands into his hair, running my fingers over his face, feeling his soft lips and tasting his tongue on mine.

Suddenly, I pulled away, looked down and saw blood. Everywhere. He was covered in it.

Gasping, I stood up. 'Oh gods, Marcus! What happened?'

He avoided my gaze.

'You should be dead!' I realised aloud. 'They flogged you!'

The corner of his lips titled upwards and he got to his feet. 'They did. They shouted abuse at me, hurled stones at me and when I was on the ground they kicked me.'

I felt my eyes fill up again, looking at his clothes. He was without sandals. His tunic was torn, in tatters, and soaked in his own blood. There were gashes and wounds everywhere on his skin that I could see.

'I found him on my way here, lying in the ditches. They had left him to rot,' Rufina said from behind, but I couldn't drag my eyes away from Marcus to look at her as she spoke. 'They must have thought he was dead.'

'But I wasn't,' he whispered, that smirk making its way onto his face again, that smugness I never thought I would see.

'Good gods,' I breathed as reality dawned on me, staring up at him.

'Yes, the good gods have given you one more chance,' Rufina said.

I turned around, embracing her tightly. 'Thank you so much.'

She squeezed me back. 'I figured that before I dedicate myself to a life of virtue again, I should get one more well-meant crime out of the way, but for someone else's sake this time.'

We all laughed at her words as we broke apart.

Catching sight of the open grave before us, I saw what devastation it was in. The earth heaped on top of the tomb after my burial was now dug up for a second time and thrown to one side.

'How did you manage all this?' I asked them.

Rufina looked beyond me at Marcus. 'Together, with help though.'

I spotted another slave behind her and then regarded the heavy slab of rock. 'But how did you move the capstone?'

She nodded at the large stick to the side of the site. 'A little leverage goes a long way, my dear.'

I grinned at her ingenuity.

She sighed as she stared at the carnage. 'Fret not. Once you two are gone, it will all be replaced as if you are still inside. My slave will do it.'

I felt Marcus' hand on my shoulder. Turning to him, the sight of him giving me a thrilling sense of elation, I kissed him firmly. 'I love you,' I whispered against his lips. I pulled away.

There was a gleam in his eyes. 'I love you too,' he murmured in reply.

Then it struck me: the three of us were standing in a ghostly graveyard, surrounded by the tombs of the worst criminals and notorious figures in history, at twilight with a super moon high in the black sky, without a plan.

'So,' I began, glancing between them anxiously. 'What do we do now? I can hardly go back to the house.'

Rufina frowned and shook her head. 'Aemilia, you cannot go back into the city at all. Not only are you no longer a Vestal, but as far as everyone is concerned, you are still beneath that slab.' She gestured to the capstone. 'And likely to be dead within the week. If you are recognised, you will be hunted down and killed.'

She took my hands and looked at me seriously. 'Despite what your father wanted, there is no future here for you anymore, for either of you, except possibly a brief and painful one. And I would much rather that, after all this effort to have your life back, you live it in painless safety. You must get as far away from Rome as you possibly can, assume new identities elsewhere and live your lives together in exile.'

I looked between them in worry. 'Can we do that? You know that wherever Augustus holds sway, we are likely to be found out. A former member of the imperial family and a former Vestal. Our accents and our mannerisms will surely give us away. Questions will be asked.'

'I know,' Rufina agreed. 'The news of your burial will be spreading throughout the world by now. And should grave robbers ever come here and discover a tomb without a body, you need to be in a land where no one has ever even heard of the Vestals. Or Rome if possible.'

I frowned. 'To uncivilised, barbarian lands?' I asked, horrified at the idea despite myself. Exile I could bear, but surviving among complete strangers with a different tongue and customs was entirely different. *Would there even be theatres and baths?*

'For the sake of your life, you cannot stay within the empire,' she repeated.

Marcus chuckled. 'Aemilia, I think you will find more barbarism here than anywhere else. And if you don't like it,' he added, shrugging, 'we can move elsewhere, possibly on the borders of the empire.'

'Although,' Rufina butted in, 'perhaps nowhere in Germania or near the Teutoburg Forest.'

I grimaced and nodded. 'Of course not.' I sighed and tried to be hopeful. 'Let us go then, to the end of the earth if necessary.' Then I turned to Rufina, for the very last time. 'Take care of them all. I won't be there to make sure they get into trouble.'

She giggled. 'Absolutely, Aemilia. Your wish is my command.' She then regarded Marcus. 'Look after her.'

'Have I not kept her alive so far?' he joked.

'Alive, yes,' she conceded. 'But from now on, try to keep her out of harm's way altogether.'

'I promise,' he answered, possibly more serious than she was.

When I had said farewell to Rufina, and we had closed over the capstone completely, I looked at Rome around me, with its torchlights keeping vigil over its inhabitants. Glancing back at Rufina, who was beckoning to her slave to return the gravesite to its former state, I turned to Marcus. He had his hand stretched out for me to take.

'So, what do we do now?' I whispered, taking hold of it.

'Follow me,' he said and pulled me after him.

I followed him through the cemetery, our only light being that of the starry heavens above.

Eventually, he stopped and knelt down on the ground, feeling around until he picked up a large urn from a graveside. He turned it over to empty it.

I gasped, 'What are you doing? That's sacrilege!'

He hushed me and continued to pour out its contents.

I stood there in horror.

He put down the urn quietly and handed me items from off the ground, but where I had expected ashes in my palms, he placed a change of clothes and the armour of a Roman guard.

I stared at him in confusion.

He gestured for me to put them on.

Realising I had few other options, I huffed and turned away, raising my stola over my head and tossing it to one side. I slipped on the tunic and the sandals before turning back around.

Marcus grinned at me and winked at me.

Realising that he had just watched me get undressed again, I resisted the urge to verbally scold him, but I did not hesitate from smacking his arm.

Then he helped me on with my armour before tucking my hair into the helmet and kissing my neck lightly. He geared himself up likewise. Then he beckoned for me to follow.

It was difficult to be quiet with the bits of metal clanging against each other, as we trudged through the graveyard, but I somehow managed it.

We neared the Colline Gate. I caught sight of the two guards already on duty sitting by the gate doors, and panic gripped my heart. I faltered, but Marcus didn't notice, continuing on. I watched in terror as he approached a guard, but, looking up and seeing me still some distance away, he gestured wildly with his hand for me to come nearer. Slowly I stepped forward. When I inspected the guards more closely, I saw they were slumped against the walls to the side of the gate, heads tilted down to their chest, asleep. Relief washed over me.

Then Marcus nudged one awake.

I nearly turned on my heels and ran, but I was so gripped by fear my feet remained rooted in one spot.

'Oi!' Marcus grunted at him. 'It's twilight. Your vigil is up.'

The guard stared up at him in confusion, rubbing his eyes. 'That's not how the rotation of the guard works,' I heard him say.

'It does if I say so,' Marcus argued. 'Now shift it before I tell the centurion you've been sleeping on the job.'

'You wouldn't dare.'

'I'd go to Prefect Gnaeus, if I thought it necessary, or the Emperor himself. Try me,' Marcus threatened.

With that, the guard stood and hurried over to his friend, shoving him awake before pushing him past us away from their post, disappearing into the night.

I looked back at Marcus who was wasting no time.

He reached up and unbolted the doors of the gate.

I hurried after him, and we slipped through the Colline Gate out into the world beyond.

Standing on the other side of Rome's walls, I saw no lights around me except for the moon and stars. The surrounding world was one of blackness. As I looked up at him, leaning his helmet-covered head against the gate and catching his breath, I realised he was all I needed.

He glanced down at me and grinned before planting a brief kiss on my lips.

I giggled with giddy relief. 'So, where are we headed to now? Beyond civilisation, did you say?'

He chuckled. 'Yes, domina.'

'And how exactly are we going to get there?' I wanted to know. 'We don't even have horses.'

Rolling his eyes, he pulled me away from the gate. 'What little faith you have in me, woman!' He gestured wildly to the roadside. There was a cart led by two horses, their hides glistening in the moonlight.

I smiled, rolling my eyes. 'You didn't plan this. You've barely been awake for half a day.'

He slumped. 'Fine, it was Rufina who organised the horses. She paid for them and everything.' He raised an eyebrow. 'But still, you should always publicly declare your faith in me, Aemilia.' He led me over. 'Not the opposite. Otherwise, people will think you've married a neglectful boar.'

'Married?' I exclaimed, pulling away. I burst out into laughter. Whether it was from shock, nerves or amusement, I did not know.

He grabbed me suddenly and pulled me close to his chest, shushing me quietly.

I silenced myself quickly. He was right – there could be guards on night-watch around the city, ready to run through any approaching travellers with their swords.

'Yes, married,' he repeated firmly in a whisper, trapping me in his embrace.

I gazed up at him in surprise. *Was he serious?*

He smirked. 'Do you think it's been easy for me to see you swan around in a bridal veil every day and not be able to call you mine? Of course, I will bloody well be marrying you,' he said, smiling back down at me. 'Only if you agree to it, obviously.'

I snorted and, breaking his hold around me, turned for the cart, but I could not keep the moronic grin off my face. 'Seriously, that is not your proposal! I am not gracing that turd of a speech with any kind of answer.'

Laughing, he hoisted me up onto the seat. Then, following suit, he turned to me. 'But you will marry me someday? I have nothing else worth living for.'

Humming thoughtfully, I kissed him. 'I'll think about it.'

'Well, I'm going to ask you every day until you do,' he warned me, gathering the reins in one hand.

'And I will keep turning you down until you ask me romantically!' I retorted with glee.

'Well, at least I know when I propose properly, you'll say yes.' As he whipped the horses into life and we rolled down the road, he chuckled and said, 'You were right.'

I frowned. 'About what?'

'I am exactly the kind of man to steal you away in the middle of the night.'

I grinned and planted a kiss on his cheek. 'Well, I am exactly the kind of girl to let you get away with it.'

There were no protective walls now, no luxury furniture or fine food, and no slaves to fetch and carry for me. There was just Marcus and me and the world. It was just the two of us, presumed ghosts, against the empire.

FINIS FABULAE

ACKNOWLEDGEMENTS

Several times I have imagined writing the acknowledgements of my first published book. So many people have shown support for my love of classics, the ancient world, and writing. Each deserves an expression of appreciation and gratitude for giving me the confidence to pursue my dream.

I thank my Latin and Greek teachers, Mr O'Dea, Mr Hughes and Mr O'Connor. They allowed me access to the ancient world and taught me the classical customs and traditions that have enabled me to visualise the settings of my stories and to describe Greek and Roman ancient history.

Deepest appreciation to Alejandro Colucci who created the front cover of *Vow* which is beautiful and perfectly captures the essence of the story. Even in my dizziest daydreams, I could not have pictured a more perfect scene. I can't stop looking at it!

Amy, my best friend, understood from the very beginning that writing was not just a hobby for me but a passion and how I want to spend my life. She has read, advised and helped me with my plotlines and character development since we were girls. She continuously shows excitement and enthusiasm for it. Without her, I probably would not be where I am today. Her opinion has always been a vital part of my process and not consulting her seems unimaginable to me.

I would like to express enormous gratitude to my boyfriend, Mark. He has always been a loving and honest ear for my ideas and has bought me copious notebooks and pens. Despite all the words in all the languages that exist, I will never be able to adequately describe the importance of his support.

The most colossal thank you has to go to my family, who have constantly furnished me with enough paper and pens to write away my hours of daylight and sometimes moonlight. My parents have always encouraged the pursuit of ambitions, no matter how high or far away they might seem. They read, analysed and corrected my drafts once they were finished. My sister, Olivia, actively helped me create a presence within online book communities. To my father, Christopher, for all his wisdom and humour, and to my mother, Nicola, for the innumerable hours of close reading and years of reassurance, I give endless words of gratitude.

My friends and family have shown tremendous patience and have given immense support and for this I will always be grateful.

A NOTE FROM THE AUTHOR

The tale of the Vestal Virgins has been told at last. I hope that you enjoyed the story. I have had the time of my life writing this book and publishing it independently. I am very proud of my debut novel, after years of writing since I was very young. *Vow* will always hold a very special place in my heart.

I have always wanted to reach this point: to write books that shed light on ancient cultures for the people today, as every historical event has had its effect. The idea of another world or one that is far away in humanity's history has always both fascinated me, even their darker aspects. Thus, I take great pleasure in writing historical fiction, focusing particularly on themes of love and on strong female characters.

I am currently studying for my BA in Classics, Ancient History and Archaeology at university in Ireland, which has provided me with all the resources and knowledge I need to write confidently about the ancient worlds of Rome and Greece.

Please leave a rating and review of *Vow* on Amazon's online bookstore.

Thank you so much for reading!

Where you can find me:
    Instagram: @katbentleywrites
    TikTok: @katbentleywrites
    Twitter: @bentleywrites

Made in the USA
Las Vegas, NV
04 November 2021